THE EMPIRE MURDERS

THE EMPIRE THEATRE MURDERS

KIT AND MARY ASTON Mysteries BOOK 1

JACK MURRAY

Books by Jack Murray

Kit and Mary Aston Series
The Affair of the Christmas Card Killer
The Chess Board Murders
The Phantom
The Frisco Falcon
The Medium Murders
The Bluebeard Club
The Tangier Tajine
The Empire Theatre Murders
The French Diplomat Affair (novella)
Haymaker's Last Fight (novelette)

DI Jellicoe Series
A Time to Kill
The Bus Stop
Trio
Dolce Vita Murders

Agatha Aston Series
Black-Eyed Nick
The Witchfinder General Murders
The Christmas Murder Mystery

Danny Shaw / Manfred Brehme WWII Series
The Shadow of War
Crusader
El Alamein

THE EMPIRE THEATRE MURDERS

KIT AND MARY ASTON Mysteries BOOK 1

JACK MURRAY

Books by Jack Murray

Kit and Mary Aston Series
The Affair of the Christmas Card Killer
The Chess Board Murders
The Phantom
The Frisco Falcon
The Medium Murders
The Bluebeard Club
The Tangier Tajine
The Empire Theatre Murders
The French Diplomat Affair (novella)
Haymaker's Last Fight (novelette)

DI Jellicoe Series
A Time to Kill
The Bus Stop
Trio
Dolce Vita Murders

Agatha Aston Series
Black-Eyed Nick
The Witchfinder General Murders
The Christmas Murder Mystery

Danny Shaw / Manfred Brehme WWII Series
The Shadow of War
Crusader
El Alamein

Copyright © 2023 by Jack Murray

All rights reserved. No part of this publication may be reproduced, distributed, or transmitted in any form or by any means, including photocopying, recording, or other electronic or mechanical methods, without the prior written permission of the publisher, except in the case of brief quotations embodied in critical reviews and certain other non-commercial uses permitted by copyright law. For permission requests, write to the publisher, addressed 'Attention: Permissions Coordinator,' at the address below.

Jackmurray99@hotmail.com

This is a work of fiction. Names, characters, businesses, places, events, locales, and incidents are either the products of the author's imagination or used in a fictitious manner. Any resemblance to actual persons, living or dead, or actual events is purely coincidental.

SBN: 9798388240255
Imprint: Independently published

Cover by Jack Murray after J.C. Leyendecker

For Monica, Lavinia, Anne, and Baby Edward

The Players

Kit Aston..................*Dashing, highly intuitive amateur detective and former spy*

Mary Aston...................*Beautiful, brave and brilliantly smart*

Rufus Watts...................*Flamboyant artist, brother of theatre owner, Tristram, son of Annie*

Tristram Watts..............*Owner of theatre, brother of Rufus, son of Annie*

Annie Watts..................*Mother of the Watts boys and orchestra member*

Eddie Matthews............*Ageing comic*

Bert Cooper..................*Young comic*

Daisy Lewis...................*Singer*

Javier Gonzalo..............*Magician*

Hector Goulding...........*Orchestra conductor*

Jane Anthony................*Magician's assistant*

Lysander Benedict........*Flamboyant, waspish theatre and arts critic*

Billy Benson................*Rival moving picture house owner*

Monteverdi Brothers...*Acrobats*

Wyman Sisters.............*Comedy cockney sisters double act*

Lucien Lemaire...........*Ventriloquist*

Romeo........................*Theatre cat, rat-catcher extraordinaire*

Two of these people will die.
Two of them have been murdered

Prologue

Folly Theatre, Manchester: February 1920

'Where is it?' he asked through lips that trembled with frustration. He stared manically around the dressing room. There wasn't much time and he'd already spent too long searching. A creaking sound distracted him for a moment. He stared up at the man hanging from the dressing room rafter. The man's face was pale, contorted and lifeless. His skin prickled with fear. This wasn't because of what he had done. It was for what he could not find.

'What have you done with it?' he snarled. There was no sympathy for the dead man, just a growing sense of despair. The stage doorman would be around soon. He'd see the light in the dressing room.

The man swore quietly but vehemently, head twisting this way and that. No likely hiding place presented itself. The book had been sitting out on the table only a couple of hours earlier. Where had he put it? His eyes darted towards the poster that the theatre manager had printed for him and his, now, ex-partner in their magic act. It had a black background with two men, one dressed in an evening suit, the other in a red, devil's costume. The man in the foreground was him, the man dressed as the devil was now swinging diabolically in front of him. Perhaps he'd be joining the dead man he depicted soon. He doubted it though.

Underneath the two men in the poster was the name of the act: "The Brothers Grimoire". The dead man had read about the name some years before. They'd agreed it would make a good, albeit slightly disquieting, name for a magic act.

It had too. For the last six months they'd worked continuously across Lancashire, Cheshire and the north of England. London would have been calling soon. Would have. Now that was all gone. He would strike out on his own. He was the star turn, not Andrew. It was *his* charisma and *his* way with an audience, that had promoters knocking on their door. So what if Andrew created the illusions. Or so he said. Sometimes, just sometimes, it seemed to him that Andrew was simply following another's ideas.

The arguments had started not long after their first engagements. It was the lack of trust from Andrew. The unwillingness to let him in on the secrets of the illusions they performed. They were all written down in that book he kept. Andrew kept everything to himself. Nothing else; only what he needed to know; only what they would do at the next show. Then Andrew would go design and build the apparatus they would use.

Andrew should have been a carpenter. He had nothing in the way of stage presence. Even dressed as the devil he radiated all the evil intent of a doll with a bow in her hair. A devil is meant to be wicked, Andrew just looked sad. Well, he was no longer sad was he? The rope creaking on the rafter echoed ominously around the dressing room.

He was growing desperate now. Where was the bloody book?

In the corner of the room was an upright sarcophagus. This was one of Andrew's more extravagant creations. He opened it. Nothing. He closed its lid. Then his eyes fixed on a small jewellery box. It was made from wood with an ornate, art nouveau trim. Moments later he opened the box. It was empty. This gave rise to yet more oaths. He shut the box and swung his head around at the room. It was enough to make a grown man cry.

He stared down at the box again. Something was not right. Had he been more of a magician and less of a showman he would have seen it immediately, but slowly a thought seeped into his mind. He held the box up and measured its depth with his eyes. Then he opened the box again. A smile crossed his face.

'You old devil,' he whispered.

He put the box down and searched for a button that would release the false bottom. He found it on the side. A lid sprung up to reveal a small leather-bound journal.

'Hard luck Andrew. Nice try,' said the man, lifting the book out of the box. He closed the inner lid and then the outer one. He had what he needed. Time to go. Against his better instincts, curiosity overcame him. He opened the journal. Across two pages he saw a diagram of an illusion. His heart jumped for joy. Then it sank immediately as he realised the instructions were written in a gibberish code. Just as he was about to explode with righteous venom towards the man he'd killed, footsteps echoed a warning in the corridor.

They were growing louder.

'Damn,' he hissed. He'd spent far too long searching for the book. The stage doorman would see the light in the dressing room; he was sure to find him. Frantically, he looked around the room. He tried to avoid looking at the man he'd killed swinging grotesquely from the rafter.

His second inspiration came just at that moment. He ran over to the sarcophagus, opened the front lid and stepped inside just as the door to the dressing room opened.

Nathaniel Magwitch had worked in theatres, man and boy, for almost fifty years. In all his time as a scene shifter, prop maker, handyman and stage door manager, he'd never seen quite anything like the sight that greeted him as he entered the dressing that evening.

Nathaniel recognised the poor man immediately. It was one half of the Brothers Grimoire act. The clue was in his costume. He was wearing a red devil's costume. A wave of nausea rose within him, and he turned away from the appalling sight. He was just about to run and find help, although he knew there was no one else in the building, when he thought he heard a noise. He forced himself to look up at Andrew Harper. He was dead. There was no mistaking the bloodless lips, the pale skin. This was death in all its glory.

Although not a brave man, he was no coward either. The shock was still upon him otherwise he might not have stepped forward and said, 'Who's there?'

Silence. The wood of the rafters creaked a little due to the suspended man. Nathaniel knew this was a different sound from what he thought he'd heard. He stepped forward towards the only thing from where the noise could have come: the Egyptian sarcophagus.

'Come out,' ordered Nathaniel, picking up a hammer that was sitting on the dressing table once used by the dead man. 'I have a weapon.'

Stealthily he approached the cabinet. Then with a sudden jerk of his arm he pulled the lid open.

The cabinet was empty.

1 Curtain Up

22 months later

Empire Theatre matinee performance, Brightmouth, October 1921

They didn't want him anymore. He could see it in their eyes. Worse. They could see it in *his*. It was painful. No, it was cruel. Once upon a time these gags would have had them rolling in the aisles. Perhaps that was the problem. He was still parlaying the same gags that he'd used a quarter of a century ago when music hall was king. Now it was variety. They said there was no difference, but Eddie Matthews knew otherwise.

Back then all he had to do was roll on stage. Didn't have to say a word. Just a look was all he needed. A bit of a dance and then a comic song. Had them in his hand he did. They stayed nestled in his palm for thirty years. Then it happened. That bloody war. The ones that came back were different. They didn't want what Eddie Matthews had. They wanted revues with their sketches and Eddie was no actor. They wanted monologues from front-of-cloth comics, not some old man singing old music hall favourites with a few gags thrown in for good measure. The men wanted filth, pure and simple. The women too. Sure they would pretend

'Come out,' ordered Nathaniel, picking up a hammer that was sitting on the dressing table once used by the dead man. 'I have a weapon.'

Stealthily he approached the cabinet. Then with a sudden jerk of his arm he pulled the lid open.

The cabinet was empty.

1 Curtain Up

22 months later

Empire Theatre matinee performance, Brightmouth, October 1921

They didn't want him anymore. He could see it in their eyes. Worse. They could see it in *his*. It was painful. No, it was cruel. Once upon a time these gags would have had them rolling in the aisles. Perhaps that was the problem. He was still parlaying the same gags that he'd used a quarter of a century ago when music hall was king. Now it was variety. They said there was no difference, but Eddie Matthews knew otherwise.

Back then all he had to do was roll on stage. Didn't have to say a word. Just a look was all he needed. A bit of a dance and then a comic song. Had them in his hand he did. They stayed nestled in his palm for thirty years. Then it happened. That bloody war. The ones that came back were different. They didn't want what Eddie Matthews had. They wanted revues with their sketches and Eddie was no actor. They wanted monologues from front-of-cloth comics, not some old man singing old music hall favourites with a few gags thrown in for good measure. The men wanted filth, pure and simple. The women too. Sure they would pretend to be shocked, yet no one laughed harder. Tarts, that's what they were.

Perhaps there was still some hope. He could see a few of them smiling. Bit older they were. Well they want filth. I'll give it to them. I've heard enough of it in my time. He glanced nervously to the side of the stage. Tristram Watts was standing there. He seemed sad rather than angry. Bert Cooper was downstairs in the changing rooms. He wouldn't hear this. To be precise, he wouldn't hear Eddie Matthews steal one of his jokes. Cooper hadn't used it in a while, and he probably bought it off another comic. If Cooper said something he'd offer him a few shillings; square him up.

An insincere smile broke out across Eddie's face. Beads of sweat were lining up like a firing squad on his forehead. Heart beating fast he launched into the gag.

'Here, sir,' said Eddie to an older gentleman near the front of the theatre. He was sitting with a woman who Eddie guessed was his wife. 'Are you married?'

'Yes,' came the reply.

'How long, sir?' asked Eddie, hopeful that he would get the right answer.

'Thirty-five years.'

This brought a few laughs and even some applause. Perfect. This was what he wanted. He had to hand it to young Cooper. The young man had good material. There were a few gags he could nick. Might freshen up the act a bit. Lord knows he needed to. This couldn't go on. Tristram Watts would have him out on his ear at this rate.

'Congratulations, sir. You'd have done less for murder,' said Eddie, looking knowingly at the audience.

A few laughs greeted this line. He'd improvised it on the spur of the moment. It was still there, he thought. Even the man and his wife were smiling.

'Why don't you stand up and tell us your name.'

The man seemed reluctant, but eventually he succumbed to some good-natured comments from the people around him or, perhaps, they were impatient for Eddie to be off and the next turn to arrive.

The man announced that he was called Fred. This news was greeted with a polite round of applause. Fred made a slight bow which brought a few laughs. It was going well. Eddie's mood, meanwhile, was somewhere between relief that things had improved and a sudden surge of hatred for young Cooper.

'Are you happy Fred?'

More laughter. Mostly men. Damn this material was good, thought Eddie. Fred glanced down at the woman beside him which brought more laughter and some hand claps. He nodded his head in an exaggerated fashion. Everyone was enjoying this. The laughs, while not loud, were sympathetic.

'You know,' said Eddie. 'I've been married nearly forty years too. Different women mind.' This brought a few laughs from the men, but the ladies seemed less impressed by this. 'I've been married to the present Mrs Matthews for twenty-one years. Couldn't be happier.'

A few women began smiling again but the laughter wasn't peaking.

'Of course that's because she left me two years ago.'

The music started up at this point which drowned out the sound of the very few laughs and some of the whistling. Bert Cooper had done this so much better. He hated

Cooper. Every step towards the wings, smiling at an audience he hated, arm outstretched, shaking his trilby in the air, was made hating these people, this theatre. He hated everyone and everything at this moment and then, to crown it all, Javier Gonzalo, the magician passed him and whispers, 'Another disaster, Eddie.'

Tristram Watts felt Eddie Matthews brush past him. He heard Gonzalo's malicious whisper and couldn't bring himself to look at the ageing comic. He suspected that Matthews would have kept his eyes fixed ahead anyway. This could go on no longer. As much as it pained him, Eddie Matthews was past it. Despite several warnings to find new material, Eddie would just sulk and drink and sulk some more. The problem with Eddie was exacerbated by Bert Cooper's effortless superiority, but this was also capsizing the show. With Bert Cooper hinting he wanted to leave already; it left him with only one comic performer, and he would lose his singer, Daisy Lewis. She and Bert were all but living together now. Where he went, she would go too. He couldn't blame either of them. Both would do well on the stage in London. Regional variety theatres were struggling with the arrival of moving pictures.

The Empire was struggling.

Javier Gonzalo was now on the stage to loud applause. Perhaps it was relief that Eddie was gone, thought Tristram sadly. His gaze fell upon the orchestra pit. He could see Hector Goulding, their ageing conductor. Just behind was the only other visible musician: his mother. Annie Watts' grey hair was tied up in a bun; her head jerked along to the rhythm of the music. The poor dear was utterly lost in the moment. How she loved music. How she loved the theatre. It had been her home for forty years or more.

How much longer, wondered her son? He turned his attention to Javier Gonzalo the undoubted star turn of the revue. Thankfully, he was showing no sign that he would leave. Where would they be without *him*?

The curtain Eddie Matthews had performed in front of had been raised to reveal a dark, brooding set with a ghost-grey fog clinging to the boards of the stage. Dominating the middle of the stage was an upright black cabinet. It looked like a large coffin.

A young woman dressed in a thin white shift appeared suddenly. Watts' gaze rested on the slender form of the young woman. She was a beauty and no mistake. While Gonzalo had a talent for illusion and genuine showmanship, the young woman certainly contributed to the act if only to keep the attention of the male audience members while Gonzalo went through his usual rigmarole. They were doing the *Spanish Inquisition* illusion for the first time. On the other side of the stage, Tristram saw Lucien Lemaire, the ventriloquist and Daisy Lewis looking on in curiosity.

Javier Gonzalo's eyes followed his beautiful assistant as she strolled past him onto the stage. His eyes weren't the only ones following her. Most of the audience did so too. This was deliberate. In fact, it was imperative. Misdirection was an important weapon in any magician's armoury. The audience was, almost certainly looking in the wrong place.

It was a lucky day for him the day he'd met Jane Anthony; lucky in more ways than one. He hoped they would share more than the stage soon. The signs were there. Persistence always pays, he thought. She was playing the part of a prisoner's lover, the two having been caught in the act of their illicit affair. Her dress captured everyone's attention; a white shift that fell to her knees. She was a good actress. The fear seemed all too real.

The orchestra struck up Gonzalo's signature tune, a slowed down *Paso doble* that the conductor, Hector Goulding, had heard while attending a bullfight in Madrid the previous year. Gonzalo did not like it much, but he had to admit that it captured the mood of his *Spanish Inquisition* illusion, and illusion was the only way to describe the trick. It was a variation of the old 'saw-the-lady-in-half'. Yet more than that. It fell into a number of magical categories including transportation, transformation, disappearance. It was a great illusion. He just wished he were able to come up with these. However, that skill lay with another, and he was dead.

The pace of the music was slow, the mood sombre. A man strode forward, dressed in the dark cape of a Grand Inquisitor. A large necklace with a crucifix dangled ominously around his neck. Underneath his large hat he wore a mask. Beside him was a guard, dressed as a Spanish soldier. The guard grabbed hold of Gonzalo and pushed him towards the sarcophagus-like black box with its golden trimmings. Then he tied Gonzalo's arms behind his back, put a gag around his mouth. Finally, a black hood was placed over Gonzalo's head.

Gonzalo played the part of a man who had been caught with Jane Anthony. He was no actor, but he managed to convey enough fear and outrage to be believable in his role, but it was Jane Anthony who had the main task of conveying the terror that the illicit lovers were feeling. Gonzalo made a token effort to struggle against his bindings but to no avail.

While all this was going on, the Grand Inquisitor said nothing. He merely directed proceedings with a wave of his arms causing his robe to flutter gracefully in the air. He radiated menace and hatred as he directed the soldier to place Gonzalo into the box. Gonzalo's lover protested in the dramatic manner of a silent movie actress, for no words were spoken. Jane Anthony was thrown to the floor by the guard. She looked on fearfully, powerless to prevent what would ensue.

The door of the box opened, and the terrified prisoner was thrown towards it. Gonzalo was forced into the box. The door closed to an almighty crash of percussion from the orchestra. Subtlety had never been Goulding's strong point, thought Gonzalo.

The pace of the *Paso doble* increased along with the tension. The Grand Inquisitor patrolled the area behind the box and then again appeared in front. He struck up dramatic poses in the manner of a bullfighter. The audience were all but booing him now, such was the level of malevolence emanating from him. The soldier disappeared and a few moments later a masked man in a white shirt appeared clutching a metal sheet with a wooden handle: the executioner had arrived.

The Grand Inquisitor strode forward to the box and opened a shutter near the top. It revealed the hooded man's head.

The executioner stepped forward.

The Grand Inquisitor waved his arms once more, sending his robes swirling around him like a whirlpool. The movement of his arms seemed to match those of Hector Goulding who was working the orchestra into a frenzy of noise that might once have been described as music but no longer. This was a visceral reading of the drama on stage.

The audience was gripped by the excitement of what they were seeing. Some of the members of the gentler sex screamed some women also. Lysander Benedict, theatre and arts critic for the local newspaper, gazed at the new illusion from Gonzalo with something approaching, but not quite reaching, a smile.

The executioner held up the sheet of metal. From his pocket he extracted an apple and threw it in the air. The metal flashed and seconds later the apple was lying in two pieces on the floor of the stage. This led to more screams. Lysander Benedict felt his pencil snap on the notebook he'd placed on his lap.

The Grand Inquisitor didn't so much walk behind the box as prance like a ballerina. The mist at the back of the stage was thicker than a London 'peasouper'. He reappeared and demanded through gesture that he take the metal sheet. The executioner was reluctant. They wrestled and the Grand Inquisitor prised it away from the executioner. The terrified young woman leapt to her feet to try and steal the murderous blade from the Grand Inquisitor. She was grabbed by the executioner and wrestled away into the wings leaving only the Grand Inquisitor and his caged prisoner.

This moment was to be his and his alone. Slowly and deliberately he put the metal sheet up to the box. He settled it into a slit in the side and then he thrust it forward with great force.

A gasp from the audience.

The black hooded head which had been visible to the audience throughout the act toppled forward and rolled towards the orchestra pit.

The theatre was in uproar. Screams filled the auditorium.

With the music at a crescendo, the Inquisitor swirled his robes and opened the door of the black box.

A headless figure stumbled forward; blood caked around the area where once a head had rested. The screams grew louder, drowning out the sound of the orchestra. The executioner reappeared and ran towards the black hooded head. He raised it up and began to pull the hood away.

'No,' came shouts from men in the audience, but they were ignored.

The black hood came off to reveal...

A lettuce.

The black hooded figure tore off his wide-brimmed hat to reveal Gonzalo. He, who only moments before had been imprisoned, had been transformed. The executioner, meanwhile, threw back his own hood to reveal that it was no longer a man, but Jane Anthony, the prisoner's lover.

The screams were now turning into applause and cheers and shouts of 'Bravo'.

Meanwhile, the headless figure rose from the ground like a spectre in the mist. To screams from the audience, it lurched forward. Then a head appeared.

It was Barney, the company dwarf.

The audience cheered the act to the rafters and Tristram Watts knew he had a hit on his hands. The only black spot on the horizon was the letters. Who was sending the vile threatening letters to everyone in the company?

2

The same day:

Sunningdale, October 1921

There comes a time in every chap's life when he must lay down his spear, or golf club and accept that it's time to return to the cave to take on the responsibilities of adding to the next generation. Charles 'Chubby' Chadderton was reaching just such an age and, frankly, it scared him.

A few of his pals had married this year: Kit had gone, 'Plum' Peters, 'Chips' Fry. Even 'Two Bob' Taylor had fallen by the wayside; the latter much to everyone's surprise, not least his own. He was still only thirty-one, yet a nagging doubt lay deep within him that either he was not marriage material or the young women he had spent time with of late were definitely not the settling down types. They were bright, they were young, and a good time was all they wanted. Chubby had reached that stage of wanting something more.

He sat glumly in the bar overlooking the eighteenth green and gazed at the foursome who were busy lining up their putts. It was a mixed foursome according to Rosie Whittington who was one of the four. He couldn't remember her exact words as he'd barely been listening.

This was, perhaps, another sign that Rosie was not the one for him. She loved golf. Chubby had once been a bit of a thrasher on the golf course, but the loss of his hand during a disagreement with a German grenade had put paid to his limited interest in the game. Gripping a golf club with a prosthetic hand did nothing for one's chipping.

He gazed at Rosie and wondered why he was less than stirred in the romantic department. She was certainly a looker, well made and tremendous fun; always the life and soul of any party even when there was no shindig to speak of. Her eyes sparkled with life, and they were directed towards Roger Fotheringhay, a six handicapper and a member of Sunningdale. He was her partner in the mixed foursomes' championship. For eighteen holes he had battered the ball around the course with a sickening malevolence. The word had reached Chubby that they were within touching distance of winning the competition.

Fotheringhay's handicap was rather like a yo-yo. It went up magically just before important club competitions, followed, post the inevitable victory, by a sharp descent in the manner of a skier racing an avalanche. At that moment he was pacing back and forward between ball and hole like an expectant father outside a delivery room.

The other couple on the green was Kit Aston and Gloria Fowles, formerly Mansfield. If anything she was even more attractive than Rosie and certainly a greater fanatic about golf. She was bent over a tricky four-footer which would have allowed Chubby an enjoyable few moments to absorb the pleasant sight of her generous disposition. At least it would have, had he not heard a young child scream in pain nearby.

Chubby turned just in time to see George Mansfield, the vile younger brother of Gloria, pulling a girl's pig tails. He missed Gloria sinking the putt. Chubby shook his head and was about to remonstrate with the young imp when he saw the husband of Gloria, Hugo Fowles, appear. His face was like thunder, as it usually was, when George came to stay with them. He caught Chubby's eye and rolled his own by way of response. Chubby sat back to enjoy what would be an entertaining and well-deserved clip round the ear for the devil child. However, his attention was diverted by the arrival of two young women.

Mary Aston shimmered into the bar, accompanied by, to Chubby's astonishment, his secretary, Miss Brooks. The two women waved to Chubby and then turned to one another in surprise. Chubby rose to his feet immediately as the young women headed towards him.

'I didn't know you knew Mary, Miss Brooks,' said Chubby, still somewhat dazed that she was at the golf club. 'Has some emergency cropped up at the office?' The office in question was the War Office in Whitehall where they both worked. Given that it was a Saturday, he couldn't quite imagine what the emergency could be.

If Chubby was confused by the arrival of his secretary, then Miss Brooks was no less taken aback.

'Oh no,' she replied, 'I was invited here today by Roger Fotheringhay. He's playing in the mixed foursomes.'

Chubby pointed to the eighteenth green, 'He's just finishing. He was playing with Kit. Sorry, how did you say you knew Mary?'

'We just met at the entrance,' said Mary Aston. 'Kate didn't know where to find the bar.'

'Kate?' said Chubby, somewhat stumped as if someone had randomly thrown a word of Swahili into a conversation about training dogs.

Mary turned to Miss Brooks and then back to Chubby, 'I rather had the impression you knew one another.'

'We work together,' explained Miss Brooks. 'I'm Mr Chadderton's secretary.'

'Ahh,' smiled Mary glancing from Chubby and then back to Miss Brooks.

'Yes, Miss Brooks and I have been working together for two years now.'

Just then two noises distracted them. They were rather different in nature, and worth dwelling on separately. From the direction of the green came a loud cheer. All eyes diverted immediately to the eighteenth green where, if the celebratory hug between Roger Fotheringhay and Rosie Whittington was any guide, evidently she had sunk a long putt that had travelled through at least two counties to reach its destination in the bottom of the hole, much to the evident satisfaction of both parties. A frown crossed the faces simultaneously of both Chubby and Miss Brooks. This was picked up by Mary.

'Do you know the name of the couple playing with Kit and Gloria?'

'Well that's Roger,' said Miss Brooks sourly.

'That's Rosie,' added Chubby in a voice that lacked its usual pep.

'Ahh,' replied Mary. She glanced at the couple on the green who were taking their celebration a little bit further than decorum, if not the rules of the Royal and Ancient, deemed acceptable in mixed foursomes. 'They seem rather pleased,' observed Mary, archly.

'Indeed,' said Chubby and Miss Brooks at the same time.

Just then, a second noise distracted the group from the joyful, if not indecorous, scenes on the green. Unseen by Mary, Chubby, Miss Brooks and most importantly, young George Mansfield, Hugo Fowles had been sneaking up on his brother-in-law in the manner of a Mohican on the warpath. After spying the young devil child pulling the hair of the young girl, Hugo Fowles was on a mission. He delivered the clip round the ear a few moments after Rosie Whittington's triumphant putt.

Young George gave a yelp and let forth a volley of words that were unlikely to have been learned from his sister. Hugo Fowles was many things, but he was not a hypocrite. There was only one place that George could have picked up such a colourful vocabulary. Hugo held his hands up to the club members who were now staring in shocked silence at the unfolding drama.

'Sorry,' said Hugo, attempting, then giving up on a smile, before snarling to the little so and so, 'Say sorry to this young girl.'

The young girl in question was Fleur Whittington, the younger sister of Rosie. She seemed somewhat unharmed by her experience and a cruel smile crossed her face as she stared at the red-faced humiliation of her tormentor. Fleur, despite only being eleven years old, was just the kind of girl who knew how to twist the knife further and twist it she would. Tears welled up in her blue eyes, a thumb was inserted in mouth; she then turned and ran over to a young, dark-haired boy to be comforted. Louis Pearson was George's arch enemy. He smiled at George and hugged Fleur.

George's misery was now complete. He glared at Hugo Fowles in a fury. Hugo lit a panatela cigar and shrugged his shoulders.

'She's a pretty young thing, isn't she?' said Hugo sporting a smile that was, if anything, even more malevolent than young Fleur's. 'Perhaps next time you want to impress a girl, George, you might try talking to her.'

With that piece of fatherly advice duly dispensed, he walked off leaving George to ponder on the mystery of the opposite sex and, more importantly, how he would extract revenge on the man his sister had been so ill-advised to marry.

'Sorry about that,' said Hugo joining Mary, Chubby and Miss Brooks. 'I rather think that Cupid's arrow has struck young George.'

'It seemed to land behind the ear,' pointed out Mary. She did not approve of violence on young children, even if it was George. She'd had previous experience with the brother of Gloria Mansfield so her sympathies were not all they might have been.

'Indeed,' agreed Hugo unabashed. He turned to Miss Brooks and held out his hand, 'I'm sorry. The name's Fowles. Hugo Fowles. My wife is on the green playing with Kit. Are you and Chubby together?' he asked, a smile crossing his face.

'Kate Brooks,' replied Miss Brooks shaking Hugo's hand. 'No, I came with Roger Fotheringhay.'

The group turned to the green where Fotheringhay and Rosie were walking off, holding hands, smiling keenly at one another. She was a rather spirited girl, noted Mary, not without approval. Such spirit when allied to an equal amount of good character could only produce a highly creditable result. Sadly, Rosie Whittington struck Mary as having a somewhat frivolous nature.

'Oh,' said Hugo. He glanced towards Mary for help.

Mary smiled and took Miss Brooks' arm. She said, 'Why don't you and I go and freshen up, Kate. Perhaps we can have a drink.'

Miss Brooks looked at Mary with some uncertainty. She asked, 'What about Roger?'

'Never mind Roger, I think you can do a lot better if you don't mind me saying.'

Mary glanced towards Chubby as she said this. This was noted by Miss Brooks who coloured a little. Despite the fact that Mary had said this in a voice loud enough to be picked up by Chubby and Hugo, it was inevitably missed by the two members of the dimmer sex. This led to a roll of the eyes from Mary. Miss Brooks chuckled, resignedly.

'Why do they make it such hard work?' sighed Mary.

'They are a mystery,' agreed Miss Brooks, but she was beginning to develop the distinct impression that a Fotheringhay-shaped bullet had been well and truly dodged.

Kit Aston's smile could not have been wider as he watched the trophy being presented to the winning couple in the mixed foursomes. The fact that it was not him mattered not. He'd had an enjoyable day on the golf course with Gloria Fowles. More importantly, he had not let the side down; they had finished a creditable third. They had played with the winning couple who had been inspired over the course of eighteen holes. No one could begrudge them the joy on their faces and the enormous hug they gave one another. No one, except Chubby and Miss Brooks that is. Kit had been alerted to the situation by Mary.

Throughout the round, he had assumed that his playing partners were together in a romantic sense given their overly enthusiastic celebration of good shots and sunk putts. It came as a surprise to hear that this was not the case. Mary's face by now was set to a frown and Chubby looked no happier. Miss Brooks, however, was smiling broadly which led Kit to wonder what, exactly, had passed between her and his wife when he'd found them sitting at the bar chatting like old friends. Now no one would ever have accused Kit Aston of being slow on the uptake but, in matters of the heart, he was perhaps no better or worse than any other chap in understanding the waves crashing around the ether.

But he got there in the end.

As he was looking at Miss Brooks two thoughts entered his consciousness simultaneously giving him a glow of satisfaction for having picked up on the machinations of a wife who had not so much sipped at the well of Jane Austen as gorged herself on it.

Miss Brooks was not wearing her usual spectacles. In all the time he had visited Chubby at the War Office, Miss Brooks had never been without her glasses. While Kit was in no way antagonistic to Salvino D'Armati's wonderful invention, or indeed their aesthetic appeal, the dimensions and thickness of the one's that Miss Brooks invariably sported had never been particularly flattering to her. Without them she was like a bird uncaged, a filly running free in the paddock. Etcetera. More importantly, she was clapping enthusiastically while standing beside a glum looking Chubby.

At this point Kit had no doubt that something was afoot. He just hoped that whatever Mary had planned, he would be able to, rather as he had today on the seventh, the ninth and a couple of the tricky par threes, keep his end up.

Presentation over, Mary went straight over to Chubby and Miss Brooks like a sprinter upon hearing the starter's pistol. Kit, who had been holding Mary's hand, was pulled along in the manner of a dog owner with a boisterous Labrador.

'Kate,' said Mary, 'are you feeling any better?'

All eyes turned to Miss Brooks who looked in the perfect vim of health. Her eyes widened like someone who had just remembered that they'd left the cooker on. Kit was now, at long last, on the same wavelength as his matchmaking wife.

'Yes, you do look rather under the weather,' added Kit, which prompted a delicate squeeze of the hand from Mary which augured well for later that evening. 'Perhaps you should consider returning home.'

Mary spun around to Kit, eyes narrowed and, it would be fair to say, the smile on her face and the love light in her eyes suggested that he should consider taking his wife away as quickly as propriety permitted. Mary turned back to Miss Brooks and said, 'Yes, Kit's right. I think that's just the ticket. Go home and wrap up warm.'

Chubby seemed thoroughly confused by what was happening. Miss Brooks had never looked better.

The penny had clearly not quite dropped. Mary decided to give matters another little push.

'Is the bus stop close by Miss Brooks?'

Miss Brooks hadn't the foggiest, as she had arrived in the caddish Fotheringhay's two-seater. Sensing that the poor woman had no earthly idea and was not fully up on where Mary was heading, Kit added, 'Yes, I think it's half a mile from the front entrance. You turn right, I believe.'

Just then, the greatest matchmaker of all, Mother Nature, decided to lend a hand. The skies opened up and rain began to hurtle down in Biblical quantities.

'I'm not sure I could leave Roger,' said Miss Brooks.

All eyes turned to Fotheringhay and Rosie who were basking all too visibly in the warm acclaim of victory. The gentleman in question was busy arranging the salt and pepper on a nearby table to demonstrate, with Rosie's assistance, how he'd got up and down from a tricky bunker. Chubby looked on unimpressed. He looked at Miss Brooks. She was even less enamoured with what she was seeing. Providentially, someone in the crowd suggested a photograph and the winning mixed foursome couple duly obliged by kissing while holding the ten-inch-high pewter award for their net seventy-three.

'I think you can leave him, don't you, Miss Brooks?' said Kit, looking on, with an unusually high level of disapproval on his face.

'But the rain?' said Miss Brooks with a voice that was halfway between hopeful and a shrug. You can lead a horse to water and all that; Chubby seemed not to be drinking from the fountain of romance. To be fair to Kit's friend, he was witnessing his delightful-looking date for the day being stolen from him by the suave six handicapper. This was enough to send any chap into a spiral of despair.

'Chubby,' said Mary suddenly, as if an idea had just arrived, unbidden, but nonetheless welcome, into her head. 'Perhaps you could give Miss Brooks a lift to the bus stop.' She laid particular emphasis on the words 'bus stop' and only just managed to stop a sardonic curl of her lip appearing. There would be a conversation with her husband later that evening with a subject something along the lines of 'Why are men so dense?'

Rain was battering the clubhouse window like a volley of machine guns on a shooting range. Roger Fotheringhay and Rosie appeared to have relinquished all restraint, egged on by the members and, suddenly, for the first time, Chubby was actually seeing Miss Brooks in a new and not unfavourable light.

'No, Miss Brooks,' said Chubby in a decisive manner. 'I shall not have you standing in the rain waiting for a bus. I shall take you home.'

Goodbyes were hastily said. Just as Miss Brooks was about to inform Fotheringhay that she was leaving, she spied Mary shaking her head and, with her eyes, directing her to the exit. That emboldened her. Moments later, Chubby whisked her away. Miss Brooks turned back long enough to see Mary giving her the thumbs up.

On their way out of the clubhouse, the possibly newly formed couple passed a rather desolate young boy, sitting on a seat outside in the rain. He was alone. The water falling in rivulets down his face was not solely the result of the torrential rain that had so suddenly descended upon this upscale slice of Berkshire.

Young George Mansfield was reflecting sadly on an afternoon that, like so many others he had experienced in his short life, had gone disastrously wrong. In a manner not unlike Chubby, he had borne witness to seeing a young girl taking his heart and cruelly stamping upon it in a highly public fashion. Perhaps for the first time he was reflecting not only on the perfidious nature of fate, but also on the possibility that he was the author of his own misfortune. Could it really be that pulling the pigtails of the newly discovered love of your life was not the ideal prelude to declaring one's feelings?

He stood up and trooped to the clubhouse window and stared dolefully inside. Sitting together at a table was Fleur Whittington and that hateful wretch, Louis Pearson. They were chatting animatedly, at least Fleur was. Louis' face had taken on that mask that most chaps must wear when listening to the one they love, talk at them. Young George, dreadfully inexperienced in matters of the heart, desperately wished that it were he who was listening to the tender words being spoken by that beautiful young princess.

In some respects, had it not been raining, Louis Pearson might have been up for swapping places with George because, by this stage, Fleur's incessant chatter was driving him to distraction. However, he caught sight of his rival looking so abjectly bedraggled outside. All at once, a cruel smile uncurled on Louis' face like a cobra emerging from a basket. He took Fleur's hand and stared into her eyes, listening to every word as if his life depended on it. When she finally paused for breath and, Lord knows, she had the lungs of a deep-sea pearl diver, he pointed to George standing outside. Fleur turned around and George's humiliation was complete.

George did the only thing that any sensible young chap would do in such a situation. He raised his hand and replicated the two-finger salute that legend tells us emanated from the English archers taunting their French rivals at the Battle of Agincourt. Fleur's eyes widened in shock, while Louis' countenance became as dark as the clouds overhead.

Whatever satisfaction George could draw from this moment was short-lived, however. To his right he heard a shriek from a young woman.

'George, what are you doing? Where have you been? We've been looking for you everywhere.'

It was his sister, Gloria. Given the fact that she was clutching a gin and tonic, to George's embittered eyes, it suggested the search had been restricted to the confines of the clubhouse bar. Standing with Gloria was that hateful beast Hugo Fowles. What had ever persuaded his sister to marry this man Lord only knew. Fowles seemed more amused than angry which, at least, suggested that nemesis would not come in the form of another clip around the ear.

George trooped over towards the couple. He was thoroughly soaked to the skin and utterly miserable. Despite his relatively tender age, he had long-since learned to shut out the lamentations of his sister when he had strayed from the path of the righteous. Gloria's free hand grabbed George's and yanked him towards the clubhouse.

As they climbed up the steps George felt a hand stray onto his shoulder. It was Hugo Fowles. For once he was not dispensing rough justice.

'Don't worry old chap. I'm not sure she was worth it,' murmured Hugo.

George looked up at his brother-in-law. Hugo seemed in earnest and, incredibly, not unsympathetic. They nodded to one another and entered into the clubhouse to the sound of the members chanting, 'kiss her, kiss her.'

It seemed apt at that moment, but George no longer cared.

3

Waterloo Station, October 1921

The train shunted suddenly causing Kit and Mary to jerk forward. It was early afternoon on the day after the golf competition. They were sitting in a train carriage at Waterloo station bound for the south coast. Having arrived in good time, they were sitting opposite one another by the window which was their favoured spot; it offered Kit a chance to stare at Mary for a couple of hours, an activity that never lost its appeal. Mary, while by no means immune to Kit's good looks, was anticipating indulging in one of her favourite train games: *who is the murderer?* The train departed. Soon, Waterloo station slowly began to recede into the distance.

'I hope you are not going to play that silly game,' said Kit, as they heard the sound of people in the train corridor.

'Can I remind you that we are embarking on a journey to the south coast to prevent a murder?' pointed out Mary, one eyebrow raised to full sardonic effect.

'Yes, I do wish Rufus had been a bit more forthcoming on what was going on.'

The train door opened, and an elderly woman entered followed by a middled-aged man with a dignified bearing that suggested a cleric.

Mary's eyes narrowed perceptibly, and Kit groaned inwardly.

A younger man entered the compartment, spied Mary and was about to plonk himself down beside her when the elderly lady beat him to the punch. He chose, instead, to sit near Kit which offered the best opportunity to attract the attention of the lovely young woman by the window. Mary groaned inwardly. She glanced at Kit and saw a look of triumph cross his face. It was clear he would not lift a finger to help her if the young buck began early attempts at mating. She would have to nip it in the bud, but this would put an end to her game.

Just then a nun entered the compartment. Mary's eyes widened and she nodded in quiet satisfaction to Kit who merely rolled his eyes.

'Is this seat free?' asked the nun. She sat beside the young man which caused a smile from Mary which she instantly regretted. The young man caught her eye, and a bond was sealed. He believed he had an ally. This would not do. Mary leaned forward, put her hand on Kit's knee and said, 'Darling, would you mind getting me my book, you know, the one on nineteenth century German poetry.'

Mary produced this ace unexpectedly much to Kit's evident dismay. It was a clever move, he conceded. Nothing was guaranteed to extinguish the love light in any man's eye more than the prospect of a young woman with an interest in any verse, never mind poetry from Germany. Sure enough by the time Kit had coldly informed her that he'd forgotten to pack it, the young man had unfolded his newspaper and begun to read the financial pages. There was always fun to be had in watching Mary rebuff love struck suitors, even in train carriages, alas this was not to be. Then providence offered Kit a compensatory gift.

'You read German poetry?' asked the nun of Mary. 'I do so love Goethe.'

Kit's eyes widened in a joy certainly not matched by Mary. Kit rose from his seat and excused himself from the carriage, just reaching the door in time before he broke out into semi-hysterical laughter.

But, laughter, they say, often comes before tears. Like Sock and Buskin, the two ancient symbols of comedy and tragedy, they coexist in an uneasy relationship. First came the comedy; tragedy awaited them as they sat on the train to the south coast.

To say the Empire Theatre had seen better days was like saying General Custer was a bit undermanned at the Little Big Horn. In addition, the overall air of gentle dilapidation was never going to be added to by the presence of policemen standing outside stopping onlookers from entering the building.

Kit and Mary's journey to the south coast town of Brightmouth had taken a couple of hours. Rather than travel to their hotel, they went straight to the theatre where they expected to meet the police artist Rufus Watts and his family, who owned the theatre. According to Rufus, the performers in the new revue had recently been sent vile letters threatening exposure for some unnamed crime.

'I fear we may be a little late,' murmured Kit as the taxi drew up outside the theatre. Despite the evidence that it was not enjoying its finest hour, the theatre still evoked a sense of nostalgia for both Kit and Mary. The theatre recalled another time; a time that had gone and would never come back; a time that had probably never existed in the first place, but Kit could recognise it, sense it, hear it and he felt unaccountably sad.

A large sign over the oak doors comprising of dozens of light bulbs proclaimed that this was indeed the 'Empire Theatre'. The building dated back to eighteen forty; it was made from red brick with stucco rendering around the edges.

'Let's find out what happened,' said Mary emerging from the taxi.

This would be less of a problem than actually being able to gain admittance to the building which was surrounded by a throng of people. Kit wandered over to a well-dressed man and made an inquiry on what was causing the commotion. Mary watched him chat to the man for a few minutes before returning with sad news.

'We are too late. The gentleman says there was a tragedy at the evening show last night.'

Mary Aston's attitude to death had formed a few years previously when she worked as a nurse near the front during the War. While not quite inured to its heartbreak, she had developed an ability to feel simultaneously both sympathy for the victim and family while avoiding any reflected trauma. Mary was no stranger to tragedy herself. She had lost both her parents during the War and just two years previously, her grandfather.

Kit and Mary's eyes met. If the tragedy was connected to the letters then it was possible they were looking at a murder. Their reactions could not have been more different. Kit had hoped that this undertaking would involve a couple of days on the south coast investigating the threatening letters which he was convinced would end the moment that the Watts family was being seen to act. He had not considered them to be genuine. The realisation that someone had lost their life while he had been at Sunningdale did not sit easily with him. Could this life have been saved had he and Mary come earlier?

Such thoughts, he realised, were absurd. He had not murdered anyone therefore no fault lay at his door. Yet the idea that a death could have been prevented gripped him. Mary seemed to read his mind. She took his hand and fixed her eyes on his.

'There's nothing we could have done. The murderer would have found a way with or without our presence.'

Kit smiled sadly. He knew Mary was right, but he felt troubled all the same. He looked around the crowd to see if there was a face that he might know, such as Rufus Watts. Instead, he saw someone else although he was not sure if this was a welcome development or not.

'Good Lord,' said Mary, whose eyes had also picked up on the same tall figure. 'Isn't that...?'

'Sergeant Wellbeloved,' said Kit in the manner of a child that has discovered his Christmas present is a pair of socks rather than a Hornby train. The man in question was tall, skinny, cadaverous, with a mouth set permanently to sneer and these were his good points. Less enchanting was his laughter which sounded like a witch cackling over a cauldron. This was a consequence of his chain-smoking which was all too visible in the nicotine-stained fingers. These same fingers had often gripped the throats of suspects who were proving less than amenable during interrogations. All in all, he was not a man who made friends easily.

Oddly, Kit did not entirely dislike him as he once had. Wellbeloved was a complex individual, and it would have been a disservice to judge him solely on the manner of his appearance. He had proven dogged and reliable, in an unreliable way, in other cases. He was a man to treat with utmost caution. However, they needed access to the theatre. Needs must, as they say.

'Sergeant Wellbeloved,' called out Kit.

Wellbeloved spun around to find the source of the voice. He seemed angry which, while not unusual, did surprise Kit. He did not remember parting with him on bad terms the last time they'd met. Then he was able to focus on Kit. The face softened. Marginally.

Kit took Mary's hand to lead her over to the man from Scotland Yard.

'Sergeant Wellbeloved,' said Kit, 'This is a surprise.'

'It's Detective Inspector now, sir,' said Wellbeloved, nodding at a police constable to allow the couple through the cordon which stretched around the front of the theatre. He led them away from the crowd.

'Rufus Watts asked us to investigate a matter involving threatening letters. Am I right in guessing we are a little bit late?'

Wellbeloved rarely smiled for the very good reason that his teeth were, if anything, even more stained than his fingers. As a result he tended to smirk which hardly enhanced his features. Smirk duly delivered, he raised his eyebrows and said, 'Yes, matters took a turn for the worse, at last night's show.'

'During the show?' asked Kit.

'During the show,' confirmed Wellbeloved. 'I'll take you to Chief Inspector Jellicoe. I think he's expecting you.'

Mary and Kit turned to one another in surprise. Perhaps it was not such a surprise Chief Inspector Jellicoe was there or that he knew they were coming. Rufus Watts, who was the police artist at Scotland Yard, would, unquestionably, have been the reason.

Wellbeloved took them through the glass-fronted doors at the front of the theatre into the marble-floored foyer. Standing with another policeman was a man who looked like a younger, plumper version of the slender Rufus Watts. Kit and Mary immediately guessed that this was the brother of the police artist. Beside him was an elderly woman who, in many respects, reminded Kit of his Aunt Agatha in terms of her age, her hair style, her physical dimensions. One obvious difference was the kindly smile that appeared to be a permanent feature on her face. This is not to say that Aunt Agatha was severe, she was that and more, but she mixed severity with a large dose of irritability, a mind sharper than a samurai's sword and a giant heart.

Kit surveyed the foyer. It was large with a ticket office on the left and walls adorned with posters advertising performances, that appeared to go back to the Victorian era. Despite having just arrived, the theatre was already casting its spell on Kit and Mary. It restored the feeling of being a child once more and drew them, willingly, into a magical make-believe world that engaged their minds, their hearts and their imagination.

The entrance of Wellbeloved along with Kit and Mary was noted by Jellicoe. He nodded to Mrs Watts and her son before walking over to join the new arrivals. His face was grave, but then it usually was. A handlebar moustache that was scarcely fashionable fifty years ago adorned his face. This gave his features a forlorn cast and did little to counteract the resemblance he bore to King George V. He was around forty years of age, a little bit shorter than Kit and, notwithstanding the heavy tweed overcoat, quite slender.

He shook hands with Kit and Mary before saying, 'We were expecting you. Rufus told me you were coming. It looks like we were too late to have stopped this tragedy.'

'What happened Chief Inspector?' asked Mary.

'Come with me into the theatre please. I'll show you.'

4

Chief Inspector Jellicoe led Kit and Mary through a set of double doors into the stalls of the auditorium. The theatre interior was smaller than many that Kit had been to in London, but no different in its layout; it was typical of the hundreds that had been built during the Victorian age.

The stalls comprised around twenty rows of seats with a staircase running either side. Above them, in a horseshoe shape, were the boxes, including a royal box near the stage, which was perhaps a triumph of hope over expectation. Above the boxes, were benches for the cheaper seats which ran along the sides and offered a progressively more restricted view as you neared the stage.

Soaring columns either side of the stage directed the eye to the ornamental work around the ceiling, parts of which were gold. Chips in the paintwork were all too visible. As they neared the steps at the side of the stage, Kit turned around. Directly facing the stage at the centre of the horseshoe was an alto-relief of Tragedy and Comedy. Tragedy and tragedy would have been more appropriate thought Kit, as they climbed up onto the stage.

The stage was bare save for the ominous-looking box which stood upright in the centre of the stage; this was where Javier Gonzalo had met his end. Jellicoe stared at the dark box and then looked meaningfully towards Kit and

Mary. It was clear, notwithstanding his previous experience with the young woman, that the chief inspector remained uncomfortable talking about murder in front of Mary.

'Is this where Mr Gonzalo met his death?' asked Mary, deciding to get matters onto a business footing. Her eyes were bright and inquisitive. Any further reservations melted away in the policeman.

'It is,' confirmed Jellicoe.

'He's now with the great magician in the sky,' added Wellbeloved mirthlessly and to no one's amusement except his own. Jellicoe glanced irritably at the detective inspector. This left Wellbeloved unmoved.

Kit and Mary walked around the box. A quick glance towards Jellicoe was met with a nod so Kit stepped towards the box and opened the lid at the front. He could see signs of dusting where the fingerprints had been lifted.

The interior of the box was much smaller than one would have expected from looking at the outside. It was well over six feet tall, yet the inside wood panelling meant that the interior height was around five feet ten. The bloodstains around the interior were unmissable and Mary wisely refrained from standing inside, despite her curiosity. Instead, she fixed her attention on the outside of the box on the point at which the blade would enter. Kit did the same from the interior. Their eyes met either side through the slit which was around an inch high. Kit turned around to view the slit on the other side. Then, he stepped back out of the box and knelt down to examine the floor.

The area beneath the box was clearly visible when he knelt down. There was an open trap door in the floor. Mary joined him in examining it. Kit's only comment was, 'I often wondered if it was something like this.'

Standing up, Kit turned to Jellicoe and asked, 'Perhaps you should tell us the grizzly details Chief Inspector.'

Jellicoe coughed and frowned. One more look towards Mary was greeted with a reassuring smile. Just as he was about to speak, they were interrupted by the sound of people entering the auditorium. It was a familiar voice.

'Ahh,' said Rufus Watts, walking towards the stage. 'I heard that you'd arrived.'

Rufus Watts was slight of dimension, enormous of ego. It was all but impossible to miss him. He wore his hair a little longer than fashion suggested advisable, his suit was a light grey with a pink shirt and a yellow bow tie. He modelled himself on the great American artist from the previous century, James Whistler both in how he dressed and his waspish sense of humour. Kit and Mary adored him.

The people on the stage watched him as he skipped along the passage by the side of the stalls. The only sound in the theatre at that moment was the clip of his cane along the floor. The cane in question had an ornate silver handle. On a previous case, it was revealed to double up as a slim swordstick rather like one Kit owned. Rufus Watts had found it to be very useful many times over the years, when his flamboyant lifestyle had placed him in precarious situations; he was a more than capable fencer when occasion required.

The little police artist made his way, quickly, up the steps and onto the stage. He exchanged kisses on both cheeks with Mary and then shook hands with Kit.

'I hope this vile murder hasn't proven too distressing for you,' said Rufus.

'I shall manage I'm sure,' said Mary.

'I was thinking of your husband, darling,' replied Rufus drily. 'Now where were we?'

'The Chief Inspector was about to tell us what happened last night. Were you here, Rufus?'

'I saw everything,' verified Rufus. 'In fact, though I say so myself, I managed the scene rather well until the police arrived. There's no question that this is no accident. Thankfully, the chief inspector concurred when I rang him last night. He came immediately.'

'Always at your command, Rufus,' murmured Jellicoe which prompted smiles in Kit and Mary.

'I trust, Chief Inspector, that you will not prevent his lordship casting his eye over these events. My mother and brother need this matter cleared up quickly. The future of the theatre depends on it,' said Rufus. For once his tone was grave.

Jellicoe and Rufus exchanged glances. There was a curt nod, and the matter was settled. The tense atmosphere was broken momentarily when everyone's eyes were diverted by a rather uncommon sight near the front of the stage in the stalls. A black and white cat came walking along the passage across from where Rufus and the others had walked. It appeared to be holding a large, rather dead, rat in its mouth. It disappeared into the orchestra pit.

'That's Romeo,' explained Rufus. 'The theatre cat.'

'He seems quite accomplished at his job,' observed Kit.

'Yes, he is,' agreed Rufus, 'Certainly he's the best we've ever had, although Othello was no slouch either.'

A moment of silent homage to the memory of the former occupant of the theatre cat position followed before Mary decided to move matters along.

'So, Chief Inspector, you were about to tell us what happened last night,' said Mary, eyebrows raised.

Jellicoe smiled at Mary and bowed slightly in acknowledgement. He said, 'Perhaps Mr Watts should do so. After all, he was here last night; he is one of our key witnesses.'

'I shall be happy to,' said Rufus. 'I'll start from when that risible so-called comedian left the stage...'

5

The Previous evening:

Empire Theatre, October 1921

The applause was muted or perhaps it was the sound of a few boos scattered around in the crowd. Rufus Watts cast his eyes in the direction of rows in the circle to see where they had come from. As far as he could tell, they were dispersed at different points in the audience. His heart sank as he took in the reaction. He glanced towards his mother who was in a slightly elevated position in the orchestra pit seated at a baby grand piano. Her face was troubled by what she heard; a face that rarely wore anything other than a smile. Rufus smiled sympathetically to her, but he was troubled.

More than troubled, he was angry. Very angry indeed. He had heard from Tristram that Eddie Matthews was complaining to him that they were out to get him. What might have been the lame excuse of a comedian long past his best rang true to Rufus. They were out to get him. But not just him. They were coming after Tristram and his mother and this was not acceptable. Kit and Mary could not come soon enough to look into this matter, and he knew exactly where the source of the problem lay. He turned to gaze up at a man sitting next to the Royal Box.

The man in question was Billy Benson. He was around the same age as Rufus Watts, which is to say he would never see forty again. His dark suit was expensive; his hair swept back from his high forehead and a pencil thin moustache hung lamely over his top lip. He wore a broad grin as if every word of Eddie Matthews had given him immense pleasure. Rufus did not doubt that he'd loved every part of the act and why wouldn't he? After all, he wanted nothing more than the Empire Theatre to fail. Eddie Matthews was just the man to help it on its inevitable journey to the graveyard of theatres. With each passing year, the number of variety theatres was diminishing, while the number of moving pictures houses grew.

Billy Benson owned the nearby Palace Picture House. He had converted it from a theatre when the boom in moving pictures had begun during the war. It was the best decision of his life. The soldiers returning home from the trenches wanted to laugh at Charlie Chaplin and Buster Keaton or be thrilled by Douglas Fairbanks or Tom Mix. People like Eddie Matthews had never been funny at the best of times and now they seemed like dinosaurs on the point of extinction.

Rufus glared at Benson until, as if he sensed the hatred emanating from the stalls, the picture house owner glanced down and met his eyes. Benson smiled cruelly before offering a military salute as if dismissing a junior officer. In some senses he was. Rufus knew as well as Benson that the Empire Theatre was on its last legs. Without an influx of cash or a smash hit show they were months, if not weeks, away from closing their doors for the last time.

Rufus tore his eyes away from Benson as he heard the moody Paso doble being struck up by the orchestra. This was the act that he had come to see. Tristram had literally bet the house on this new magician, Javier Gonzalo. When Rufus had arrived earlier, Tristram was almost in tears with relief and excitement at what he'd seen in the matinee performance earlier that day and the manner in which it had been acclaimed by the audience.

The theatre was only as good as the acts performing and Javier Gonzalo was from the very top of the profession, or soon would be. Something would have to be done about Eddie Matthews though, but Rufus also suspected foul play with regard to the unfunny funny man. There was no question, they were out to get him. He was the weak link in the show and Billy Benson had his men in the audience giving Matthews the bird. Rufus had no doubt that Benson was also the source of the vile letters that had circulated around the cast of performers. Thank goodness Kit and Mary were due to arrive tomorrow.

The curtain was up now to reveal a dark stage with a threatening mist clinging to the stage and a single black box standing upright like a Satanic tombstone. He settled back and felt himself relax as he watched the fog swirl around the malevolent-looking cabinet in the middle of the stage. A masked man in a black cape appeared. Gonzalo followed, dressed in a white shirt and breeches. With him was a beautiful, young and scantily dressed woman wearing a white shift. Rufus recognised a hit when he saw one. He began to feel both better, but also nervous as the drama onstage unfolded. Rufus could not see his brother, but he had no doubt that he would be standing in the wings as usual; a mother hen overseeing her chicks.

His mother, meanwhile, was lost in the music. Her head swayed from side to side as she bashed the piano keys dramatically. Tears welled up in his eyes as he thought of her and her lifelong love affair with theatre. He would make it his mission to ensure that they would never lose this theatre.

The prisoner had now been gagged, tied up and a hood placed over his head. Soon he was in the box. There seemed to be genuine terror in the eyes of his assistant. She could certainly act, thought Rufus, impressed. Meanwhile, Gonzalo was displaying his acting props. The black box had been spun around to reveal that the magician was now in the box with a black hood over his head. He was moving from side to side and even above the music Rufus could almost imagine the sound of him kicking the box.

The executioner had made a great play of slicing through the apple. Seconds later the blade had been wrestled from him. By now, the audience was in a frenzy. The drama seemed all too real. The head inside the box was jerking from side to side. Probably some clockwork mechanism, imagined Rufus.

As the audience screams grew louder, several things happened at once. The executioner who had wrestled Gonzalo's lover away from the Grand Inquisitor came back on stage followed by the actress and a dwarf. It was if they were trying to stop the execution.

Rufus had not been given advance warning of what happened in the act. He had wanted to enjoy the surprise and thrill as it happened. This felt wrong. It was as if something in the illusion had gone wrong. He rose to his feet. The whole audience was on its feet.

Too late.

The blade sliced through the box and completed its deadly business to the crash of cymbals from an orchestra who were unaware of what had taken place above them on stage.

6

'The black-hooded head came rolling towards the orchestra pit. I think they must have stopped playing at that point because all I could hear were screams,' said Rufus Watts in conclusion.

There were a few moments of silence and then all eyes turned to the deadly black box still dominating the centre of the stage.

'How horrible. The poor man' replied Mary which probably summarised well what everyone was thinking.

Kit walked over to the box once more. Kneeling down he took a brief look at the castors fixed to the bottom before rising. Then with a brief glance in the direction of Jellicoe, which was met with a nod, Kit rolled the black box away to examine the trap door or, to be more precise, the hatch through which Javier Gonzalo had intended escaping.

Mary joined him in staring down. A chute led down to the dark area underneath the stage. The illusion certainly seemed a lot less magical now. Kit returned to the large box to inspect, once more, the interior.

'So if I'm right, ' he announced, 'Gonzalo enters the cabinet. While all of the spinning is going on, he has quickly freed himself from his loosely tied bonds. He places a lettuce disguised in a hood on a shelf to make it seem like it is someone's head. He was then meant to open the trap door in the box, which obviously opened outwards as there is no room to move inside. He would slide down the chute underneath the stage where he would quickly change into the Grand Inquisitor's costume. Then he would rush up onto the stage to take the place of the actor who was wearing that costume. Presumably, the other performers were providing some form of misdirection while all of this was going on.'

Jellicoe nodded as did Watts.

'The act concluded with Gonzalo revealing himself as the Grand Inquisitor, Jane Anthony, his assistant becomes the executioner and Barney, a dwarf, steps out of the cabinet,' finished Jellicoe.

'What became of the two men who were on the stage with Gonzalo?' asked Kit.

'The soldier and the executioner were played by the two members of an acrobat act, the Monteverdis - Gian Luca Monteverdi and Enrico Monteverdi,' explained Jellicoe. 'The only person to touch the cabinet during the illusion is Enrico Monteverdi. He plays the soldier and then the executioner. His role is to spin the cabinet around on its castors to show the audience that it is solid on all sides. Then, I believe, it comes to rest facing the audience who see the open hatch and the hooded head. The prisoner uses his foot to press down a small, tilted mirror at the front which fills the gap between the cabinet and the castor wheels. This hides the fact that he is about to escape from the box into the chute. The audience think they are seeing the floor of the stage when in fact it a mirror is reflecting it back to them. Rather clever.'

Kit walked around the cabinet and then moved it back to its original spot. Then he turned to Chief Inspector

Jellicoe and said, 'So the only people on stage at any point before the tragedy were Gonzalo, Miss Anthony and the Monteverdi brothers?'

'Yes, during the act,' replied Jellicoe. 'Whenever Barney saw that the hatch door from the cabinet had not opened, he realised that Gonzalo was in danger.

'And who was underneath the stage? You mentioned Barney. Anyone else?' asked Kit.

'According to Barney there were a couple of other people with him. Eddie Matthews descended the same steps that Gonzalo was meant to use having just finished his act, so he was there. The ventriloquist, Lucien Lemaire, was there too, near the door that leads to the greenroom,' said Jellicoe. 'He was the next act to follow Gonzalo after the intermission.'

Kit glanced towards Mary who was desperately trying not to catch his eyes. Mary had long held a view that ventriloquists were a little mad and susceptible to schizophrenia. She had absolutely no evidence to support this, but the lack of such particulars in no way held her back, or Aunt Agatha, who agreed with her on this topic.

'It seems strange that he was below stage if there was an intermission,' observed Kit.

Jellicoe nodded at this and seemed to be taking a mental note to ask Lemaire why indeed he had been there at that time.

'What about the orchestra?' asked Kit. 'Are they able to access the area underneath the stage?'

'They can, through a door,' said Jellicoe, 'But no one left the orchestra pit after the performance began. This means they would not have been able to effect any act that could lock Gonzalo in the cabinet.'

'I see,' said Kit. 'Who wheeled the cabinet on stage originally, before the curtain went up?'

'Gonzalo and Gian Luca Monteverdi. They did this while Eddie Matthews was performing...'

'Dying you mean,' said Rufus Watts. This was met with a frown from Jellicoe, but the Chief Inspector was well used to the waspish humour of the Scotland Yard police artist. 'Performing on stage,' continued Jellicoe. 'He is what is known as a front of cloth comic. He stands near the audience, just above the orchestra pit. Behind him is one of the curtains, not the main one. His act allows the stage to be set up behind the curtain. In this case, it was Gonzalo and Monteverdi. Miss Anthony was in the wings but did not touch the cabinet at any point in the moments before the act began.'

'Shall we go underneath the stage?' asked Mary. 'I'd rather like to see what it's like down there.'

This eminently sensible suggestion was greeted with nods and the group went towards the side of the stage and down a spiral staircase that led directly underneath. It was an area with no natural light except from the hatch above them which opened directly under the cabinet. Wellbeloved led the way as he was familiar with the area now. He found the light switch and soon there was a dim glow from a bulb. It revealed quite a large space with a door at one end and a fire escape at the other. There were a number of boxes and chairs dotted around the area. In the centre was the chute. It was around three feet long and allowed a rapid exit from the trap door in the stage.

Kit turned to Jellicoe just to confirm rather than ask, 'And this hatch was always open.'

'Yes,' replied Jellicoe. 'The stage trap door was open. This was confirmed by Barney, Matthews and Lemaire. Gonzalo was trapped inside the cabinet by the fact that his escape door would not open when he released the catch.'

'But at the moment, the only thing that makes us think that a murder may have taken place is the fact that threatening letters were sent to all the performers. Is it possible this may have been a tragic accident and that the two matters are utterly unrelated?' asked Kit.

'It was no accident,' said Rufus firmly. 'I'm sure of it.'

'I'm inclined to agree with Mr Watts,' said Jellicoe. 'We examined the cabinet this morning. The latch works well enough. We tested it a few times. At the moment, we have no idea why it did not work during the illusion.'

'Is it possible that when they wheeled the cabinet on, that it was not positioned perfectly over the opening in the stage. That would have stopped the door on the inside opening,' suggested Mary.

'No,' said Jellicoe. 'There is a latch on the stage that fixes the cabinet in place. The audience cannot see it, but the people on stage can. Also, I believe Barney would have given the alert earlier had he seen that the cabinet was not perfectly aligned to the chute.'

'Assuming he's not the murderer,' said Mary.

'This we will establish, but there were at least two checks, from those above, on stage and Barney below, regarding the positioning of the cabinet. They would all have to be in league for this murder to be accomplished successfully,' said Jellicoe before adding, 'We are not ruling this out, of course, but I find it unlikely.'

'Where are the other performers now?' asked Mary.

'They are staying at Mrs Harrison's Theatrical Digs,' said Rufus Watts. 'None of the performers are from the area.'

'May I see the statements from the people you've questioned,' asked Kit.

Jellicoe nodded. There was some hesitation in his manner. Although he liked and admired Kit Aston, he was still policeman enough to resent slightly the involvement of someone from outside the force in any investigation. Yet it could not be denied that they had worked well together in the past and they could not afford to prolong their inquiries. Quite aside from the potential risk of another murder, albeit a low one in his view, there was the need to re-open the theatre. The Watts family could not afford for the theatre to remain closed indefinitely. Unquestionably, Kit Aston would be a useful ally no matter what.

'We can furnish you with the statements,' confirmed Jellicoe. 'How would you like to proceed?'

Kit glanced at Mary before saying, 'Perhaps Mary and I could retire to our hotel. We can re-join you later and meet your family, Rufus. After that I'd like to meet the performers so that I can understand more about what happened.'

Mary frowned at this. Eyes narrowed she said, 'Do you mean, we, not I?'

Kit smiled to Mary. He loved the fact that she had immediately picked up on how he had expressed the next step of the plan. She was his equal in every way, yet society still denied her the opportunities that men took for granted. What a waste, thought Kit.

An idea had formed which involved Mary. Whilst he would not insist she do as he bid; it was difficult to escape such an implication. Mary could choose what she would do. That would never change in their marriage. The trick was piquing her curiosity enough so that it removed any objection in her mind. That process had already started and would continue, under various nefarious means, back at the hotel. All was fair in love and amateur detection...

'I think we should talk about that, my dear, back at the hotel,' said Kit with a grin.

'The answer's no,' said Mary, but she was half-laughing as she said this.

'You don't know what I'm about to suggest.'

'I think I do,' said Mary with a wicked grin.

'It may not be needed darling, but I think we should at least give ourselves this option.'

'No.'

Rufus Watts' patience was not considered among his best qualities. Therefore it was of little surprise when he interrupted Kit and Mary with the question on everyone else's mind.

'What in Heaven's name are you talking about?' he asked exasperatedly.

'I was merely suggesting to Mary that she may need to join the cast of the revue,' replied Kit. 'Live cheek by jowl with the performers.'

'Working undercover,' said Rufus giving a slow approving nod.

'No,' said Mary, a little unconvincingly it must be reported.

7 Intermission I – The Deserter

October 1916

He lay in his bunk, like the others, cowering. Bunk? In reality it was a hole cut into the side of a trench wall. The officers had bunks. He had mud. The bombardment was getting worse now. The noise was obviously louder. It would end soon. Then they would be called.

The bloody Hun had started the bombardment just as he'd fallen, exhausted, into his makeshift bed following a night on duty. It was rotten luck, but then again, wasn't the whole bloody war rotten luck for anyone fool enough to be in it? And he was in it all right, up to his neck. The sensation of drowning is not solely the experience of someone in water. You can be on dry land too, yet feel the icy waters slowly rise around you, taking you to it and away, away, away...

The thought of leaving was hardly an original one. Every man jack of them wanted out. It seemed to him the only way to escape was by ambulance or cart. In one you were alive, what was left of you. In the other you were one of a dozen bodies piled high.

No longer was it possible to use picket duty to buy your ticket to Blighty. The tacit agreement between each side to shoot the fingers off a smoker in the opposing trench had long since been exposed by the brass. You were as likely to end in prison as Blighty. Or worse, a firing squad.

There seemed to be no choice. Stick it out until the Hun finally got him or...

Was there really an 'or'?

No. Don't even think about it. Just get on with the business of slowly dying, day by day or succumbing to madness. What was it he'd said the other day that had the men laughing: it's either a bullet or Bedlam for me. He should write that down. Make a song of it. If he ever got out alive it would bring the house down.

Like he used to do.

As ideas for lyrics came into his head, the call came. The thuggish sergeant screamed into their faces. It was time to make ready or something like that. It was difficult to hear his exact words, not that it mattered. The sergeant may not have had much of a turn of phrase, but the message was abundantly clear: get out of bed, the attack has started.

He rolled over in order to climb down from his dugout, arse first. Then it happened. Well something did. He hadn't a clue. One minute he was attempting to climb down into the trench. The next he was under several feet of mud and dirt and other stuff that he didn't want to think about.

It's difficult to scream when your mouth is full of trench mud. He didn't panic. No, it was something else again; a higher order of terror where you don't know what you are doing. You cease to be human. You become a frenzy.

Maybe it was seconds, maybe minutes, but soon he had burrowed his way out of his sludge prison like an agoraphobic mole. His ears were ringing, but he was fairly sure the bombardment had ended. He looked around him. It was carnage. The trench no longer existed nor did the dozen men who had been milling around only seconds before. He realised that the trench wall was gone. His eyes were still a little blurred from the dirt and the tears, but he could just about make out a line of men, quarter of a mile away, advancing quickly towards his position. He didn't stop to pick up a gun. Another idea occurred to him. He went over to the one recognisable dead body in the mess around him.

'Sorry, mate,' he said. There was no time for a prayer never mind a eulogy.

He didn't look back.

He just ran. And he didn't stop running until he reached England.

8

Kit and Mary returned to the theatre around four in the afternoon. During their two hours at the hotel all manner of bids and suggestions were attempted, rebuffed, conceded until compromise was reached. Mary was still not entirely happy about what she had agreed to, but the manner in which Kit had tried to persuade her was not without recommendation. The prospect of joining the company as a new act was not something one undertook lightly.

'The last time I did something like this, I ended up half-dressed on stage in an American nightclub.'

Kit smiled fondly at the memory. This had occurred on a case in San Francisco when they were not yet married. The sight that Kit had beheld that evening was utterly entrancing and certainly had him looking forward to their future together.

'I seem to remember that it was your idea to audition,' pointed out Kit. 'I was against it.'

This stopped Mary in her tracks for a moment. This much was true, although Aunt Agatha had also had a hand in the idea. That said, if she'd known what she would be required to wear, or almost wear, it might have given her pause for thought. Anyway, that was the past. British music hall and variety was a world away from a seedy nightclub on the outskirts of San Francisco.

She hoped.

There to greet them was Rufus Watts. With him was the man they had seen earlier when they first arrived in the foyer.

'My younger brother Tristram,' said Rufus to Kit and Mary. 'Tristram, may I introduce Lord Kit Aston and his charming wife, Mary.'

'Lord...' said Tristram before Kit held his hand up and smiled.

'Please call me Kit.'

'I'm sorry for the loss of Mr Gonzalo,' said Mary. 'I'm sure this has been quite a shock for all of you and just about the last thing this, or probably any, theatre would need.'

They spent a minute commiserating with Tristram on what was happening and then Kit brought up the topic of their plan. Rufus felt his mood immediately improve at the prospect that Kit had a plan of attack.

Tristram seemed to have taken the death of Gonzalo much better in his stride. To Kit's eyes he didn't seem so put out about the tragedy as one might have thought. Perhaps it was the prospect that the notoriety from the murder might result in a boost at the box office. Given that Gonzalo was the star attraction, had he not been decapitated mid act, they were going to need all the help they could get.

'I'm sorry that we could not come yesterday,' said Kit.

'You couldn't have done anything, I suspect. The suddenness of what happened so soon after those awful letters caught us all on the hop.'

'Well, perhaps,' said Kit, who still felt an irrational sense of responsibility for what had happened. 'As Rufus will have told you, we have worked with Scotland Yard before, a number of times. I think the Chief Inspector has moved beyond tolerating our involvement to welcoming it. Almost.'

'Assuredly,' said Rufus. 'He's a dour old goat, but he likes you and you know it.'

Kit tried not to blush at this but gave it up as a bad job. Moving on, he said, 'I think that there may be some merit in myself, and Mary not being seen as part of the investigation. To this end I have a suggestion.'

Tristram raised one eyebrow, Rufus two.

Kit continued, 'I think it would make sense if Mary joined the company. I can attest to the fact that she has a wonderful singing voice, and she has had experience singing in a nightclub.'

'I was semi naked at that time,' said Mary with a frown.

'I suspect that wasn't the only semi in the room,' observed Rufus with a twinkle in his eye. Kit certainly wasn't about to dispute that. He grinned in response but decided against adding to the schoolboy humour.

'I think it would make sense if you said that you are adding Mary to the bill at the request of myself. You can suggest to the others that I am some sort of angel who is looking to invest in the theatre and that Mary is my girlfriend. I'm trying to turn her into a star.'

'Strange place to start,' said Tristram casting eyes around the foyer of his own theatre.

Kit and Mary both smiled at this. It appeared Tristram, like Rufus, had an affably acerbic sense of humour. They were very much alike, unquestionably. Each had clear blue eyes and an aquiline nose that suggested nobility. Tristram had shorter hair and was physically a little broader. Paradoxically, he appeared to be a little less theatrical than his brother, but this was relative. Sarah Bernhardt at her most tragic would have seemed recessive in comparison to Rufus Watts.

'I suspect the sooner we can restart performances the better it will be for you. The show must go on, as they say.'

'It certainly needs to,' said Tristram, flicking his eyes in the direction of Rufus. 'Do you think that the Chief Inspector will be amenable to this?'

'I'll see what I can do,' said Kit, not wishing to commit too much, too soon. 'How is everyone taking this?'

'They are all shocked, naturally. The letters were one thing, but I don't think any of us believed it would result in murder. At worst we thought it would be a bit of mudslinging. I think once the shock wears off there may be some grief. Gonzalo was by no means popular, but he was respected, I think.'

'Can we see one of the letters?' asked Mary.

'Of course,' said Tristram. 'I wasn't sent one myself. They only went to the performers. They all said the same thing. I'll show you if you come this way.'

They followed Tristram past the box office towards a door marked 'Manager's Office'. Tristram opened the door and allowed the others to enter. Inside, sitting behind one of the desks, was an elderly woman.

'Mama,' said Tristram, with emphasis on the second syllable, 'This is Kit and Mary, the friends of Rufus.'

Mrs Watts eyes widened. If pushed, Kit would have described her reaction as something approximating hope. He felt a stab, not of guilt this time, but of anxiety. He sensed much depended on what he was able to accomplish. She was on her feet immediately and around the desk to greet the newcomers.

'I'm so happy you have said you will help us,' said Mrs Watts. Kit's first impression of her as an older, kindlier version of his aunt was in no way diluted upon acquaintance. She seemed to smile as much with her eyes as her mouth. Both he and Mary liked her immediately, especially when she took Mary's two hands in hers and proclaimed her the most beautiful girl she'd ever seen.

'I won't argue with you there, Mrs Watts,' said Kit.

'I insist you call me Annie. Mrs Watts makes me seem rather ancient.'

This resulted in a kind-hearted roll of the eyes from her two sons.

'Mother is seventy-nine going on twenty-three. Please excuse her,' said Rufus in a haughty voice that could not disguise his affection. She seemed to be the polar opposite in her utter lack of conceit.

'Well, now that we're all together,' said Mrs Watts, 'why don't I make a cup of tea.'

'Ah, tea,' said Tristram, 'I wondered how long it would take before you made that suggestion. She's definitely slowing down Rufus.'

'I'd noticed,' replied Rufus archly.

Mrs Watts ignored her two sons, as usual. While she went off to rustle up some tea and, as it turned out, some sandwiches, Kit and Mary inspected the playbills in the office. At one point Kit turned around and asked, 'Can you tell me who is on the current bill; the running order?'

Tristram answered, 'We open with the Wyman Sisters. They perform some songs and cockney patter. Neither are from London. Then we have our first comedian, Eddie Matthews.'

'Comedian?' said Rufus archly.

'Yes, well, I can't disagree there. He doesn't tell jokes so much as say things that are meant to be funny and true. At this point, the audience are in a good mood, so it does just about pass muster and thankfully he is not on too long. He introduces Daisy Lewis. She sings some comic songs and dances a little. She's good and always puts the house in a good mood. After him we have the Monteverdi Brothers, they're Italian, from Rome. Then Eddie Matthews returns to do a little bit more front of curtain business which allowed Gonzalo and the brothers a chance to set up the Spanish Inquisition illusion.'

'Do you have stage hands?'

'The Monteverdi brothers also act as stagehands,' explained Tristram. 'It's extra money for them and saves us a little. We lost many of our employees during the War, either to fight or because business declined so much. Mother runs the ticket office these days.'

'I see,' said Kit and felt a stab of guilt once more for forcing Tristram to reveal just how straitened were the circumstances of the theatre.

'The Spanish Inquisition act takes us to the intermission. We have a small bar upstairs which I run with mother. Then it's back for the second half of the show.'

'You mentioned a ventriloquist?' prompted Kit.

'Yes Lucien Lemaire finishes the show with his dummy, Charlie.'

'What part of France does Monsieur Lemaire come from?' asked Mary.

'Doncaster, darling,' replied Tristram.

'Ah,' said Mary, 'I don't think I've been to that part of France.'

'Daisy Lewis follows. She does a few songs and then she is joined by our comedian, Bert Cooper.'

'How does it work having two comedians on the bill?' asked Mary.

'Trust me darling,' interjected Rufus. 'There's only one comedian on the bill. Bert is rather good, I must say.'

'He's probably the star of the show alongside Gonzalo,' agreed Tristram. 'Definitely destined for bigger things. So was Gonzalo until...'

There was a moment of silence while they thought of the young magician.

'Anyway, that's our troupe. Eddie Matthews aside, it's quite a strong bill, but we could use another singer, although not of comic songs. Daisy does that rather well and we don't want to over egg things. Can you sing more serious songs, Mary? Love songs perhaps? I'm sure the men will simply adore you,' said Tristram approvingly.

Mary smiled gracefully but did not say anything to this. Instead, she answered the question, 'Well how about, *You Made Me Love You*, or *Let Me Call You Sweetheart*, or *I'm Forever Blowing Bubbles*?'

The smile on Tristram's face grew wider as he heard Mary mention these songs.

'Do you know *After the Ball*? I do love that song,' asked Tristram.

Mary nodded, 'Yes I know the song. I'm sure I could do it.'

'Capital,' clapped Tristram. 'Well, I think after we have finished the tea that mother will insist we drink, we can then run through of some of those songs. Lord only knows when we'll be able to start up again, though.'

Mrs Watts was a well-oiled machine in the art of tea-making. She returned less than ten minutes later from a kitchen behind the office with a tray containing a bone china tea pot. The cups and saucers were stacked rather precariously, but she managed with aplomb. She set the tray down, unpacked it and then returned to the kitchen to collect an enormous plate of sandwiches.

As they took the tea, Tristram went to his desk to look for the threatening letter. Kit explained further what he had in mind.

'I gather that the performers are all staying at the same theatrical digs.'

'Yes, the inimitable Mrs Harrison,' replied Rufus.

'She sounds as if she is an interesting character.'

'Not a bad sort,' said Tristram, clutching a letter in his hand. 'Rather like a dragon, but she keeps them all in line. We've used her for years. Why do you ask?'

'Apparently, my lord and master wants me to stay there,' said Mary, folding her arms. She had a half smile on her face. 'I'm to go deep under cover.' These last words were said with just a touch of drama to them, every syllable enunciated with theatrical relish.

'Do you really think that the letters, or the death of Gonzalo, are connected with this group?' asked Tristram. His face, never mind the tone of his voice, expressed severe doubts about this.

Kit smiled and acknowledged the scepticism in Tristram's voice.

'There are two considerations: firstly, you can never tell. The murderer could be one of us. There is no rule that says a murderer must look like Bill Sykes or carry a club. Secondly, and this part may interest you, I spoke with the

Chief Inspector just before I came out this afternoon, he's staying at the same hotel. He agreed to open the theatre again if we can have Mary staying at the digs. It's rather dependent on this. Do you think Mrs Harrison will have space?'

Tristram perked up a little at this.

'Well, I think Mary, unless you sound like a foghorn with a frog in its throat, your audition is a foregone conclusion.'

'You've heard me sing then?' said Mary with a grin.

At this point Tristram went over to Kit and handed him one of the letters that had been sent to the performers.

'The letters are all the same. Daisy gave me hers. She and Bert are, shall we say, sweethearts. Mrs Harrison turns a blind eye to such matters as we're such good customers.'

Mary glanced towards Kit with one eyebrow raised hopefully. Kit shook his head which was met with a frown.

'Are there any single men in the company?' asked Mary of Tristram with a wicked gleam in her eye.

'I imagine Lemaire, and the Monteverdi brothers will be butting heads in no time when you arrive. I'm sure Mrs Harrison has room for you.'

Kit meanwhile was studying the letter and the envelope in which it had been posted. There wasn't much to study.

'It was posted locally,' pointed out Tristram.

Kit handed the typed letter to Mary. It read:

I KNOW WHAT YOU ARE.

I WILL EXPOSE YOU.

9

Mary looked up at Kit. In fact all eyes turned to Kit after the contents of the note had been revealed. Mrs Watts held a sandwich to her mouth but did not bite as she waited for the man her son had lionised to say something profound that would shed new light on what had happened and instantly solve their problems.

Kit's eyes roamed around the room. He smiled and shrugged.

'It looks like you have both a murderer and a blackmailer or...'

'It's the same man,' added Rufus.

'Or woman,' said Mary, true to form. Kit smiled at his wife and nodded.

'Or woman.'

This brief volley of thoughts served only as a prelude to silence while the group consumed the delicious cucumber sandwiches and tea prepared by Mrs Watts. When they had finished they turned expectantly once more to Kit.

'Shall we give Mary a chance to show you what a delightful singer she is?'

Mary's eyes narrowed at this, but she realised that her husband was not mocking her.

'Don't build your hopes up too much. Remember, I may not have a chance to perform. This performance is only to reassure you that I'm not a complete nincompoop.'

The group made their way inside to the auditorium. Mrs Watts took her place at the piano while the others sat down in the stalls and fixed hopeful gazes on Mary as she climbed the steps and glided to the centre of the stage.

'What song would you like my dear?' asked Mrs Watts, with that inevitable smile.

Tristram Watts piped up at this point, 'Perhaps *After the Ball*. I was thinking that if Mary's singing voice is as delightful as her speaking voice we could end the show with this number.'

'Jolly good,' replied Mrs Watts. 'I do so love that song.'

Mary was now standing in the middle facing her audience. Although the stage was relatively small, she looked a tiny figure to Kit. If she was nervous, she was hiding it well, he thought. She smiled and rolled her eyes. Mrs Watts began the intro to the song.

Kit glanced down at his hands. They were gripping the arms of the seat as if he were afraid he would fall off.

Mary sang, '*A little maiden...*'

Kit and the others immediately began to relax. Mary's voice rang out clear as crystal, devoid of any mannerism. In combination with her tiny physical presence and fragile beauty, it gave the song an additional layer of melancholy. By the end of the song, the family Watts was collectively weeping much to Kit's surprise. They broke out into spontaneous applause when she sang the final note with a clarity of diction that owed as much to her natural inheritance as the years spent with a governess and then finishing school.

The audition was an outstanding success. Mary descended the steps to more applause and something even more welcome from Kit which drew a wolf whistle from Tristram. Rufus shook his head disapprovingly at his younger brother. Mrs Watts came over and embraced Mary.

'My dear that was so beautiful. I think it's the best rendition of the song I've ever heard,' she said and there were tears in her eyes.

The sight of tears in one woman is almost sure to bring tears to another in much the same way as a man breaking wind among a group of men will almost certainly...well, you get the idea.

'My dear Mary,' said Rufus, 'I really had no idea you had such a sweet voice.'

To which Tristram added, 'What a pity you're married to this lucky man. I could use someone like you.'

Mary made a mock curtsy and glanced wryly at Kit.

'Well, if things don't work out with this one, at least I'll have something to fall back on.'

Kit was simply too happy that she had performed so well to worry about the usual teasing that every husband must endure stoically to ensure peace in the household. However, now that Mary's role as a potential new recruit to the show had been established, they needed to, as Aunt Agatha might say, get a move on.

'I think perhaps we should install Mary at the digs so that she can begin that end of the investigation,' said Kit.

'One, thing,' suggested Tristram. 'Shouldn't we have a stage name for Mary?'

'Mary Frost,' said Mary. She met Kit's eyes as she said this and for a moment there was more than a hint of emotion behind them. Mary was the daughter, that Agatha had never had.

Tristram drove Mary from the hotel to Mrs Harrison's digs which was a quarter of a mile away, located just off the sea front. The car was a six-year-old Vauxhall that was clearly Tristram's pride and joy. Rufus refused to travel in it. Unlike his brother, he had no interest in cars whereas outside of the theatre, they were a passion for his younger brother. His greatest regret in life was the fact that the two interests that he loved most were almost irreconcilable.

A life in theatre was all consuming yet offered very little by way of financial reward; certainly not enough to indulge oneself in the latest cars. The wealth of the Watts family was entirely tied up in the theatre building, which they owned. Its value was declining year after year as new forms of entertainment came along which meant that their industry was dying a slow death. As they drove, they passed both the Empire Theatre and the Palace Moving Picture House.

'The Palace is owned by Billy Benson. Evil man,' said Tristram. 'He's made several offers over the years to buy us. Offers us less each time.'

'It sounds as if he's rubbing it in,' said Mary, saddened at the very real prospect that Annie Watts might no longer be sat by her piano, lost in the music she was playing.

'He is. Bad, bad man. I think he's the one that circulated those vile letters,' claimed Tristram.

'But surely he wouldn't stoop to murder?'

Even for Tristram, this was probably an accusation too far. Equally, he could not bring himself to say anything that might offer even the faintest of praise to the hateful man. His solution was to huff a little.

A few minutes later they pulled up outside a four storey, red brick villa. There was a small, printed sign that read: *Harrison's Guest House*. Having left, reluctantly, the five-star opulence of the Grand Hotel, the guest house offered a more modest accommodation for Mary. However, she was excited or nervous; or both. The idea of, once more, working on a case was always welcome. Even the prospect of singing on stage held little fear for her as she had done so, on many occasions, at her finishing school. Working undercover gave her more cause for anxiety.

The first time she had worked undercover had been eighteen months previously when she and Kit had been on the trail of 'The Phantom'. Mary genuinely felt remorse at having to mislead people in the household where she had adopted the role of a maid. Now she would be required to do the same again with people who probably had committed no crime. She steeled herself for the few days ahead and, of course, she would miss Kit. Horribly. Oddly, she was not afraid, despite the potential risk that there was a murderer in the house. Although it was on her mind, it was the night or two in a bed without her husband that made her feel most lonely.

Tristram carried Mary's bags into the digs where they were greeted by a woman in her forties whom Mary took to be Mrs Harrison. She clearly had once been quite a beauty and retained a slender not ungraceful demeanour.

'Mrs Harrison, here is the young lady I was telling you about, Mary Frost.'

Mrs Harrison cast her eyes over Mary and seemed to approve. Mary's appearance suggested, while she was not likely to be a trouble maker, the same might not be said for how some members of the house would react.

'Is she alone?' she asked turning her attention to Tristram.

'Yes. Her fiancé will not be joining her.'

Mary had taken the precaution of removing her wedding ring but keeping the engagement ring intact. This, she hoped would act as a deterrent for any attempts at romance from the young men in the house.

'I might have to put Henry outside her room just in case,' said Mrs Harrison thoughtfully.

Mary smiled and raised an eyebrow at this. 'Henry?' she asked.

'Henry is a St Bernard. He belongs to the Wyman Sisters. They won't mind. What he lacks in belligerence he compensates for in size and an overwhelming affability. I think he would lick an intruder to death,' said Tristram.

'I am sure I shall be safe,' grinned Mary, following Mrs Harrison through the front door into a large hallway with dark brown wallpaper.

'I'll take you up to your room. We dine at seven on the dot. I hope you like apple tart.'

'It's on the menu every night,' added Tristram.

'Hush you,' said Mrs Harrison, but there was a twitch at the side of her mouth that belied any implied grievance.

They trudged up the stairs to the top floor. Mary was in a garret room with a dormer window. It was chillier than an Antarctic outdoor swimming bath. The room had a brass bedstead, a jug and a bowl for washing, a pitcher, a pine wardrobe that looked like a coffin and a tiny gas fire . It was thoroughly cheerless.

'Charming,' said Mary cheerfully.

Mrs Harrison and Tristram both looked at her as if she were clinically insane.

'I'm glad you like it. It's all we had left,' was Mrs Harrison's only comment as she left the room.

'Are you sure Mary?' said Tristram. He looked around the room with some scepticism. 'I suppose it's not quite what you're used to.'

'I shall be fine,' answered Mary with more confidence than she was feeling. Tristram left her at this point, conscious that it was now nearing seven in the evening and dinner would be served. He intended staying long enough to introduce her but drew the line at remaining in the room while she changed.

Mary had a rather winning flair, in Kit's book, for not taking too long to dress, unlike her sister Esther. After a quick wash, she changed before skipping down the stairs to the corridor outside the dining room where she met Tristram. Inside, there was a lot of noise, not all of it happy. The rest of the company were clearly feeling the strain of the last twenty-four hours.

Tristram gave her an encouraging smile as she descended the stairs. Taking both of her hands in his, he said, 'Final chance.'

'Nonsense,' said Mary, with a grin.

They entered the room and all chat stopped abruptly. Every eye in the room was giving Mary the once over. In the case of Lemaire and the Monteverdi brothers, it was a thrice over. Tristram had outdone himself in their opinion. The presence of an engagement ring was noted and duly ignored by the three young men.

With the three men was an older man that Mary took to be Eddie Matthews. At the far end of the table was another man, in his thirties, sitting with an attractive woman who was a little younger. Mary recognised Bert Cooper and Daisy Lewis from the picture on the playbill. The picture did Miss Lewis no favours. She was certainly more attractive in real life, despite the frown that was being thrown in the direction of her boyfriend, Cooper.

Sitting in another corner were two women who Mary took to be the Wyman Sisters. They didn't look in the least bit related. Susan Wyman was around thirty years of age, slender with a hard face that had seen a lot of life and hadn't liked much of what she saw. She removed a cigarette that appeared to be a permanent fixture in her mouth and blew a smoke ring towards the ceiling. Jackie Wyman was built on lavish lines. No expense had been spared to clothe her or feed her for that matter. Of the two 'sisters' she seemed friendlier. She had a plump pink face with a pert nose. Sitting at her feet was a St Bernard.

'This is Henry,' said the lady. Henry gave a loud snore as if to announce himself. 'My name is Jackie, and this is Susan.'

'Well. Isn't this nice,' said Tristram. 'Anyway, boys and girls, may I introduce Mary Frost. She will be joining the revue as clearly we are going to have to make some adjustments with the sad death of our friend Javier. The show must go on. Mary is a divine singer. She auditioned earlier and brought tears to my mother's eyes when she sang *After the Ball*. She will be a very welcome addition to our troupe when we re-open.'

'When will that be?' asked Eddie Matthews, his voice was full of scornful scepticism. He was a man in his sixties with a long, narrow face, a cynical eye and deep crevices either side of his nose that ran down to his mouth. For a comedian, he appeared to have no idea what a smile should be, nor to have practised it very often.

'Very soon, I hope,' said Tristram. 'I'm sure that the accident will be quickly dealt with by Chief Inspector Jellicoe. He strikes me as a very capable man.'

This was certainly the impression of the people at the table. The tension in the room seemed palpable and not solely the result of an attractive new arrival. Mary could see taut faces and narrowed eyes. Behind these eyes lay secrets, but was one of them really a murderer?

'Then why are we being treated like common criminals,' asked Daisy Lewis. Her voice was pleasant, without any sign of rank. She might have been a governess or a doctor's daughter.

'Well I'm sure that's not the case,' said Tristram. 'Anyway, let's welcome Mary to our bosom, I'm sure she will be a popular addition to the show.' He glanced in the direction of the three young men. There was little in their eyes that suggested anything other than complete agreement. 'On that note, I shall leave Mary in your capable hands.'

Tristram departed and Mary took up the empty seat beside Eddie Matthews. She noted that Jane Anthony was not amongst them. Perhaps she was still mourning the loss of her partner and who knows what else, surmised Mary.

All eyes were on Mary now.

'Well, I'm pleased to meet you all,' said Mary, a tad more nervously than she'd intended. 'I'm sorry it has happened in such tragic circumstances.'

This was met with some approval from Daisy Lewis, although it was clear the three young men were barely listening to what she had to say.

'Where have you played before, my dear?' asked Daisy.

Thankfully, Kit had prepared her for such a line of questioning. They had agreed that she would be caught out if she mentioned any British theatres. Best to keep to the truth, or at least, some of it.

'America,' replied Mary, secure in the certain knowledge that no one would have played Lehane's in San Francisco before. The surprised reaction relaxed her, and she began to talk about her time there. She smiled gleefully as an idea occurred to her about how Kit would pay for coming up with this undercover scheme. Why should she be the only one to put on an act? Over the next few days she realised that they were all putting on an act of one sort or another.

The dinner gong rang just then. Everyone rose wearily to their feet.

'What is the food like here?' asked Mary brightly.

'I hope you like apple tart,' replied Bert Cooper with a friendly wink.

10

While Mary was just minutes away from sampling Mrs Harrison's one and only dessert, Kit was feeling decidedly despondent at the prospect of a night away from Mary. It was one thing to come up with these plans, but quite another to carry them out without some personal sacrifice. In this case, it was a feeling of nervousness about putting Mary in a situation where she was potentially at risk, albeit a small one, in Kit's judgement. Aside from that, he missed her. A night away from Mary was a night he would never have back.

The company of Jellicoe at dinner was welcome but no compensation. Wellbeloved had taken the opportunity to gain some sea air, fish and chips and who knows what entertainment that a seaside town might provide? Jellicoe decided not to ask lest he received an answer.

By now, Kit had been able to review the case files which included pen portraits of the company, along with details of their whereabouts when the tragic event unfolded. Aside from Rufus Watts and a man called Lysander Benedict, a local arts critic, no statements had been taken from the audience in the auditorium. None were considered suspects as there were no instances of any of the audience having been near the stage at any time during or before the performance. For this reason, they had been sent home without any of their details being obtained. As far as Jellicoe and Wellbeloved were concerned, the case, if there was one, centred on those performers who had been on or near the stage at the time of the performance.

'Does this mean you are excluding Bert Cooper from your list of suspects, chief inspector?' asked Kit, as he perused the file of the comedian. It was situated to the right of a rather tasty vegetable broth starter.

'Not excluding exactly. At the moment there doesn't seem to be any case for him or, indeed, Daisy Lewis, to answer,' said Jellicoe. 'Not only had neither of them met Gonzalo prior to this revue, they were not in the theatre when the death occurred. Both were across the road with Billy Benson for a quick drink at The Docker's Fist. We are, of course, checking their histories back at the Yard.'

'So we are left with the people who were on or near the stage at the time, Miss Anthony and the Monteverdi brothers as well as, below the stage, Eddie Matthews, Lucien Lemaire and Barney Hallett.'

'And Gonzalo himself,' pointed out Jellicoe.

'Let's start with him, shall we. Javier Gonzalo, real name Graham Gibson,' said Kit, glancing up at Jellicoe as he said this. The policeman smiled but said nothing.

'Not quite so exotic. So Mr Gibson was from Manchester. He worked in various theatres in the north as a magician and then the War came. He joined up in nineteen sixteen, survived somehow and then returned to what he had been doing pre-war. At this point, he joined another magician. I wonder if they met during the War because it says that Gibson often worked entertaining the troops near the front. Anyway, they went their separate ways last year and Gibson became Javier Gonzalo. He moved down south where he met Jane Anthony and Barney Hallett; they became part of his act.' Then Kit added sadly with a shake of his head, 'he was thirty-one years of age. Imagine. He survived the hell of France only to lose his life in what may have been a tragic accident.'

Jellicoe merely nodded at this as he was negotiating his soup; the task was made somewhat difficult by his large, dripping moustache, which gave him a forlorn countenance. Kit, meanwhile, glanced over Jane Anthony's file.

'Jane Anthony is twenty-nine. I see she's a war widow. Lost her husband in nineteen seventeen. Took to the stage soon after. Met Gonzalo last year. Where was she before?' asked Kit.

Jellicoe replied, 'She was an actress before she married her husband. She returned to acting the year after his death but,' said Jellicoe sadly, 'there was a lot of competition. The War caused too many young women to become widows. She decided to try her hand at variety and worked in a number of places she says before she met Gonzalo at the end of nineteen twenty. There is some question over whether they were sweethearts or not. Miss Anthony's reaction to his death suggests they were, but we have not inquired too deeply on that point.'

Kit picked up the file on the acrobat brothers. He said, 'The Monteverdi brothers, I see, came over from Italy early in nineteen twenty. They started off in a circus but moved into variety, as it offered more money. They were both on stage before and during the act, like Miss Anthony.'

'Yes, they both act as stagehands. They help with the other acts if props or scenery need to be moved. They're both in their twenties and very strong, as you may imagine.'

'I do hope Mary won't be troubled by them,' said Kit, a frown creasing his forehead.

'Are you not stereotyping Italians somewhat?' said Jellicoe with a half-smile.

'Probably. I doubt the country objects to being seen as Latin lovers, though,' observed Kit wryly. 'What do you think of Eddie Matthews? It sounds like he is on borrowed time if Rufus Watts' opinion is any guide. Which it usually is.'

'Rather a sour individual. There is a fetid air about him. He's been in the business a long time, so there is quite a bit of checking to do on him. That said, neither he nor the others have had any recent convictions. There are some problems with this of course.'

Kit smiled at this and filled in the rest of the thought, 'I imagine stage names make all of this something of a challenge.'

'Correct,' said Jellicoe, finishing his soup and wiping his moustache with the napkin. 'We can't be certain that the names they are giving us are the truth. I don't think Eddie Matthews has changed his name in decades, but who knows about the Monteverdi brothers or Lemaire.'

'Ah yes, our French friend who hails from Doncaster. I take it he is not French.'

'Actually his father is French. A chef apparently. Lemaire hasn't seen him since he was a child. He ran off with a waitress.'

Kit raised an eyebrow, 'I'm trying hard not to stereotype the French, but I must confess to having difficulty.'

Jellicoe chuckled.

'Lemaire, like the others in the revue, is a young man. He didn't fight in the War. I'm not sure if this was for physical reasons or if he was a conscientious objector. Cooper did fight in the War, I might add. Managed to survive unscathed. Of course, all of this has to be verified.'

'And Lemaire was below stage with Barney and Matthews, waiting his turn.'

'Yes. Strange that he was not in the green room like the others, but he says that he wanted to have a sense of the atmosphere.'

'Who was in the green room when the death occurred?' asked Kit, flicking through the statements.

'The Wyman Sisters, they're not sisters by the way. Susan Parrish and Jackie Rutherford formed a double act during the War. They did some entertaining of the troops; singing songs and comedy dialogues as two cockney women.'

'Have they or any of the others worked together before with Gonzalo, I wonder?' mused Kit. 'If they haven't, then...'

'Motive becomes a problem. I agree, it's important to know. We're looking into that back at the Yard,' said Jellicoe smiling. Kit noted the smile. 'Initial statements suggest many have worked together before and with the dead man.'

'What is amusing you?' asked Kit, smiling.

Jellicoe's face coloured slightly before he answered. 'As it happens, the person doing the research on this is my son. He's joined the detective ranks.'

'Congratulations, best of luck to him,' said Kit. 'I hope he can unearth a motive from his inquiries. Without a sensible motive we must, once again, consider the idea of an accident.'

'The threatening notes?' asked Jellicoe, as he helped a waiter take his soup plate.

'Perhaps there was a plan to blackmail one or some of the performers, but this doesn't mean the tragedy was a planned murder. The blackmailer may have been as surprised as anyone,' suggested Kit.

'Plausible,' admitted Jellicoe, 'and yet...'

'Yes, and yet. I'm not sure I believe it either,' said Kit. 'But then how did the murderer stop Gonzalo escaping from the cabinet without there being a device in the trap door to achieve this and in full view of the audience and their fellow performers. I must admit, I'm a bit stumped, on that one, at the moment.'

'That's not what I want to hear, dear boy,' said a voice from behind Kit. It was Rufus Watts, dressed in a cream suit and pink tie which made him stand out somewhat from the other men in the dining room of the hotel, who were all wearing black tie and dinner suits.

'Ah Rufus you're late,' said Jellicoe although not unkindly.

'I'm an artist,' explained Rufus, 'the rules and customs demanded of policemen and minor nobility...'

'Thanks Rufus,' said Kit with a smile.

'Minor nobility,' continued the diminutive artist, who looked as if he were shaping up to expostulate on a favoured topic, 'do not apply to a group of people that inspire, educate and help everyone gain insight into their own emotions, their culture and the nature of existence.'

'And I thought you just sketched criminals, Rufus, forgive me,' said Kit, grinning.

'Only to make money. Now, what have you ordered for me?'

'Humble pie wasn't on the menu, alas,' replied Kit.

'Never eaten it, never shall,' said Rufus decisively. 'By the way, I was speaking to our local arts critic, Lysander Benedict. He rather fancies himself in the amateur sleuth line. He says that he has some information that may shed some light on motive. Unless we are nearer finding our killer, chief inspector, now that our dashing amateur sleuth, from minor nobility, has joined the hunt, perhaps we should listen to the windbag.'

'Friend of yours?' asked Kit.

'Blood brothers,' said Rufus. 'So, we really have no ideas at the moment?'

'None,' said Kit and Jellicoe in unison.

'Just as well that I arranged for him to come down to the theatre tomorrow morning to tell us what he knows. I must warn you, though, he's a frightful man. Very full of himself. I can't abide people like that.'

'Afraid of the competition, Rufus?' asked Kit, with a smile.

While this chit chat was taking place, former sergeant, now Detective Inspector, Wellbeloved was sitting just down from the theatrical digs. He held a newspaper containing what remained of the excellent fish and chips he'd ordered earlier. This was not the first time he'd staked out a house. It would not be the last time either. To this end, he had purchased, many years ago, a lightweight stool that he took with him when the occasion demanded. In a case where leads were at a premium and his ability to beat a confession was now completely circumscribed, there was nothing left for him but to sit and wait for something to happen.

Something usually did.

He had taken the precaution of wrapping up warm, but the night's chill soon began to permeate the several layers of clothing he was wearing. This was not going to be a comfortable night. He stretched his long legs out on the pavement and kept his eyes fixed on the large house. He'd give it until two in the morning and then return to the hotel.

Or perhaps not. He'd noticed a house on his way to the digs that possibly had some potential for a man like himself. It would warm him up no end, he was sure. Just then he felt a spot of rain. He pulled the hat over his head and buried his hands in his pocket and prayed that the cloud would pass quickly.

As it turned out, he didn't have to wait until the early hours of the morning for events to take a dramatic turn. Instead, around nine in the evening, just as Wellbeloved was feeling increasingly like one of Scott's men in the Antarctic, a taxi drew up outside Mrs Harrison's guest house. Wellbeloved tried to rise to his feet, but a combination of age and cold meant that his limbs would not obey the flood of instructions coming from his brain. He was forced to watch helplessly as a man emerged from the house clutching a suitcase.

Moments later, he was in the taxi and, no doubt, off to a train station to catch a train that would take him to any one of a number of towns on the line up to London. Wellbeloved watched as Bert Cooper, the comedian, sped away and no amount of swearing on the part of the detective was going to stop him escaping the clutches of the law.

11

The wind sighed through the trees as Mary Aston and the rest of the troupe walked along the street that led to the sea front. They were only a short distance from the theatre, but the cold wind was already stinging their faces. The call had come, around eight in the morning, that they were to attend a meeting with the police at the theatre. Under any normal circumstance, this might have spelled the end of the show. However, these were not normal circumstances for a number of reasons of which the death of Gonzalo was only one and not the most recent, either.

By now, everyone was aware that Bert Cooper had departed the digs under suspicious circumstances. The screams of Daisy Lewis had been the clue to this. They trudged towards the theatre under a black belly of sky that perfectly reflected the mood of the company. Jane Anthony was being comforted by Lucien Lemaire and had not yet been introduced to Mary, although she did, from time to time, cast glances in her direction.

They reached the theatre. Not for the first time did Mary reflect on how sad it looked alongside the bright, shiny art deco newness of the Palace moving picture house, just across the street. It seemed symbolic of the fortunes of the two forms of entertainment.

Tristram greeted them in the foyer. Standing with Tristram was Kit and Chief Inspector Jellicoe. There was no sign of Wellbeloved. In fact, he was still in bed having earned a lie in, following the escape of Cooper. The detective inspector had managed to move his long legs to find a taxi to make it to the railway station. However, he was just too late. Cooper had timed his flight from the digs to perfection. The train departed with him on board with Wellbeloved staring forlornly at an empty platform.

A series of phone calls followed over the next few hours, to police stations on the line, some were more successful than others in finding anyone to answer. The train's arrival at Waterloo resulted in a thorough search, but Cooper had either disguised himself before evading capture or had got off the train at one of the major towns on the line. From somewhere like Guildford it was entirely possible for him to catch another train. In short, realised Wellbeloved, he could be anywhere. Wellbeloved had been commended by Jellicoe for his prompt action and no blame was attached to the big policeman for Cooper absconding.

It was a grim Tristram Watts that the company saw when they congregated in the foyer. He had now lost not one, but two of his star turns. A plan was in place for the loss of Cooper. This had been anticipated, but not the suddenness of his departure. Gonzalo, however, would be more difficult to replace notwithstanding the very attractive addition of Mary Aston. He still had the problem of Eddie Matthews' declining appeal to manage. For all he knew, the veteran might even demand a bigger billing now, despite the public's limited interest in his act.

'Good morning everyone, well perhaps "good" is stretching things a tad. I think you're all aware that Bert Cooper has decided to leave us at somewhat short notice.'

This was greeted with a sniff from Daisy Lewis who was still clearly upset by what had happened.

'I'm sorry Daisy,' said Tristram in a kindly voice. 'I know you were close. Chief Inspector Jellicoe would like to speak to you in a few moments, but first I would like to introduce Mr Alston. Mr Alston and I are discussing projects for the future.'

Mary had gone straight to Kit when they had arrived in the foyer and hugged him. The reason for the rather demonstrative display was twofold. There was enough in the reaction of the Monteverdi brothers and Lucien Lemaire, the previous evening, to suggest that she would probably be the subject of their attention sooner rather than later. She hoped that such obvious affection might act to nip in the bud any actions from a mischievous Cupid. There was also a second, more pressing, reason.

'I told them you were American,' whispered Mary. Kit caught the wicked gleam in her eye and smiled back at her in an "I'll-get-you-back-for-this" way.

'Where from?' asked Kit *sotto voce*.

Mary shrugged in an "It's-your-problem-now" manner.

'Mr Alston would you like to say a few words?' asked Tristram. Rufus and Annie Watts appeared from the office at this moment just as Kit began to speak.

'Well, I declare this is quite a state we find ourselves in,' said Kit in the manner of a southern gentleman addressing his Confederate troops, on the eve of Gettysburg. He stared directly at Mary as he said this. Mary's eyes widened in alarm; the joke was being well and truly turned back on her. She wondered how long she would survive without exploding into laughter. Knowing Kit as she did, he would push every button he could to ensure that she suffered.

Even now, she could see Jellicoe shuffling a little, Tristram was about to have a stroke and Rufus Watts had immediately turned tail and left the office. Annie Watts looked confused but maintained the saintly smile that never seemed to leave her face.

'I would like to say to you all that I dearly wish to stand with you. This is a charmin' theatre and you good folk surely do seem like people that I, and my precious Mary, could get on with.'

It took a few moments for Tristram to recover from the shock of what he'd just heard. Despite his flamboyant appearance, unlike his brother, or his mother for that matter, he was not a man who appreciated spontaneity. He was a planner. He liked things to be neat, ordered and, as far as possible, rational.

'Very good,' said Tristram at long last. 'Chief Inspector Jellicoe, would you care to update us on the progress of the investigation and the events of last night?'

Jellicoe nodded and then began to speak. There was an air about Jellicoe that almost everyone who met him understood immediately. He radiated both seriousness and competence in equal measure. He was no one's fool and only a fool would try and prove otherwise.

'Thank you Mr Watts and Mr...Alston. First of all, may I once again offer my condolences for the loss of your colleague, Mr Gonzalo. With regard to Mr Cooper, we know that he caught the train towards London, but he has managed to evade our officers so far. I do not think he will be able to manage this for long.'

At this point Eddie Matthews interjected.

'Does this mean that the investigation is over?'

'Why do you ask that Mr Matthews?' asked Jellicoe, who knew perfectly well why the comedian had posed this question.

'Well it's obvious innit? Cooper killed Gonzalo or whatever his name was and did a runner.'

Jane Anthony glared at Matthews in a rage. Mary guessed the comment "whatever his name was" had been a little too disrespectful for the man she worked with. Mary could see tears glisten in the eyes of the young woman.

'No, Mr Matthews, our investigations will continue, for the moment. However, given the events of last night and also, with respect to Mr Watts and his theatre, we think it only right that you are allowed to re-open.'

This was greeted with rueful smiles or, in Jane Anthony's case, anger. The reaction was not as enthusiastic as Tristram would have hoped but given the circumstances it was hardly a surprise. He would have to chat with Jane and Barney separately to make them see that despite their loss, he had a business to run and people to employ. Many people, in fact.

Jellicoe waited a few moments then addressed Daisy Lewis specifically, 'Miss Lewis, would it be possible to meet with you again in Mr Watts' office. I know Detective Inspector Wellbeloved spoke with you already. I would like to understand more from you about what happened last night.'

'Why don't we go to the stage, and we'll discuss what we do now, while the chief inspector and Daisy go through last night's events,' suggested Tristram.

As they moved into the theatre auditorium, Kit turned to Mary and said, 'American?'

'Southern gentleman?' replied Mary with a grin. Then her face became more serious, 'I was in a bit of a bind. As we agreed, I said that I'd only performed in America. I gave them some cock and bull story about my family moving to San Francisco. Then Daisy asked me if you were American too, so I said yes. It made more sense.'

'Fair enough,' conceded Kit. 'I didn't think of that. Oh well, did you give them my Christian name.'

'Chauncey,' replied Mary, beginning to giggle again.

The group were now sitting in a semi-circle on the stage. Facing them were Kit and Tristram. The theatre owner stood up from his seat. He was clutching a piece of paper and a pencil.

'I was having a think about the running order of the show. Just to tell you, I have a young man coming later that my mother and I saw during the summer at a concert party on the front. His name's Miller and he's rather good. He's just finished one show, so he can spare us a few weeks before his next engagement. I had intended putting him in Javier's slot, but now I can see we'll have to put him in Bert's. Lucien, I will move you to Javier's slot and we'll add Mary into yours. Mary, as you will see in a few moments, is a rather fine singer and she will do a wonderful job, I am sure. In fact, I am thinking that when Mary does her turn she can be joined by Daisy to duet on a few rousing numbers at the end. I think their voices would work beautifully together and I doubt the men in the audience will be complaining. Are there any questions?'

'Are you bringing anyone else in?' asked Matthews. 'Seems to me we have a lot of comedians.'

Tristram fixed his eyes on Matthews and ardently wished that the man he was looking at was one of them.

'We'll see, Eddie, we'll see. I think you raise a good point. Looking at some jugglers. Jane, perhaps we can have a chat later about what you want to do. Obviously, we will continue to pay you for the length of the engagement but perhaps, when you feel ready, there is something that you may be able to contribute.'

Mary glanced over at Jane Anthony once more. There was no question she was a rather beautiful girl with bubbling blonde hair and large, brown eyes. She seemed more composed now, yet Mary could sense that her emotions were not far from the surface. Her hands were clasped together, and she seemed to be using them to hold herself together. Or she was in prayer.

'Thank you Tristram,' she whispered, not trusting her voice to go any louder. Tristram smiled kind-heartedly while Daisy Lewis reached over and clasped her wrist.

Tristram turned his attention to Mary, 'I think, for now, it might be an idea, if Mary is willing, that we hear from her.'

Mary nodded to this. She had anticipated just such a request. She felt ready to perform. It had been a year since her last, rather unconventional, performance in San Francisco. Before that she had sung regularly at the frequent school concerts. Although, she felt a little apprehensive about singing in front of genuine professionals, whose assessment would probably not be uncritical, she had enough belief in her ability to cope with the level of scrutiny to be faced.

The rest of the troupe rose from their seats and made their way to the stalls to view the performance. As it happened, another performance was taking place in the wings that stopped everyone for a few moments. Romeo, the theatre cat, was taking a well-earned break from rat-catching. His attention was taken by some rope hanging from the curtain. This was greeted with a few chuckles which helped considerably towards lightening the gloom that had descended on everyone. Even Jane Anthony was able to smile at Romeo's antics.

While the troupe settled in their seats, Mary walked to the centre of the stage. All eyes were on her. She glanced towards Mrs Watts who smiled reassuringly to her. Moments later, her hands began to caress the keys of the piano – the opening bars of *After the Ball.*

Mary began to sing as she had the day before. Ignoring the looks on the faces of the men, it was all too clear what they were thinking, she risked a glance towards the four young women who were sitting together. Three of them, including Jane Anthony, smiled back at her in encouragement. Only Susan Parrish remained impassive. She dragged on her cigarette, as if it contained the last oxygen in the room. Three out of four supporters among the women wasn't bad. She felt more relaxed now. Even thoughts of her deception were forgotten as the song's wistful melody and her delivery took over. It was all in a good cause, for their safety.

The end of the song was greeted by warm applause. Tristram went over to Mary and took both her hands in his.

'Well, I think you'll agree that Mary will make a fine addition to the show.

Lucien Lemaire, Eddie Matthews and the Monteverdi brothers could not have agreed more.

12 Intermission II – The Prostitute

August 1917

It had been two weeks. Two weeks since her life had ended. Yet she knew it would happen this way. Women know. They feel things that men can never feel; sense things that they can never sense. She'd known, the minute that his papers came through, that he would march to his death. They would throw him towards a merciless enemy as they had thrown so many hundreds of thousands of others.

How she hated the war. It had taken everything from her. Everything. Happiness would be a memory now. Her life was over; it was lying dead in the mud of some farmer's field in France.

What would she do now? The rent had to be paid, she was already in arrears. The widow's pension was not enough. Not that they cared. She had to find work.

Soon.

This presented a second problem. She had no experience in all of the usual things women did like domestic service or factory work or, or, or... It didn't matter what she thought of, she would have no idea what to do. Being an actress might prepare you to be a servant in a play, but in real life she would have no idea what to do.

One of her friends had mentioned that they needed women on buses; they also needed postal workers. She wouldn't go into a factory, though. She'd heard how women were treated there. No, there was a limit.

A knock at the door.

Instinctively, she looked around her one room flat. It was tidy. She couldn't abide clutter. Yet, perhaps on this occasion it might have served her well. Her heart was heavy with foreboding as she went to the door.

'Who is it?'

'It's Len.'

Tears began to well up in her eyes. She would have to open the door to him. What choice did she have? He had keys anyway. She twisted the key and stood back to let Len in.

Len was tall, rather burly, but a not unattractive man in his early forties. He was also a rather wealthy landlord. Her landlord.

'Hello, my love, how are you these days?' said Len in a voice dripping with counterfeit care.

'Well, you know Len, it's still so tough.'

Len took her hand before she could pull it away. She was afraid now. Something in his eyes. How he was looking at her. She was used to this of course, but it never felt comfortable, especially not since Mick had been killed. No man had dared cast a glance her way, then. Mick could handle himself. The silly boy! Thought he could take on the Kaiser and his lot.

'Have you found work yet,' asked Len, concern flickering in his eyes.

'I'm looking. I'll go to a couple of places tomorrow.'

'It's just,' he paused for a moment, trying to pretend he was concerned for her welfare. 'It's been a couple of weeks now. You're behind.'

'I know Len, I'll try.'

Len nodded, but his face was a mask now. She sensed it was coming. It was there in his posture. In his eyes.

'There's ways of course.'

'What do you mean?' she said, then cursed herself for giving him the opportunity.

'You know what I mean.'

13

Lysander Benedict and Rufus Watts stared at one another, like two main street gunfighters who had chosen to wear the same outfit that day. Their disdain was mutual, deeply felt and probably satisfying to both. Benedict wore a light suit, sported a light grey cloak with silver-silk lining and had a thick black cane with a silver knob that almost certainly did not contain a blade like Rufus'. He was a similar age to Rufus which is to say nearer fifty than forty. He had a thin moustache and heavy face that sat atop a thick neck, supported by a bulky body and short legs.

'Rufus, my dear friend, how are you and the family coping?'

'As you may imagine, Lysander. Enough of that. I have a bone to pick with you, Lysander,' replied Rufus.

'Oh really?' Benedict was all holy innocence.

'Yes, old girl,' said Rufus, 'You profess no great liking for Billy Benson and his moving pictures and yet you persist in giving us the more awful reviews. Whose side are you on?'

'I'm always on the side of art, Rufus, as you know.'

'Do I?'

'Yes. While I will concede Gonzalo had something about him, at least until he and his head went their separate ways, may he rest in peace and I did write this, I'm afraid the rest of the show is a bit of a hit and miss affair. Eddie Matthews? The less said about him the better.'

'I wish you'd taken your own advice,' retorted Rufus sharply. He held the newspaper up in front of him and read from the review by Benedict, '*When Thoreau wrote that the mass of men lead lives of quiet desperation, he must have had the unfortunate experience of the audience watching Eddie Matthews' act in mind...*'

'So far, so true,' said Benedict, unapologetically, but Rufus was not finished yet. He rustled the paper to interrupt any further sanctimony from Benedict.

'*Daisy Lewis is an attractive, well-meaning performer with a voice that would adorn any baby's bath time.*'

Benedict had the grace to blush at this before commenting, 'I was rather pleased with that line. But come on Rufus, I was complimentary about everyone else, including Miss Daisy. I rather liked her act as you well know.'

Tristram arrived in the office accompanied by Kit and Jellicoe. He made no effort to hide the scowl on his face as he greeted the newspaper critic with a curt nod that was only just on the right side of civility.

'So Lysander,' said Tristram, 'Now that you've made your fashionably late entrance to the case, what have you to tell us?'

Whatever, Lysander was about to say, was interrupted by the arrival of Annie Watts carrying a trayful of tea. She seemed genuinely delighted to see Benedict, which caused much eye rolling from her sons.

'I hope you haven't laced the tea with too much arsenic, mother. This nice policeman might shut us down again,' said Tristram.

After a few minutes, while they group enjoyed the tea and sandwiches, an expectant silence fell. Just as nature abhors a vacuum, Lysander Benedict and the two Watts boys have even less regard for silence. Soon a few prompts from Rufus saw Benedict draw a rather extravagant handkerchief from his breast pocket, delicately dab the side of his mouth, nod pointedly in the direction of Mrs Watts before turning to the rest of the group to address them.

'Notwithstanding my success as a theatre critic,' began Benedict portentously which drew a snort from Tristram, ignored by the speaker, who continued, 'I once harboured some ambition to treading the boards myself. Initially, I thought about acting.'

There was no question that the fruitiness of Benedict's wine-encrusted speaking voice would have been a welcome addition to any minor repertory company.

'Sadly, theatre's loss was arts criticism's gain,' said Rufus sourly.

'Indeed,' agreed Benedict, ignoring the sarcasm. 'Not only acting, but you will also be interested to learn that I showed great promise in the area of prestidigitation. As you will have seen from the sad loss of our friend Gonzalo, or Graham Gibson as he was once known.'

This caused a few eyebrows to be raised around the table in surprise that the theatre critic was aware of the magician's real name.

'Yes, you seem somewhat taken aback that I know of our dear friend's former name. You see, I have been following his career with interest for a few years now. Among people like me who are interested in this area, Gonzalo or Gibson was certainly one of the more promising practitioners of the art. Did you know for example that he was in a double act soon after the end of the War?'

Can there be anything more satisfying than asking a question to which you know the answer to but no one else seems to have a clue about? There was a collective shaking of heads which drew an enormous smile of satisfaction from Benedict while the two Watts brothers scowled.

'Oh indeed, he was in a double act called, rather dubiously I always thought, the Brothers Grimoire. This of course is a play on the fairy tale writers and a book of spells. I gather they stole the name from some Germans.'

Kit frowned at this. There was something in his memory about the name. Perhaps something that his Aunt Agatha had mentioned. He did not have time to recall more as Benedict was forging on relentlessly.

'Yes, the Brothers Grimoire built up quite a following in Manchester, Blackpool and Southport. Just as they were about to make their bid for success in London, one of the brothers committed suicide. That left Gibson with a range of successful illusions to do himself and also without having to share the profits. There was always some suspicion over the events surrounding the death of Andrew Harper.'

'From the police?' asked Jellicoe sharply.

'Alas not, chief inspector. I gather they were not a very inquiring lot up there. They took the suicide at face value. There was a suicide note. Harper was known to be a depressive. It was, to all intents and purposes, an open and shut case.'

'But you did not think so?' asked Jellicoe.

Benedict gave a shrug. Then he opened his arms expansively which prompted an audible groan from Tristram.

'As a gifted amateur in the art of prestidigitation, I have more insight into the art than most. Magic became the dominant interest of my life when I was young. I realised from an early age that the wonder of magic was not so much in the illusion itself, as the way it was dressed up and the skill with which it was performed. I imagine I would have been rather good at this, but I had no talent, believe it or not, for envisaging illusions. I think that Gonzalo and I were alike in this regard if what I understand is true. I gather it was Harper who created most of the illusions. So, his death may or may not have been murder. Had it not been for the convenient suicide note, it may also have been considered a tragic accident.'

'How so?' asked Jellicoe.

'He hanged himself. I gather that this was an illusion they were considering introducing into their act – the Hanged Man or some such nonsense. Not in very good taste, but it would have been a first.

Jellicoe and Kit exchanged glances. This would need to be followed up. Kit was already thinking about his valet, Harry Miller, who was still in London.

'How on earth could they hang someone and not kill them,' asked Jellicoe.

'Oh, I think you'll find there's always a way, chief inspector. It's well accepted within the world of magic that the bigger the trick, the more banal the solution.

As he was saying this, the arts critic fished out from his pocket a newspaper cutting and handed it to Jellicoe.

'Of course one cannot know now,' said Benedict, his mouth curling up to emphasise how such matters are beyond the ken of mere mortal men such as himself. 'This article was sent to me by a young friend in Manchester who shares an interest in illusion. He was deeply saddened by the young man's passing. He felt that there was enough doubt around the circumstances of the suicide to warrant at least something, other than a cursory investigation, that your colleagues up north considered sufficient.'

Jellicoe ignored the barb while he read the article. He handed it over to Kit, who had Rufus and Tristram either side of him, to read.

'More tea?' asked Mrs Watts in the meantime. If her sons abhorred silence then she had an equal if not greater revulsion for social gatherings that were not being oiled by liberal quantities of tea.

Kit read the article carefully. The newspaper was the Manchester Guardian dated 18th May 1920.

Tragic Suicide of Young Magician

The Funeral took place today of Andrew Harper, one half of the popular illusionist act, The Brothers Grimoire. Mr Harper was found hanged in his dressing room at the Folly Theatre. Mr Harper had been known to suffer bouts of depression since returning from the War early in 1919. Police have confirmed that they are not pursuing any investigation as Mr Harper provided a suicide note before taking his own life.

Mr Harper is survived by a twin sibling who was not present at the funeral today and who had not yet been contacted by the police. The funeral was organised and paid for by Mr Graham Gibson, the other half of the Brothers Grimoire. Mr Gibson was said to be distraught at the funeral today.

Kit looked up from the article, his attention was directed towards Jellicoe. The stern cast of the policeman's features was, if anything, even sterner having read the piece.

Then Jellicoe turned to the newspaper arts critic. With barely contained fury he said, 'Why have you waited until now to show us this?'

Benedict was slightly taken aback by the rather aggressive tone of Jellicoe. He stuttered a reply, 'It took a little time to locate the article.'

'Then why didn't you mention it when you spoke to Detective Inspector Wellbeloved when you saw him yesterday.'

'Well, I, I was going to, but I thought it better that I find the article first. I wanted to make sure my facts were correct.'

'Why break the habit of a lifetime, Lysander?' asked Tristram, archly.

This was met with a sharp look from Mrs Watts who did not take kindly to unkind remarks from her children although, thought Kit with a smile, she should really be used to it by now.

'I think I shall leave you in the capable if rather rude hands of my children, gentlemen,' said Annie Watts. 'We have a show to run.' She looked meaningfully at her two children and then departed.

Jellicoe sighed at the prospect of the new avenue of inquiry that had just opened up. However, Kit was already thinking ahead. He noted the reaction of Jellicoe which was all too comprehensible. The chief inspector was here as a favour for Rufus Watts. This was going to add complexity and require more resources than he could reasonably spare. Kit had his suggestion ready.

'Chief inspector, I know this is a little bit unusual for all the reasons that you already appreciate, but perhaps I could help a little with regard to looking into what occurred in Manchester.'

Jellicoe frowned for a moment and then a light entered his eyes followed by an ever so slight smile.

'Are you proposing we avail ourselves of the services of Mr Miller?' asked Jellicoe.

'Yes, I am,' answered Kit. 'Without, I may add, resorting to his particular set of skills.'

Kit was referring to the fact that before the War, his valet, Harry Miller, had been a reasonably successful burglar. The War and his rescue of Kit Aston, one night a couple of weeks before Christmas 1917, had changed his life forever.

'What do you propose?'

'Harry could go up to Manchester and meet with people in the police there to understand the particulars of the case. You would need to warn them in advance of course. Then he could try and find the twin brother of this young magician. One could argue that if Gonzalo or Gibson were murdered then the twin brother would have a clear motive. Revenge. Harry could certainly research more about this and speak to people in the local theatres, where the Brothers Grimoire would have worked.'

While Kit was speaking, Rufus was nodding his ahead in agreement. Having met Harry Miller on many occasions, he had little doubt that the little Londoner was highly capable and would quickly get to the bottom of what had happened in Manchester.

'Very well,' responded Jellicoe, although there was some reluctance in his voice. He was in a bind. There was just not the men to put on this case which still might turn out only to have been a tragic accident, notwithstanding the threatening notes and the sudden disappearance of Bert Cooper.

Kit, meanwhile, was pondering the words of the newspaper critic. Gonzalo, if Benedict was to be believed, was potentially, a murderer. Yet what was the motive for killing his partner in the act? Especially as it seemed they had complimentary skills. One was a showman, the other was a man who suffered from depression, but who created the tricks that the act used. Both had equally important roles in making the act a success. Illusions are rarely original. Even Kit appreciated that, it was all in the presentation; the theatre you create around a simple piece of misdirection. Nothing about what had happened in Manchester made any sense. Was this all misdirection?

The meeting ended on this point. While Lysander Benedict sauntered off, no doubt to write up a column about how he was helping the police, Kit accompanied Tristram and Rufus back into the auditorium.

14

Hector Goulding and the orchestra had arrived a little earlier for band call. They comprised the conductor Goulding, Annie Watts on piano along with a violinist, a cellist, a trumpeter and a percussionist.

Mary was on stage with Daisy Lewis. Both were deep in discussion, each clutching sheet music. Goulding was standing with them. The mood appeared quite relaxed. Kit suspected that Mary had already won her spurs with the other performers. Quite aside from the fact that she really did have a pleasant voice, her personality and sense of humour would always be a winning combination. Daisy Lewis seemed to have recovered from the shock of Cooper leaving her. This, of course, raised some questions in Kit's mind, but he hoped that Mary would be able to find out more on this.

He watched as Mary and Daisy duetted wonderfully on a few songs made famous during the War: *A Long way to Tipperary, Pack Up Your Troubles (In Your Old Kit Bag)*, and *For Me and My Gal,* with the latter's lyrics remade for female singers. Their voices blended delightfully. Mary's wistful and delicate delivery complemented Daisy's deeper, earthier voice. It was clear that Daisy Lewis was quite enjoying singing with her. Perhaps it was helping to take her mind off what had happened, mused Kit.

When they had finished, Tristram called from his seat in the stalls that, as it was after twelve thirty now, they could break for lunch. Then he turned to Kit and Rufus.

'You know if Mary ever fancies to make a go of this...'

'I'll let her know,' laughed Kit, but he was feeling rather proud. Now, he had to remember to revert to the character of Chauncy Alston that Mary had mischievously lumbered him with. He rose to greet Mary and be introduced to Hector Goulding.

Goulding was tall, slender and made every effort to appear elegant. He was in his early sixties but seemed older. A moustache reluctantly adorned his lip. His raised, aquiline nose gave every appearance of being owned by a snob, which was confirmed the moment he spoke.

'How do you do, sir,' said Kit in his southern gentleman guise.

Goulding eyed him suspiciously, before replying, 'Charmed, I'm sure.'

Kit ignored this and ploughed on, 'I must say my gal Mary sure sounded pretty good up there to these ol' ears of mine.'

Goulding glanced at Mary, with only the merest hint that he was in any way impressed.

'She'll do,' he said before wandering off to join someone less boring than Kit; probably himself. Kit glanced at Mary and the Watts brothers. They were fighting losing battles against holding back their laughter.

'You've met Mr Goulding now. What do you think?' asked Rufus, eyes twinkling with mischief.

The departure of Lysander Benedict following his revelations allowed Kit the opportunity to explore the theatre a little bit more in the company of Rufus Watts while his brother and mother returned to the auditorium to recommence the rehearsals for the re-opening of the show on the next night.

They walked around past the stage door, at the side of the theatre, to a narrow alley at the back. There was a large doorway to allow for scenery to be moved in or out. The brown paint was peeling off the door which was met by a we-really-should-do-something-about-that comment from Rufus.

The air was salt-stained and fresh with the smell of fish, wafting in from the harbour. As they neared the stage door, three youths spilled out onto the street from a pub near the corner. As Kit and Rufus passed them, one of them broke wind so ferociously that it was a wonder he managed to avoid taking off into the air. The three youths erupted into hysterical laughter.

'Friends of yours?' asked Kit as they reached the stage door.

'Oh yes,' replied Rufus, 'I'm seeing them later for cocktails and canapés.'

Kit was happy to return inside through the stage door. It was here that Kit met Ezra Bertram, the ageing occupant of the position of stage door keeper. He also doubled up as lighting manager, although he no longer worked as a stagehand. He gazed benignly at Kit over his half-moon spectacles.

'Arthritis, I can't lift much anymore,' explained Ezra to Kit as he and Rufus walked into his office. Kit noted that the office led to another room in which he could see a single, unmade bed peeking out. At the foot of the bed was Romeo the cat who was happily lapping up some milk from a plate. 'Have you met Romeo?' asked Ezra with a broad grin. He still had some teeth left. Some. Kit put his age at anywhere between sixty and ninety. He was keen to ask if this was where he lived, however did not want to appear rude. Thankfully, Ezra was only too glad to fill the gap in Kit's knowledge.

'I've been at the theatre fifty-one years, man and boy. Joined when I left school at twelve. Mr and Mrs Watts have always looked after me, allowing me to stay here and everything,' he said, almost welling up with tears. 'Now it's Mr Tristram who runs things. There are no better people on this planet sir. None.'

'I'm inclined to agree with you, Ezra,' said Kit. He reverted to his southern accent but suspected that it might be lost on Ezra who seemed a simple soul.

Kit risked a glance in the direction of Rufus. The artist seemed to be welling up a little. He smiled towards Ezra then said, 'Ezra was like a second father to us.'

'Oh they were terrible boys, they were. Always up to something,' laughed Ezra, fondly.

Just then they heard a noise coming from the small room that appeared to be Ezra's sleeping accommodation. It was a man's voice.

'Ah, I see Barney has joined the land of the living once more,' said Rufus drily.

'Barney sleeps here?' exclaimed Kit, somewhat taken aback by the news. He had yet to meet the other member of the magic act that had gone so badly wrong.

'Yes,' replied Rufus nodding. 'Mrs Harrison has something of a phobia about people like Barney. He's used to it. You don't mind Ezra, do you?'

'No,' laughed Ezra, 'It's nice to have the company. Much as I love Romeo, he's not a talker.'

107

Romeo walked past them to return to his work. They followed his progress back to work down the corridor that led towards the stage. Barney appeared at the door. He eyed Kit suspiciously.

Barney Hallett had dark hair with flecks of grey appearing. He was just a shade under four feet six. To Kit's eyes, he seemed a little the worse for wear. This was confirmed a few moments later by Ezra.

'You had one too many last night, old friend.'

Barney groaned, rubbed his head and replied, 'Don't remind me.'

'Barney, meet Mr Alston. He is looking at investing in the theatre,' said Rufus, conscious he had not formally introduced Kit yet.

Kit shook hands with Barney and, with more of a hint of the southern drawl he had adopted earlier, said, 'Pleased to meet you. I'm sorry about Mr Gonzalo. What happened exactly?'

Barney paused for a minute, and he seemed to become a little emotional, as the events flashed in front of him once more.

'It was terrible Mr Alston. I was underneath the stage waiting for him to fall through the chute.'

'Who else was there?' asked Kit.

'Eddie Matthews appeared. His act had just finished. We chatted for a moment. It was difficult to hear him over the music. I have to use that as my guide for what point they are in the act. I could also hear the wheels of the cabinet above me. Then just when Javier was supposed to come down, nothing happened. I could hear him kicking at the trap door of the cabinet. That's when Eddie Matthews said, "Something's wrong, Barney." I knew he was right.'

'So what did you do?' pressed Kit, forgetting his accent for a minute.

'There are stairs up to the wings on either side. I went up the side where the Monteverdi boys were. I shouted to them that Javier was trapped but, well, we were too late to stop what happened.'

'Do you know what stopped the door from opening?' asked Kit.

'That's just it, there was no reason why it should have been stuck.'

'Perhaps, you can show me, I'm rather curious about this,' asked Kit. Barney nodded at this. Then Kit turned to Rufus and Ezra. 'Where can I send some telegrams? I need to give Harry Miller some information and book him a room.'

Ezra piped up at this point, 'Let me sir. Just wait a moment.' He left the group for a moment and opened the stage door that Kit had entered through just a few minutes earlier. Putting his fingers to his lips he gave a piercing whistle.

'Never been able to do that,' said Kit.

Rufus seemed unimpressed, 'I'm not quite sure why you would want such an accomplishment, dear boy.'

Kit shrugged and smiled, 'You never know when these things might be useful.'

The raised eyebrow from Rufus suggested 'never' was the only answer to this question.

A minute later Ezra reappeared back inside. With him was a boy of about twelve years old wearing a baker boy cap and denim dungarees. He was also, unusually for this part of the world, black.

'Meet Joshua, gentlemen. Joshua, this is Mr Alston. I think you know Mr Rufus.'

Joshua's smile was wide, and he touched his cap.

'Hello gentlemen.'

'Joshua, this Mr Alston is from your mother's part of the world.'

Kit was surprised that his accent had proved so convincing, and he scolded himself for doubting Ezra's ability to guess its provenance.

'Joshua,' said Kit, a little nervously adopting his southern accent once more. 'Would you mind running to the telegraph office and sending a couple of telegrams for me?'

'Yes sir,' grinned Joshua.

Kit went into Ezra's office and found some paper. He quickly scribbled the messages and handed them to Joshua along with some money.

Joshua looked at the money and frowned. He said, 'This is way too much sir for these telegrams.'

'I know,' said Kit. 'The rest is for you.'

The boy's eyes widened, and he laughed out loud.

'Mr Rufus, you should watch young Joshua dance sometime. I've never seen anything quite like it,' said Ezra, proudly. Rufus was surprised by this and put his hand on Joshua's shoulder.

'Do you dance young man?'

'Yes,' exclaimed Joshua. Like most young boys, he took the view that it was better to speak in exclamations rather than the dull monotone of adults. Kit wondered when he had lost that innocent desire to proclaim to the world what he was thinking rather than disguise it with words. 'I love to dance. My mum sings to me every night and I dance.'

'Well, perhaps we should look at you sometime,' murmured Rufus with a smile. Then he added, 'Now hurry along.'

A tall young man of eighteen by the name of Jez Barker, who earlier had so distinguished himself with his intestinal pyrotechnics, spied Joshua exit the stage door. He dug an elbow into his shorter and arguably, even less intellectually enhanced friend, Stan 'the man' Taylor and pointed to Joshua. Their third friend, Mick Houston was already chuckling.

This was a gift from heaven. The young black kid was a regular subject of their wit and repartee. As yet this had not spilled over into anything more than a few comments about Joshua's personal hygiene.

'Shall we chuck 'im in the bin, Jez?' asked Stan, always eager to please the unofficial leader of their group.

'Don't be stupid, Stan,' said Mick, who was the unofficial second-in-command, although he never acknowledged his place in the ranks.

'Mick's right, Stan,' came the murmured reply from Jez. Too many people. Plenty of time to have fun.

By tacit agreement they accepted there would be little opportunity, on this occasion, for greater sport, other than a few well-chosen comments along lines already developed previously.

*

Kit watched Joshua walk outside. Up ahead, he saw the three youths eyeing Joshua closely. As expected, a few moments later the youths began shouting abuse at Joshua about his colour. Ezra darted outside immediately, shouting, 'Clear off you little blighters.'

Tristram shook his head then glanced towards Kit and saw that his eyes were blazing. Ezra returned, flushed and angry. He said, 'Happens a lot. They run off and I'm too old to catch them. Young Joshua seems used to it.'

Kit was appalled. He turned to Rufus with an expression that had changed dramatically. His anger had turned to ice. Rufus frowned before smiling, 'What are you thinking?'

Kit murmured thoughtfully, 'I have an idea on how to put a stop to this.'

Kit was reluctant to add to this rather enigmatic reply. He and Rufus took their leave of Ezra to follow Barney. The corridor, like much of the theatre, had framed playbills on the walls, some dated back to the 1880's. Every so often Kit would stop at one and comment on an artist that he might have seen.

They stopped and glanced into the empty dressing rooms. Then Rufus pointed to the green room where the artists waited for their turn to perform. The room was small but comfortable. There were several armchairs and a sofa. Kit nodded and they moved onwards to the door that led through to the area immediately beneath the stage. Barney took them through what had happened from his point of view. He stood directly beneath the trap door on the other side of the chute.

'I was here, waiting for Javier to come through,' said Barney. He pointed to a small step ladder directly under the escape hatch in the stage. 'I use this to climb into the cabinet.'

'Where were Matthews and Lemaire?'

'Lemaire had just entered; he was standing by the door,' said Barney pointing, 'and Matthews was on the other side near me.'

Kit nodded without saying anything to this. He walked over to the chute and looked up. Using the step ladder he climbed up and popped his head through the trap door. His eyes were now level with the stage in the gap between the cabinet and the stage; half his head was below the stage, the other half above. The gap was around two to three inches. All he could see were the castor wheels of the cabinet. There was singing on stage. It sounded like Daisy Lewis was rehearsing one of her numbers, *Oh by Jingo*, a song with nonsense lyrics that demanded much of the performer. Daisy Lewis handled it with a practised ease that impressed Kit immensely.

Kit ducked back below stage. Rufus raised his eyebrows in a questioning manner. It was greeted with a shake of the head. Inspiration had not struck yet.

The music finished up above and there was a low murmur of voices among the performers. Then Kit heard two sets of footsteps on the stage. They were now standing above and front of Kit.

'Boys and girls,' announced Tristram, 'I'd like to present our new, stand-in comedian. This is Max Miller. I've seen him a number of times in concert parties, and I think he will be a wonderful addition to our show.' Max was greeted with a muffled round of applause.

Kit turned to Rufus and Barney, 'Have you seen him?'

Rufus shook his head, but Barney nodded and smiled.

'I have. He's young, a bit near the knuckle but a good turn. Certainly better than Eddie Matthews. Mind you, I've been to funerals that were more fun than watching that man.'

15

Mid-afternoon found Harry Miller, Kit Aston's valet, on a train heading up to Manchester. It had taken him less than an hour to pack an overnight bag and reach London St Pancras just in time to board the train. The journey would take a little over three hours. He was to stay at the Midland Hotel. Kit would send instructions on what he was to do.

It felt good to be working on a case once more. Over the last six months he had been questioning just how much he wanted to be in service. As much as he admired Kit Aston and despite his deep fondness for Mary, service was not something that came naturally to him. He was a Londoner with that city's wicked sense of humour and lack of reverence for authority. Yet for the last couple of years he had led a life that had not lacked for excitement and travel. Interspersed with these adventures, were periods of ennui that he knew Kit Aston felt as much as he did. Both were men of action and it certainly looked as if Mary had acquired a taste for adventure too.

Perhaps, following the brush with death he'd experienced a few months ago in Tangier, a period of reflection and inactivity had been just what he needed. The cravings had returned now. They would be staved off by this new case, if that's what it was, but they would never go away now, he accepted.

Mile after mile of green countryside, silvery grey skies and smoke-stained northern towns swept past him until he was finally pulling in to Manchester Central Station. Despite having stayed at the best hotels since working in service for Kit Aston, Miller never felt anything less than a thrill when walking into grand hotels knowing that he was there as a guest. He strolled through the hotel like he owned the place although he was not someone who would forget who he was or from where he had come. A part of him would always be Harry Miller, former burglar. Oddly, he wanted never to lose that. Kit certainly didn't want him to lose this, given the number of times he'd called upon his uncommon skills for breaking and entering in the cause of their investigations.

A telegram from Kit was waiting for him when he arrived at the hotel. It gave a phone number to ring at seven in the evening, when Kit could brief him fully on what was needed. This left Miller with an hour to stroll around the centre of Manchester.

The hour passed very quickly and soon he requested a call to the number Kit had given him. When he was put through, a familiar voice came on the line.

'Hello, Harry are you safely ensconced?'

'Hello sir,' replied Harry. 'Yes, it's a lovely hotel. Looking forward to dinner here.'

They chatted for a minute about the hotel before Kit got down to business for the next day.

'Chief Inspector Jellicoe has arranged for you to see his counterpart in Manchester, a Chief Inspector Sheridan. He's has been apprised of what happened down here. He led the original investigation into the death of Andrew Harper, which is to say he did nothing. Clearly, we want to keep him on our side so try and find out as much as you can about the people that Harper and this chap, Gibson, knew. They will tell you more than this chump of a detective. Also, try and find out if he ever found this missing twin of Harper.'

'Will do, sir. Anything else?'

'Yes, go to the Folly Theatre if you can. That's where Harper and Gonzalo were working as the Brothers Grimoire when he killed himself or was killed. See if you can pick up anything from them. Finally, the reporter at the Manchester Guardian is a chap named Pat Tully. He wrote the article about Harper's funeral. Speak to him and perhaps even the theatre critic. Who knows? They may be able to help us.'

After this, Kit updated Miller about the progress of the investigation which was a fairly short conversation. The call ended after fifteen minutes to allow Miller to go to the restaurant and order the most expensive meal, while Kit would dine without Mary, worrying still about her working undercover at the theatrical digs.

By eight-thirty, Miller had finished his meal. He was at a loose end so decided to take a walk into the city and, perhaps, catch a show. A quick enquiry with the receptionist provided him with directions to the Folly Theatre which was nearby on Peter Street.

Miller headed out into the night. It was a short walk to the theatre. A large sign left the viewer in no doubt that this was the Folly Theatre. Miller hoped that his expedition would prove anything but. He went over to the playbill.

Headlining the show was "the cheeky, cheery and chubby" Billy Danvers. This looked right up Miller's street. The show was probably underway, but the prospect of seeing some of the speciality acts which included a strongman, and a juggler didn't stir him much. He bought a ticket and peeked his head through at the act on the stage. The current act was a drummer beating seven bells out of a variety of drums around him. Miller decided to give this a miss and headed upstairs to the bar. He wasn't alone. Half the audience appeared to have used the appearance of the drummer to extend the intermission by a few minutes in order to finish off their drinks.

After Miller had bought a pint of ale, he wandered around the edge of the bar area scanning the various framed playbills to see if any featured the Brothers Grimoire. He found one near the exit.

The playbill was a lavish affair. The Brothers Grimoire was written in gothic script at the bottom. The picture on the bill showed two magicians, one dressed in tails seemed like the hero of in a moving picture. He was holding out his arms while a rather scantily dressed young woman floated between them. The other man in the picture was the very personification of Satan himself. His face was red, and he had horns protruding from his head. Good and evil appeared to be in a battle to win the young woman. Underneath the main headline featuring the Brothers Grimoire, was a support act, Madame Svengali, the witch of Metis.

When Miller finally took his seat, he was in time to see the end of an act featuring a rather large lady singing an aria from an opera that Miller had no intention, on the evidence before him, of ever going to see.

At last the headline turn showed up on stage to great applause from the audience. Billy Danvers was just as Miller imagined him to be. Short, plump and dressed in a light suit with thick stripes and light grey bowler hat. His nose had been rouged slightly to enhance the image of being a clown. Miller decided he would be the judge of that. The comic grinned broadly while waving his hands to get the people to stop clapping. When the applause died down he chuckled a little before he began to speak.

'I see there a few ladies in the room. Now I was thinking this was more for the gentlemen.'

This brought a few anticipatory laughs from the women in the audience. Miller was in the grand circle and could see there were quite a few in the audience.

'I've just come over from the hotel. When I checked in today, I found a lady's nightdress lying on the bed. Hey, hey, what's this, I thought, so I rang the bell. For what? To ask them to take it away? No. To ask them to fill it in.'

The crowd roared in laughter; in Miller it provoked a smile but not much more. Hopefully, things would get better.

'I came here by train. I'm not saying it was a bit late, but on that line you don't need a watch, you need an almanac.'

Miller chuckled at this. He settled back to enjoy the show.

16

Kit's initial impression that Mary and Daisy Lewis had hit it off onstage was proving to be every bit as accurate off the stage too. Mary's natural vivacity, openness and sympathy meant women were often drawn to her.

At dinner that evening, the whole of the troupe showed up, including Jane Anthony who had, thus far, kept away from the others. Expressions of condolence were, once more, forthcoming, but there was something rather forced about it all now. Mary sensed they were waiting for the funeral the next day and then they just wanted to get on with their lives.

The show must go on had been a phrase left unuttered, yet Mary could sense its presence in the room. It was there in the praise for Mary and Daisy's duet, it was hung over the discussion about the new comic, Max Miller, who had appeared earlier at the theatre before returning to his home in Brighton. The people around her, Mary realised, truly lived and breathed their way of life. It was a vocation no less than being a priest, a teacher, or a nurse. Once more, she felt a stab of guilt about her deceit.

The presence of Jane Anthony subdued conversation. No one wanted to say the wrong thing. Perhaps sensing this, Jane retired early to bed before the arrival of the inevitable apple tart with custard. Mary was disappointed as the brief conversation she'd had with Jane gave her the impression that she was both friendly and thoughtful. When she left to return to her room, it seemed to act rather in the manner of a pin being pulled out of a grenade.

'I'm surprised the coppers are letting us back to do the show,' began the ever-sour Eddie Matthews.

'Why do you say that?' asked Lucien Lemaire, only half-interested. His attention had been on Mary for most of the meal.

'Oh come on Lemaire, let's face it, one of us garrotted poor Gonzalo in that cabinet. Had to be one of us and that one of us is sitting in the room,' announced Matthews to the shock of the others at the table. Noting his impact he added, rather unnecessarily, 'One of us is a murderer.' In the moments before the storm broke he fixed his eyes on Daisy Lewis and sneered, 'Or maybe he escaped last night.'

Lemaire saw his opportunity. Observing the look of shock on Daisy's face, which seemed genuine enough to Mary, who was sitting beside her at the table. He snarled at the ageing comic, 'Shut your mouth or I will shut it for you.'

'Permanently?' retorted Matthews, a sly grin on his face. This was swiftly followed by a laugh that resembled a lemon in that it was intense, bright and very bitter.'

Mary immediately snapped at Matthews, 'How dare you. What kind of a man are you? How can you be so insensitive?'

Lemaire lowered his voice, conscious that the conversation would be carrying up through the ceiling to Jane Anthony who boarded directly above them. 'There is absolutely no way that someone in this company killed Gonzalo. It had to be someone from the outside.'

'How?' laughed Matthews, not making any attempt to be quiet. 'One of us killed him. It's as plain as your fake French accent.'

'Keep your voice down, Matthews,' said the elder Monteverdi brother, Gian Luca, pointing up to the ceiling.

'What do I care what she thinks? Crocodile tears from that one. I've shed enough of them in my time to know what they look like.'

Lemaire stalked over to Matthews and stood over him. It seemed the thing to do now and he didn't expect Matthews would put up much of a show if he were threatened. Meanwhile, he hoped that the charming Mary would see what a real man looked like rather than that southern American fop she was with. He snarled at the old comedian, 'You are a miserable little man aren't you. While that poor woman mourns the loss of Javier...'

'Graham, you mean,' butted in Matthews.

This somewhat took the wind out of Lemaire's sails for the minute, but he had a girl to impress and *mon Dieu* he was going to do so.

'You should apologise to us all for your vile insinuations,' roared Lemaire.

'You can go to the devil. You're all talk and no fight,' responded Matthews, but his voice was lower now, and he looked like he wanted an end to an argument he regretted starting.

Mary fixed her eyes on him. Something in his manner suggested he knew something. Perhaps he just was born with a sly look on his face but, unquestionably, there was a certainty in what he'd said that made her wonder if, perhaps, he'd seen something.

Lemaire still had a girl to show off to, though. Just as he was taking a deep breath in order to ratchet up the volume a little bit more, Mrs Harrison entered the room, like a German Commandant at a prison camp. The expression on her face, which was somewhere in the no-man's-land occupied by incandescent fury and murder, was enough to silence the ventriloquist, much to his evident frustration. Whatever minor victory he had hoped to gain, through his bullying of the contemptible comedian, had been ripped from his hands by the fearsome landlady of the house.

Mrs Harrison proceeded to lay down the law in no uncertain terms thereby further undermining Lemaire in the eyes of all. He retired to his seat, beaten but unbowed. When Mrs Harrison had retired to her quarters, Matthews decided to risk another, less controversial remark.

'We'll need the police outside to control the crowds tomorrow night, just you see.' As it turned out, the police were in force the next night, but not for the reasons that Eddie Matthews would either have expected or, indeed, welcomed.

The group wisely left any further thoughts on the investigation unspoken. Daisy Lewis decided to retire for the night. Her departure saw conversation turn to the new comic who had performed a little of his act for the troupe earlier at the rehearsals.

'What do you think of Max Miller, Mr Matthews?' asked Enrico Monteverdi. He was the younger of the brothers. The elder Monteverdi was all stature while Enrico was all sinew with dark hair and looks that Douglas Fairbanks would have killed for. The elder brother, Gian Luca was chattier and much more self-confident. He was the strong man in the act and one of the best jugglers that

Mary had ever seen. While the brother's eyes often darted towards Mary, Gian Luca mostly ignored her.

Matthews seemed relieved at the change of subject. It was also an opportunity to indulge in one of his favourite past times, discussing and dismissing other acts as inferior. In fact, Mary had rather enjoyed the cheekiness of Max Miller, but remained silent as Matthews dismantled the act.

'Typical of the new breed of comic. Relies a little too much on muck if you ask me.'

'Rubbish,' said Lemaire, still sore from earlier.

Jackie agreed. She said, 'I think he'll be a star. Yes he was a bit near the knuckle, but it was implied, never explicit.'

'True,' acknowledged Matthews, trying not to resume any argument, 'but it's the whole act. Don't hear me wrong. I enjoyed parts of it. He has potential. I says to him afterwards there were bits he could improve. Bit of rephrasing here, more subtlety there. Better set ups. There's potential all right and the crowd are with him. No one is out to get a young comic like they're out for me.'

There was a collective rolling of eyes at this. This was a favourite subject for Matthews, his belief in the existence of mysterious persecutors who were organised and out to give him the bird. From what Mary had seen of him, she could see the audience no longer found him funny. Perhaps they never had. Watching him go through his act was uncomfortable; one felt embarrassed for the old man. Perhaps children might find it funny, an old, red-nosed comic manically waving his arms around and talking gibberish; Mary didn't find it in the least bit amusing and nor did the audience. There was despair in his eyes when he performed. It was all so sad.

Mary excused herself soon afterwards and went to her room. On the stairs she met Jane Anthony. Her eyes were red from the tears. Mary immediately took her hand.

'I'm sorry if you heard what they were saying.'

Jane nodded but did not reply.

'Mr Matthews is fairly free with his opinions, isn't he?' said Mary.

A harder glint appeared in the young woman's eyes.

'Oh yes. He always has something to say. He thinks he knows everything. It was an accident. A horrible, tragic accident. Can't people see that?' cried Jane. 'Instead, I must listen to vile innuendo and answer the most awful questions from the police.'

Mary decided not to comment on this. They parted and Mary went to her room while Jane entered the bathroom. Mary read for a while before deciding to leave the room to freshen up. There was only one bathroom in the villa with another outside. She descended the stairs and went into the kitchen, passing Henry the St Bernard on the way. He looked up from his bowl with an air of apology. Mary stroked him behind the ear before reaching for the torch that Mrs Harrison provided for those who had to go the lavatory in the garden. The torch barely made any impression on the blackness of the night. She pulled her dressing gown around her as she picked her way along a path. Then she heard a noise behind her. Mary spun around.

From up above, she saw light in a window with a head peeking through. She recognised Mrs Harrison despite her hair being in a net.

'Are you going to the lavatory?' shouted Mrs Harrison.

Mary replied, 'Yes'.

'Well don't go in that one luv, that's the neighbour's and we're not speaking.'

'Oh,' said Mary, half smiling. 'I'll bear that in mind.'

'Move a little to your left,' advised the landlady. Then the window shut, and the light went off.

A few minutes later, as Mary walked back down the garden, she saw the orange glow of a cigarette. A man was smoking near the kitchen door of the villa. When she drew nearer the door, she saw that it was Lucien Lemaire.

'Hello Miss Mary,' said Lemaire, in a voice that was dripping honey.

'Hello Mr Lemaire,' said Mary. She proffered the torch. 'Do you need this?'

Lemaire looked her over in a rather obvious manner. 'Are you talking just about the torch?'

Mary smiled and tilted her head. She handed Lemaire the torch and went to move past him.

'Excuse me, Mr Lemaire.'

Lemaire's arm shot out, blocking Mary's way to the door.

'Not so fast Miss Mary. Are you sure you wouldn't like to stay a little longer?'

'No, Mr Lemaire. I would not like to stay. Excuse me.'

'Call me Lucien. What are you afraid of?' asked Lemaire, a slow grin appearing on his face. Mary could see that he was a man that could be considered attractive. Clearly, Lemaire had that impression of himself too and appeared to believe it was shared by every female that had ever cast their eyes on him.

'For all I know Mr Lemaire,' replied Mary, 'You could be a killer.'

'Only of ladies' hearts,' responded Lemaire, although a flicker of desperation was in his eyes as if, even he, realised that this line was unlikely to do anything for him, except make him look foolish. He laughed nervously, 'I'm jesting of course.'

'I hope so, Mr Lemaire. Now if you will please move, I am rather tired,' said Mary.

Lemaire moved his arm from the doorway to let Mary pass. As she entered the kitchen she heard him say, 'You can do better than that southern fop, Miss Mary. A lot better.'

Mary imagined that Kit might agree with him on that point, as Chauncey Alston, notwithstanding his unquestionable good looks, was not a character to steal ladies' hearts. She smiled to herself but kept moving lest the ventriloquist think her interested. Another thought had struck her. Kit was keen that Mary try and search the rooms. They had yet to uncover a concrete motive for the murder. This seemed a good opportunity, particularly as Jellicoe had not been able to gain approval to search any of the rooms except Gonzalo's.

She hurried up the stairs. Checking to see if anyone was in the corridor, she opened the door to Lemaire's room very quietly. The light was already on. She stepped inside the room.

The first thing she saw almost made her scream. Sitting upright on the bed was Charlie, Lucien Lemaire's dummy. It had a malevolent grin on its face as if it knew what Mary was intending to do. She crept forward, not taking her eyes off the diabolic figure. Keeping away from the window, she stole over to the drawers. She knew it was her imagination, but throughout her time in the room, she had the peculiar sensation that the dummy was staring at her. She kept her attention fixed on likely hiding places for anything that might be of interest.

The top drawer revealed socks and some other things that Mary had little desire to investigate further. The next few drawers were filled with assorted clothes. Inside the wardrobe, were hung a couple of suits with a couple of pairs of shoes at the bottom. There was a desk near the window. She crouched down and opened one of the drawers. Inside, was the same piece of paper she had seen in Tristram's office, the threatening note.

Torchlight outside attracted her attention. Lemaire was on the way back. Mary hastily shut the drawer and crept back towards the door. Just as she was about to open it, she heard a creak in the corridor. Someone was outside. It sounded like whoever had been in the bathroom had just left it. By the heaviness of the tread, Mary guessed that it was a man.

Mary held her breath. A tremor raced through her body. She felt the fabric of her dress against her skin. The seconds ticked by as she waited for the man to return to his room. At this point, Mary felt like screaming at him to get a move on. She heard Lemaire downstairs now talking with someone. Still the man remained in the corridor if the creaking of the floorboards was any guide. In fact, unless she missed her guess, he was outside the room.

Mary's heart was racing like a Derby winner just as it passes the post. The man outside seemed unsure about what he wanted to do. Lemaire was ascending the stairs now.

'Hello Gian Luca,' said Lemaire casually in a low voice. 'If you're hoping to make a pass at Miss Mary, I can tell you, you're too late.'

'What do you mean?' asked the elder Monteverdi.

'Oh, I'm too much of a gentleman to say. I just met her in the garden a few minutes ago. Let's just say she gripped my torch and a light shone into the darkness.'

Mary felt like gripping the ventriloquist's neck when she heard this scandalous smear. Men! She had always known Kit was different, but this was, even by the fairly low standards she expected from the species, particularly outrageous. To lie so blatantly and besmirch a young woman's reputation so casually, was beyond the pale.

Monteverdi laughed at this, a little uneasily in Mary's view. The only problem with such a shameful and barefaced lie was that it would soon seem to be true when Lemaire entered the room. She could hardly claim it was a mistake. Just as she was thinking of making herself comfortable underneath the bed, salvation was at hand.

'Do you fancy a brandy? It's still a little early,' said Lemaire.

'Very well,' replied Gian Luca. 'Enrico's in a foul mood. I'll leave him to his bad temper.'

With that, the two men began to descend the stairs. As soon as they were away, Mary skipped out of the room breathing a sigh of relief.

And ran right into Eddie Matthews.

17

The next morning:

'What did you say?' asked Kit, laughing. He was sitting facing Mary in Tristram's office.

'I nearly fainted, I can tell you,' replied Mary, half chuckling. 'Well, he gave me a bit of a look, so I said, well, it seems Mr Lemaire has missed his chance. Then I walked off.'

'Did Matthews say anything?'

'No, he just gave a laugh that was, shall we say, lascivious in nature.'

It was around nine in the morning. Kit and Mary were sitting with Jellicoe in the office. Mary had shared the events of the night before. Despite Kit's offer, Mary deemed it prudent not to assassinate Lemaire, especially given that Chief Inspector Jellicoe was presently drinking his third cup of tea from Annie Watts.

Jellicoe, it must be said, was somewhat unsure that he wanted to hear about Mary's uncommon, probably unlawful, search of Lemaire's room. On the other hand, his superintendent back at Scotland Yard was asking questions about when he would return. Crime did not stop, he said, just because he was sunning himself by the seaside. Just to emphasise this point, the rain rattled against the office window. Sunning himself; indeed.

'Where is Tristram and, come to think of it, Rufus?'

'Well, it's a little early in the morning for Rufus, but Tristram is down in the auditorium. We met a young man yesterday when you were rehearsing. According to Ezra, he's a rather extraordinary dancer. He's due anytime soon.'

'I should like to see him,' said Mary.

Kit turned to Jellicoe and asked, 'And how are Detective Inspector Wellbeloved's inquiries progressing?'

'Slowly. We now have a picture of who has worked with who and when. From this we can establish if anyone could have had a motive dating back to prior engagements.'

'So what are the connections between the various performers?'

'Gonzalo has worked with most everyone at one time or another. He worked with Matthews in Manchester when he was with the Brothers Grimoire. In fact, he was on the same bill at the time of Andrew Harper's death. He worked more recently in Brighton with Lemaire. The Monteverdi Brothers were there too. Matthews was working at that theatre too but left just as Gonzalo joined. Barney Hallett only teamed up with Gonzalo when he was in Brighton. Daisy Lewis and our friend Cooper, who is still at large, by the way, worked with Gonzalo in Eastbourne just after Christmas this year. They've worked with all of the others too, I gather. The Wyman Sisters were on the same bill.'

None of this seemed to move them much further on, but at least they could now be certain that everyone had, if not a motive, then an opportunity to have a reason through their prior association with the magician.

'I can't believe Cooper will evade capture much longer. In which case we can have a nice long chat with him about his reasons for jumping ship,' said Jellicoe although the sense of frustration about how long it was taking was evident.

'I've had some thoughts on that, chief inspector,' said Kit.

Mary's eyes narrowed at this, and she fixed them on Kit. The frown which went with it suggested that Kit was perilously close to a brief incarceration in the dog house, a location all too familiar to that breed of man universally known as "husband".

'Go on,' said Mary in a dangerously slow voice that, in any other situation, might have reasonably been considered as seductive.

'Yes, well,' said Kit laughing nervously. He realised any attempt to treat her reaction as a source of humour was unlikely to help his cause, so he wisely decided to get on with what he had to say. 'I wonder if our friend Cooper will be so easy to catch. If I'm right, I think he has done a rather good job of evading capture for quite some time.'

'How do you mean?' asked Jellicoe.

'I mean that his departure came rather as a surprise especially given that his alibi of being in the pub with Lysander Benedict meant he was just about bottom of the list of suspects. This had me thinking that there may be other reasons why he would be keen to avoid a police investigation. In such circumstances, it's normal to dig into people's pasts. What if Cooper was an army deserter? I knew quite a few that did. They would swap their identifications with boys that had died and then they would be off. Half the time, I didn't know where I was when things became a little bit hot. Bullets and bombs can befuddle you jolly quickly, I can tell you.'

Jellicoe nodded at this, and a smile crinkled the corner of his eyes although his drooping moustache made him seem forlorn. Kit risked a glance at Mary. She was resting her chin on her hand, a hint of a frown caressing her eyebrows.

'It only came to me last night,' said Kit before adding with a wry smile, 'while you were romancing Mr Lemaire.'

History did not have a chance to register Mary's response, as there was a knock at the door. Ezra entered and said, 'Young Joshua is here with his mother.'

'Ah excellent,' said Kit.

'Is Joshua's mother a member of the US Cavalry?' asked Mary.

'It would seem so,' said Kit rising from his seat. 'Will you join us chief inspector?' Jellicoe shook his head and pointed to a report that had been sent down from London by Wellbeloved. It contained more of the detail that Jellicoe had briefly summarised a few moments earlier. This was greeted with a sympathetic smile from Kit who added, 'If there's anything else of interest let me know.'

Ezra led Kit and Mary down to the auditorium. While they walked, Kit said, 'This should be interesting. The young lad's mother, Mrs Walker, is American.' This was greeted by delighted laughter from Mary and a clap of the hands. She was going to enjoy this all the more now. Kit smiled, 'Thank you for the support.'

'You're welcome,' said Mary.

As they entered the auditorium, they saw Tristram and Annie Watts, as well as the orchestra conductor, Hector Goulding, standing on the stage with Joshua and his mother.

Mary glanced up at Kit when she saw that Joshua and his mother were black.

'I wonder if Mrs Walker is from the south,' said Mary.

'I've been wondering the same thing myself, darling. I was rather hoping there would be no one else around. As Mr Goulding is there, I suppose I should maintain the deception.'

Kit and Mary climbed up to the stage where Tristram introduced Mrs Walker to them.

'Mr Alston this is young Joshua's mother, Mrs Walker. May I also introduce Miss Mary Frost,' said Tristram.

'I gather you are from my part of the world,' said Mrs Walker to Kit. She had a soft southern accent.

'I surely am,' said Kit, his eyes widening in horror at what he must have sounded like.

Mrs Walker's eyes widened also, but she maintained some composure. She was a tall, very handsome lady in her mid-thirties. She raised a sceptical eyebrow in the manner of a woman that had long since given up trying to understand the ways of the island race.

'Whereabouts do you come from?' asked Mrs Walker, a half-smile on her face.

'Charleston,' said Kit hopefully.

Mrs Walker chuckled at this, 'Why I'm from Charleston myself.'

Mary started coughing at this point, at least that's what she hoped it sounded like.

'Do you know the Beauregard-Simpsons?' asked Kit, half in desperation. Every drawn-out southern syllable was a dagger in his heart. By now, he was keenly aware that Tristram, too, was on the point of exploding with laughter.

'I've heard many good things about them.'

'I'm relieved to hear it,' said Kit who was relieved that the game was not up. Tristram decided to put Kit out of his misery by suggesting that they retire to the seats while Annie Watts and Hector Goulding, who was an accomplished violinist, played for young Joshua.

As they took their seats, Kit leaned in towards Mrs Walker to whisper to her. She held her hands up and grinned, 'I'm sure you have your reasons, sir.'

'I do. My apologies for butchering the accent.'

Hector Goulding now had a violin in his hand, and he appraised the twelve-year-old boy.

'Well, young man, what shall we play you.'

'Can you play ragtime music sir?' asked Joshua without a trace of nervousness. He was still dressed in his dungarees, but he had new shoes on, Kit noted. The previous day he'd worn a pair of very old boots that looked a size too big for him.

'Of course I know ragtime,' sniffed Golding. 'Would *Alexander's Rag Time Band* be acceptable?'

Joshua's eyes lit up and he nodded his head furiously.

'Very well,' said Goulding. He glanced towards Mrs Watts who had not stopped smiling throughout. She nodded to him and began the introduction.

The music started and so did Joshua. The smile never left his face nor those looking on as his feet miraculously came alive and became one with the melody. As Mrs Watts and Golding played the music, Joshua's tap dancing became its percussive beat.

Kit risked a glance at Mrs Walker and Mary who was sitting on the other side of Joshua's mother. Tears streamed down both their faces as they stared up at the stage. Kit returned his attention to Joshua. His feet were pumping out the rhythm of the music, his arms swayed too, but only to the point where they enhanced rather than distracted from the beat. When the music subsided, Joshua added an impromptu few steps and then bowed. The acclaim was immediate. Tristram was on his feet immediately shouting 'bravo'.

Joshua bowed once more and then put his arm out to acknowledge the two musicians. Annie Watts was in tears while Golding remained as reserved as ever, but there was just a flicker of a smile as he nodded to the young dancer.

'I'm not sure I need to see any more to convince me that young Joshua will not only be in the show tonight, but that he will have a great career in this business if he so chooses,' said Tristram.

Mary was, by now, comforting a very proud and emotional mother. A second performance was demanded, and Joshua's reading of W.C. Handy's *St Louis Blues* was another showstopper in Kit's view.

When they had finished Joshua came down from the stage with a smile as wide as the English Channel. He was hugged by his mother. Then he shook hands with Tristram and Hector Golding who appeared to be showing just a hint of warmth that hitherto had been absent in his demeanour.

Kit glanced down at Joshua's tap shoes. He said, 'They look new.'

At this point, tears welled up once more in Mrs Walker's eyes. She glanced towards the stage door manager, Ezra. The old man shrugged and grinned ruefully, 'Well, I couldn't very well let the lad dance in those clodhopper boots, could I?'

'Well done Ezra,' murmured Kit. The old man blushed a little and waggled the hair of his protégé.

'Well done, Joshua,' replied the stage door manager modestly.

Mary took Mrs Walker's hand and said, 'You should be very proud.' Mrs Walker was proud beyond words just at that moment. She nodded and smiled. Mary was curious, as ever, and decided to jump in where Kit had feared to tread. 'Has Joshua left school?'

Mrs Walker sighed before replying, 'He was at school, but it's not easy. He's different. His no-good wretch of a father is long gone and then there's his colour.' Mary squeezed Mrs Walker's hand. However, Mrs Walker had not finished, 'I teach him what I can in the evenings, but during the day I let him be. I have my work and he has a number of clients on the sea front. They know he's a good boy and they trust him.'

'He is a good boy,' assured Mary. 'What do you do Mrs Walker?'

'I work as a seamstress. I was a lady's maid. I came over with Mr and Mrs Andrews. We lived in London. It was a big house, mighty fine. Then when the flu took dear old Mrs Andrews, well, Mr Andrews just couldn't bear to stay in the place, so he went back home to the States. He offered to take me back too. He said he'd find something for us at the old house. I said thank you but no. It's not been easy for Joshua here, but it's a might better than it would be over there, Miss Mary. They don't treat our kind very well over there. Kids disappear. I didn't want that for my Joshua. He's happy here, too. Some treat him badly, but most are so nice, I could cry. Mr Ezra for example. Mrs Watts and Mr Tristram, too. They always got something for him to do. Mr Benson, too. He's not a nice man like Mr Tristram,

Joshua says, but he looks after his people, and he had no prejudice for my boy. That's plenty good in my book.'

Mary was surprised at the speech she had heard, although she frowned when she heard about Billy Benson.

'I gather Mr Benson is keen to take over the Empire and turn it into a picture house. Joshua needs to be careful Mr Benson doesn't use him to find out things about the Empire.'

Mrs Walker smiled and turned to Mary, 'Oh, my Joshua knows all about that. He says Mr Benson is a hard man, but not completely unkind; he never asks about the Empire. If anything, it's the other way around. Mr Rufus is a terrible man for this, but Joshua knows to say nothing.'

Mary laughed at this. She said, 'Yes, Rufus is a terrible man, but his heart is in the right place. Did Joshua know Mr Gonzalo?'

'He did. I don't think Joshua liked him very much. Most of the people here are very nice to him because they see him around all the time, but some are less kind than others. Mr Gonzalo thought a might too much about himself according to Joshua. He thinks that the others didn't have a good opinion of him either, particularly Mr Lemaire or Mr Cooper. He was the star of the show, and they didn't much like that. No, they didn't much like that at all from what I hear, Miss Mary.'

When Joshua left with Ezra and Mrs Walker to find something suitable to wear for the afternoon rehearsal, Kit, Mary and Tristram returned to the office. Mary updated them on what Mrs Walker had said, which Tristram confirmed with a roll of the eye and a dismissive comment about 'artistes'.

As they walked away from the stage, Kit said, 'I sent my friend, Chubby, a telegram yesterday thanks to young Joshua. Chubby works at the War Office, Tristram. He can look into Mr Cooper's file for us. With any luck, he'll be on the job now as we speak.

Just at that moment a few hundred miles away, Chubby was, indeed, on the job, but perhaps not in the way that Kit had imagined, although he would thoroughly have approved.

The last few days since Chubby had taken Miss Brooks home from Sunningdale Golf Club had seen an extraordinary transformation in their working relationship. This was symbolised very much in Chubby occasionally calling Miss Brooks by her first name, Kate. Remembering to call her by her Christian name was still proving a little more difficult than one would have imagined for a man who was now spending at least one hour a day kissing said young woman. While referring to her as Miss Brooks was not exactly a passion killer, she was thankfully just as enthusiastic about the turn of events, if not more so than Chubby. However, it was still something that she had to regularly remind him of.

While his friends were walking through the auditorium, Chubby was holding the telegram in one, prosthetic, hand and Miss Brooks in the other. No doubt in time, Chubby would bring to bear his native intelligence and sense of dedication to the task, but for the moment, with Miss Brooks staring up into his eyes, it was very much a case of first things first.

139

18

If Tristram had been in Manchester with Harry Miller, he would have been the first to acknowledge that 'artistes' were not the only species of man to have a good opinion of their own abilities. Such regard, in opposition to every known fact, was in the realm of most men and none more so than those who occupied senior positions in the police force. While Chief Inspector Jellicoe was certainly an exception to the breed, Chief Inspector Sheridan, in Miller's humble opinion, had stepped off the pages of a semi-comic novel.

They had agreed to meet at the hotel. Aside from the fact that Miller always felt distinctly uncomfortable in police stations and had been forced to stay a night or two in several, it suited the chief inspector who lived near to the hotel.

Sheridan was a large man dressed in a checked suit that would have seemed more appropriate on the Folly's stage from the night before. Missing was the hint of a red nose to indicate that nothing he said should be regarded with anything other than an easy-going good humour. It's absence and the stentorian features of the policeman suggested that good fellowship and assistance were the last things on Sheridan's mind.

'Why has Jellicoe asked you to investigate? I sent him the file,' snapped Sheridan.

Sheridan's opening gambit made Miller's heart sink. He avoided responding directly to this. Instead, he adopted the manner of a man who does not have a lot of time.

'If we could get down to business, sir,' retorted Miller. He had observed in a number of the nobles he'd worked with over the years; how effective the high hand could be in dealing with petty officialdom. Sheridan's eyebrow snapped upwards like a greyhound out of the trap. 'This comes from higher up than Jellicoe, I can assure you sir,' added Miller, with just enough sarcasm in his voice to put Sheridan on his guard.

Sheridan was no one's pushover, though. He leaned forward and asked sceptically, 'What do you mean?'

'Anarchists,' replied Miller.

Sheridan sat back and exhaled. This was a different matter. Despite the fact that he could see no connection between a magic act and subversion, unlike the tiresome Suffragettes, there was no point in looking naïve.

'I see,' he said, clearly not seeing anything. 'What do you want to know about the death of Andrew Harper?'

'Was there any suspicion of foul play?'

'None. It was suicide.'

'Why do you say that?'

'The suicide note was something of a clue,' said Sheridan, more than a hint of mockery in his voice. Miller felt his temper rising.

'Does the suspicious death of his former partner in the Brothers Grimoire act give you cause to reconsider that opinion?' asked Miller before adding quickly, 'I'm sure the original verdict from the coroner made sense at the time.'

'No.'

Miller felt a strong urge to throttle the man in front of him. He decided on a different tack.

'Were you ever able to contact the twin sibling of Mr Harper?'

'No.'

'Did you try?'

Sheridan eyed Miller for a moment before replying, 'No.'

'Why not?' asked Miller who had now decided to forego all civility.

'Why should I?'

'Didn't they have a right to know?'

'I'm sure they did, but that was left with the lawyer.'

'Lawyer?' asked Miller, a little surprised.

'Yes, chap called Lacey. From Lacey, Lacey and Kemp. They're in town. He was in charge of all that. Ask him.'

Miller decided to have one more attempt at prising an answer from Sheridan on the death of Harper.

'Did anyone have a motive for killing Harper?' asked Miller more in hope than expectation.

'I've no idea,' replied Sheridan shamelessly. 'Not his partner that's for sure.'

'Why not?' pressed Miller.

'He paid for the funeral. Not sure I'd want to kill my partner then spring for the cost of burying him. Harper was the brains behind the act. Gibson was just the front man. Unfortunately, Harper was a depressive. I've seen lots of their type top themselves. Make no mistake, this was suicide.'

It was a fair point, but nonetheless it did not mean that Gonzalo / Gibson did not have a hand in the death of

Harper. There seemed little prospect that he would gain much more from the detective, so, after finding out where he could find the firm of Lacey, Lacey and Kemp, he bid Sheridan an unfond farewell.

When they had parted, Miller made his way back into the city. Along the way, he passed the Folly Theatre once more. On the off chance that someone might be around he walked to the entrance but there was no sign of life. As it was only nine thirty, this was no great surprise. He wandered around to the side. The stage door entrance was also shut. Rather than assume no one was there, he rapped on the door. It took a minute or two, but the door opened to reveal a man in his sixties, slight of build but not unwelcoming in his manner.

'Hello?' he asked. One of the particular peculiarities of the English language is how any sentence can be turned into a question by a mere inflexion of voice.

'Good morning, my name is Miller. I was hoping I could chat to someone about the death of one of the Brothers Grimoire. I don't suppose you remember this act?' asked Miller disingenuously.

'Do I remember them?' replied stage door man, Nathaniel Magwitch. 'I'm the one what found poor Mr Harper.' Naturally, he remembered the Brothers Grimoire very well.

A cup of tea later, for this is how time is measured in England, Miller listened to the older man recount the events of that evening.

'They were a great turn, Mr Miller. We used to sell out when they were on the programme. I've been watching acts for forty years or more and I can tell a good 'un.'

'Why were they so good?' asked Miller, genuinely fascinated.

'Look, I know it's all a fix. I've been watching magicians long enough. But they put on a show, and it were clever too. I didn't know some of the tricks; they were new to me. Not just that, it was the show they made around it all. Different class it was.'

'Did you know them well?'

'No, not really,' said Nathaniel. 'The chap that died was very quiet, not very sociable. Thoughtful sort. The other one was more, well, not sure really. Not a nice man, I would say. Very charismatic on stage, but not very nice off it. At school I'd have called him a bully.'

'Did he bully the other chap?'

'Yes. Yes, I'd say he did. Mr Harper was different. Just very quiet.'

'Did you know that he had a twin?'

'No,' replied Nathaniel. 'News to me.'

'Did they have friends in the company?'

'No,' said Nathaniel firmly. 'Mr Gibson was very firm on this. I think he was afraid that the secrets to their tricks would be given away, although Mr Harper was quite friendly with Madame Svengali.'

'What was her real name?' asked Miller.

'No one knows. She spoke only with Mr Harper, and she kept herself to herself. Good turn, also. She had a mind reading act. Never knew how she did it.'

'Did Mr Gibson speak much with her.'

'She didn't like him; kept out of his way. I thought that she and Mr Harper were sweethearts, but then I wasn't sure.'

'Did they have any friends among the performers?' asked Miller.

'No, not particularly. They kept themselves to themselves. There was only the two of them. They didn't use any girls this time around. Nothing like that. Another show they did, there was a girl who was in a levitation act. Never knew her name. Nice girl. A widow, I gather, poor thing.'

'What kind of tricks did they do? I saw the levitation poster upstairs' pressed Miller.

'Well, I've never seen nothing like them. They also did a trick where they cut a man's head off. Another one they made a man disappear. The levitation was my favourite. When you see it though, it's all, well, I shouldn't say. It's a bit of a con, really. Clever, mind. Mr Gibson always made a big show of it to give him his due. Mr Harper just ran around and played the devil.'

The older man seemed genuinely in awe of these tricks. Miller was less interested in the tricks themselves and moved the conversation on before the old man went into too much detail.

'So you don't think they were good friends, do you?' asked Miller.

'No, I wouldn't have said. They argued from time to time, but you know what performers are like,' answered Nathaniel.

'Did either of them have family? You know, like children, wives, brothers, or sisters?'

'Sorry, I never saw anyone visit them. They were quite secretive. I suppose it goes with their profession. They didn't seem to trust anyone.'

Miller decided there wasn't much more to be gained from the stage door man, so he thanked him and was about to make his way back onto the street when a thought occurred to him.

'I don't suppose you have any spare playbills that feature the Brothers Grimoire?' asked Miller.

Nathaniel said he did and disappeared upstairs. He returned a few minutes later clutching three playbills. Two of them Miller had seen; the third playbill was a more general advertisement from when they were not a headline act.

The weather in Manchester, from the few times Miller had been to visit, rarely varied from grey and brooding. He wrapped the coat around himself and made his way towards the law firm which was a few streets away. His mood was as overcast as the sky. He didn't seem to have uncovered much that would help with the investigation on the south coast. This was disappointing but, he supposed, a part of the life of being a detective. You collected random pieces of information together; some of the pieces would be useful, others would not be, except in the sense that by their elimination you slowly moved towards the right solution.

Lacey, Lacey and Kemp occupied a dark brick building in the centre. A few years before, he would have felt trepidation at entering such a place, but now, having spent so much time with Kit Aston, important people held no fear for him. Besides which, he had seen such people in the trenches. They had acted as stupidly, as bravely or as cravenly as anyone else. They were not special or different or, for that matter, better.

'May I see Mr Lacey?' asked Miller of the man at the front desk.

'We have two Mr Laceys. Do you have a preference?' he sniffed, sizing Miller up with one look and deciding he was not much impressed with what he saw.

'I have been asked by Scotland Yard to speak to Mr Lacey in connection with the death of a performer, a magician, last year. His name was Andrew Harper. The man who was his partner, in the act known as the Brothers Grimoire, has recently died under very tragic circumstances. The police are investigating the matter and have asked me to make some inquiries of the Mr Lacey who handled the estate of Mr Harper.'

The man disappeared through a door leaving Miller to wait in the reception. He sat down on a Chesterfield sofa. A couple of minutes later the man reappeared.

'Mr Lacey will see you now. He can only spare you five minutes as he has a client appointment at ten.'

Miller thanked the man and followed him through the door into an ante room. A young woman was sitting at a desk with a typewriter. Her hair was tied up in a bun and she wore spectacles. Unquestionably, she was rather attractive. She ignored Miller so he ignored her, too. That would teach her.

Mr Lacey's office was large with high ceilings. Two sides of the office were filled with books: all legal tomes. A few original oil paintings adorned the free spaces on the wall. Lacey sat with his back to a large window. He rose to greet Miller. Lacey was in his forties and had an air of self-importance. He gripped the inner lapel of his coat with one hand while gesturing for Miller to sit down.

'Good morning,' said Lacey. He did not offer to shake hands, so Miller made no attempt to do so either. 'I gather you are seeking information about Mr Harper. May I ask what your connection to him is?'

Miller briefly explained the circumstances that had brought him to Manchester. Lacey nodded but did not respond. When Miller had finished, Lacey made a point of being seen to weigh in his mind how much he should reveal to the man that he had never met before who claimed all manner of connection with Scotland Yard.

'You say Sheridan sent you?'

'He did not exactly send me. The chief inspector seemed to have very little interest in the case or, indeed, in helping me. I think he just wanted to be rid of me,' replied Miller, honestly.

This brought the merest hint of a smile from Lacey and perhaps convinced the lawyer to be helpful. Sheridan was not a man one wanted to keep company with.

'That sounds like Sheridan all right. Very well, specifically what do you want to know?'

'Do you think Andrew Harper was murdered?'

Lacey's eye brows shot up at this. He sat back in his chair and stroked his chin.

'You certainly don't beat about the bush. So you think there is a possibility that the deaths of the two former Brothers Grimoire are linked. Interesting. Well, we'll never know about Mr Harper, thanks to the inept handling of the case by our friend Sheridan.'

'What do you know of the case that might help us?'

'Mr Harper was a troubled young man. He grew up in a Barnardo's care home and suffered greatly from depression. I gather his parents had abandoned him which may have contributed to his illness. We have no way of tracing them; I might add. I did not know Mr Harper personally. I was only asked to handle the estate, what there was of it.'

'Who asked you to do this?'

'Mr Gibson,' replied Lacey.

'I understand that he had a twin. Were you ever able to locate him?' asked Miller.

'Her, Mr Miller. He had a twin sister. She died a month or two after Mr Harper.'

Miller was astounded by this news. He leaned forward to ask the question that was burning in his mind, but Lacey anticipated what he wanted to know.

'She died of a pulmonary tuberculosis, Mr Miller. There can be no doubt of this. I have not been to the grave myself, but according to the lady I spoke to at her lodgings, I believe she was buried in the municipal cemetery on Barlow Moor Road. It's rather a large cemetery so you may need to inquire as to where the grave is located.' The lawyer scribbled a note down on a piece of paper and handed it to Miller. 'That's the address of the cemetery and also the lodgings where she lived.'

Miller sat back, a little deflated and not a little sad. Two young people, who had been abandoned, who had then grown up in care homes only to die at a young age. Life could be so cruel. And death.

'I'm sorry not to be of more help. Sadly, I cannot furnish you with any suspects or motives for your current inquiry,' said Lacey. Miller nodded a thank you and departed almost immediately.

Miller returned to the hotel unsure of what to do next. It was a few hours before his train departed, so he had some time left in which to check on the details shared by Lacey. He ordered a taxi to take him to the cemetery.

Just before midday, Miller found himself staring at the grave of Eliza Harper. There was no birthdate. Instead, it read "1892?". The date of her death was 21st July 1920. The dark cloud overhead seemed to envelop Miller as he gazed at the headstone. Spots of rain began to pitter patter on his hat. He looked up to the heavens and wondered why such things could happen.

There was nothing to be done for them now. The twins were at peace, he hoped; perhaps they were together once more, in another place. The feeling that had overcome him at Lacey's returned: an overwhelming sense of despair for two young people who had never been given a chance. It felt like the air was being crushed from his lungs, not just because he was sad for the brother and sister. He realised that it was for himself too and this thought appalled him. Life was for living; it was a gift that had to be embraced, cherished and consumed voraciously.

He trudged away from the cemetery back towards the waiting taxi. His train was not until two in the afternoon. There was one more call to make.

19. Intermission III – The Queer

March 1919

He sat in a dark corner with a face blazing like a roaring fire on a winter's evening. Those eyes, that mouth, the utter grace of the movement had him enraptured. His life had changed in the moment their eyes met. Both knew what must follow. It was as certain as the seasons.

Breathe, he said to himself. Even such a simple thing as respiration was difficult. How foolish he must look and yet the smile on the other's face was one of sympathy. Perhaps he was not alone in feeling his senses spiralling out of control.

I want to spirit you away from this place, from this world. Go somewhere that we can be together, alone. He shifted his gaze slowly away from the object of his desire towards the old man. They were holding hands surreptitiously. Who was he? What was he? He glanced towards the eyes that had so beguiled him. Dark, brooding and yet there was humour there. It concealed itself at the corner of the eye. A crinkle.

It gave him hope.

The dancing had started. All around him, men were dancing with all of the grace and restraint of whirling dervishes. It was madness. A happy madness. Had the police come at this point there would have been bloodshed.

Their sort were not wanted here or anywhere else.

And what were they doing that was so wrong? It was just love. Why shouldn't they love who they wanted? He looked into those dark eyes again and knew he was falling into them, drowning. Happily.

His eyes.

And then the police came.

A dozen uniformed men burst through the doors of the underground cellar. Mayhem. Their sticks were out, and they were hitting anything that moved. He didn't stop to think. His fists began to clear a path through the pandemonium. There were a dozen policemen with sticks, but what they had not considered, these fascist louts, was the fact they were facing treble that number of men. Many of them were young and, my goodness, they were angry. A furious, collective strength ripped through.

They fought back.

The battle, because that's what it was, began to change in favour of the people fighting for their lives. When you are fighting for life, love and freedom, it endows you with a courage that you do not normally possess. When you know you're going to die, inhibition dies first. The fear had drained from them once they had made the decision to fight. In its place was exhilaration.

Across the room he saw the young man that had so enraptured him being attacked by one of the uniformed thugs. All thought left him. In its place was hatred. He tore across the room and leapt onto the policeman, knocking him against a table. The policeman crashed to the floor unconscious. His eyes sought out those of the young man.

He had fallen to the ground. All thought was gone now. He grabbed the young man's hand and yanked him away from trouble. The old man, cowering underneath a table, didn't look up. They barged past another policeman, running up the upstairs and into the night. They skipped down the lane. Laughing.
Free.
But no one is ever truly free.

20

Early afternoon saw the arrival of moving picture house impresario and businessman, Billy Benson. He was the sort of man you heard before you saw and saw before you listened. His sense of dress was as loud as his voice and he was a man that liked to be noticed and heard, in that order. This made him more like the Watts brothers than any of the individuals concerned would care to have admitted. Conflict was inevitable as the three egos sought ascendancy within the small world of a British seaside town.

Chief Inspector Jellicoe, who was using Tristram's office as his crime room, decided, wisely, to vacate the building when he saw the larger-than-life Benson explode through the door. He had already interviewed him following the death of Gonzalo / Gibson and had concluded that Benson had nothing to say and had spent a great deal of Jellicoe's precious time saying it.

Kit, on the other hand, was genuinely curious to meet a man that Rufus had spent five minutes during the previous evening on an eloquent, heartfelt and bitingly funny character assassination. On first appearance, Benson certainly suggested he was going to live down to Rufus' estimation of his personality. Before Kit could be properly introduced, Annie Watts appeared.

'Billy, how nice to see you. Would you like a cup of tea?' she asked, a kindly smile on her face. There was not a trace of animosity in this remarkable woman, Kit realised. Benson bowed to Mrs Watts, took her hand and kissed it. She blushed and said, 'You are a naughty boy.'

'Madame you are and always will be my queen,' said Benson, grandly. He glanced slyly at Rufus as he said this.

'Only room for one queen here, my dear,' said Rufus unabashedly. 'What do you want William? The answer's "no" by the way.'

Benson sat down facing Tristram who was seated on one side of the desk with Rufus standing by him, leaning with two hands on his cane. Benson smiled at this and then fixed his eyes on Kit. He held his hand out and said, 'Well as my friends appear in no rush to introduce us, I'll do the honours. The name's Billy Benson. I run the picture house over the road.'

'Yes, I passed it. Very impressive building.'

'It's the future,' said Benson pointedly. 'I believe I'm right in thinking that you are Lord Kit Aston?'

This certainly surprised the Watts brothers and Kit, although he gave no sign that this was the case.

'Yes,' replied Kit. He glanced towards Rufus before adding, 'Rufus and I have worked together before.'

Benson's beaming red face took on a more serious mien. He nodded and said in a grave voice, 'Yes, bad business. Very bad business.'

'Are you making a point or commiserating William?' asked Rufus.

Benson paused for a moment and then he smiled broadly, 'Both,' he admitted. 'I feel sorry for your loss

Rufus, Tristram, I really do. We've had enough death to last several lifetimes as you well know.'

Kit noticed that both Rufus and Tristram grew more serious at this, and they nodded to Benson, whose voice had choked slightly. There was a moment of silence and then the picture house owner continued, 'But face facts. Music hall is dead, and variety is dying. If we don't kill you off then radio will.'

Tristram bristled at this and snapped back, 'I think you'll find there's life still left in this corpse. Why don't you give watching Theda Bara hamming it up a miss tonight and come along and watch some live entertainment. You might be surprised.'

'I daresay I will like it, but the fact remains, and you know it, you can't keep going forever. There's no profit in this.'

There, indeed, was the rub. The Empire Theatre was only just surviving. Had the Watts family not already owned the theatre, then they would have long since given it up. The War followed by the Spanish flu had all but crippled their income. Now, just as things were looking up in the country, new forms of entertainment were either stopping people from going out or diverting them elsewhere. Then there were the acts themselves. For a theatre to survive it needed stars. While Daisy Lewis and Bert Cooper were very much on the way up, as Gonzalo had been until his untimely death, Eddie Matthews was on another trajectory and Lucien Lemaire was simply a speciality act just like the Monteverdi pair.

Kit listened intently. There was nothing new in what he heard, but to hear the stark reality was still unsettling. Rufus and Tristram had never denied there were problems; it was all too visible in the peeling paintwork, the hint of disrepair and now, in the gloating of their chief rival. Or perhaps gloating was too strong, reflected Kit. There was a hint of sadness in Benson's voice too. It seemed to Kit he wanted to help them, but the pride of the Watts family was not something to be trifled with. Just then, Annie Watts arrived with a tray of tea and some sandwiches. Benson, not just Tristram and Rufus, looked at her fondly.

It was a distressing realisation that this indefatigable lady, this proud family, would not be able to hold back the tide of change forever. They would lose. Billy Benson, far from being the villain of the piece, was merely the messenger.

While they drank their tea, the brothers updated Benson on the new acts who were joining the show that night.

'I've seen Miller,' said Benson. 'Raw but funny. He's a good turn. You did well there.' Tristram gestured with his hand that it was a mere trifle for him to attract such talent. 'And you say young Joshua is going to do a turn?'

'He is,' said Annie Watts. 'He's a dancer that boy.'

As they enjoyed the afternoon tea, Kit decided to bring up something he'd noticed in the statements provided by the performers following the death of Gonzalo.

'I gather, Mr Benson, that you were backstage on the night that Gonzalo died.'

If Benson was surprised by this remark he hid it well. However, both Rufus and Tristram were donning armour and searching for the nearest spear.

'What on earth were you doing there?' demanded Tristram, territorially.

Benson feigned an innocent air.

'Yes, it's true I popped backstage to see Bert Cooper to invite him for a drink. I have a private engagement, a birthday party coming up, if you must know. I wanted to ask him if he would do a turn for me. I'm not trying to poach your performers, trust me. I'll stick to Mr Chaplin and Miss Pickford if you don't mind,' said Benson. Rufus put his hands in the air and widened his eyes to mimic a silent movie actress. 'Very funny Rufus. You really should be on stage. Hopefully, you'll have a better scriptwriter. Anyway, I left the backstage area long before the show began. It weren't me guv.'

When the sandwiches were finished and there were a good many of them, Benson took this as his cue to leave. After Benson had departed, Kit turned to the brothers and asked, 'Do you really believe he was responsible for the letter?'

Something in Kit's accusatory tone made the two men hesitate. They met each other's gaze. Then Rufus shrugged.

'I suppose it's easy to blame him.'

'And boo and hiss,' added Tristram unabashedly.

Mrs Watts' face took on a stern countenance.

'I hope you have not been casting aspersions against Billy. Those vile letters would never have come from him, and you know it. Anyone with eyes can see that it's not his style.'

Her sons seemed a little sheepish at this point. They would neither of them see forty again, yet they were never too young to earn a public rebuke from a mother concerned by misbehaviour.

'Let's have none of this sort of talk again,' said Mrs Watts, effectively closing down any further denunciation of their rival.

'Well, if it wasn't him then who did send those notes?' said Rufus in exasperation.

Kit spoke up at this point, 'It was one of the troupe. I'm sure of it. I have some thoughts on this, but I don't want to say much now. Let me think a little bit more about it. In the meantime, I wouldn't mind having a look at the dressing rooms again.'

'It's the smell of the greasepaint, Tristram,' proclaimed Rufus. 'He can't resist it.'

Rather than walk through the auditorium where the performers were rehearsing, Kit and the brothers walked around the side of the building. It was raining gently now, and the wind was whipping in off the sea which made it decidedly too cold to return via that route.

Ezra greeted them warmly and led them through to the dressing rooms. There were two – one for the male performers and one for the ladies. He unlocked the ladies' dressing room first. It was not the largest of rooms. There were three tables with a seat and a mirror against the wall. The mirror was framed by light bulbs, some of which blinked before giving up the ghost.

'Ah yes,' said Tristram with a little embarrassment. 'You did mention that we need to buy some more lights.'

The room was spotlessly clean and smelled of lavender. Kit looked in some of the cupboards which contained various dresses and costumes.

'The police searched these, sir,' said Ezra, unsure of what to say while Kit was poking through various garments.

'I'm sure they did. I was just curious.'

They left the ladies' dressing room and went into the men's dressing room. This was in a very different state. Slightly larger, with one additional table and mirror, it looked as if a tornado had hit town. Kit raised one eyebrow to Tristram and smiled.

'We really are a different species,' sniffed Rufus disapprovingly.

Kit looked around the dressing room but without much idea of what he was looking for or, indeed, what might be out of place or missing. This was something he liked to do in cases where there seemed no obvious thing to do next. He shifted his gaze around the room as if trying to photograph every detail. His eyes settled on a whisky bottle sitting on one table. As if reading his mind, Tristram said, 'Eddie Matthews. He's not a big drinker, thankfully. Probably just needs a stiffener before he goes on. Lord knows, I need one after he's been on. I'm sure he does, too.'

Romeo the cat entered the room as the four men were just leaving. He climbed up onto one of the chairs and curled up for a late afternoon rest following a hard day rat-catching.

'Nice for some,' said Tristram eyeing their feline employee wryly.

21

Detective Inspector Wellbeloved returned to the theatre, the bearer of bad news and yet more bad news. Although he had definitively established the network of interrelationships between the performers based on their statements, cross-referenced with calls to the theatres where they had performed, nothing suggested any kind of conspiracy against either of the Brothers Grimoire. This worried Jellicoe less than the other piece of news from Wellbeloved. The chief inspector was being recalled. He had to return that evening leaving Wellbeloved in charge of the investigation. There was also growing pressure on Rufus Watts to return, too. All in all, the outlook was a little bleaker than it had been earlier.

Kit studied the big policeman closely. It would be fair to say that his feelings towards Wellbeloved were guided by Jellicoe. When they had first met, Jellicoe had given the impression that Wellbeloved was a little too keen on obtaining evidence through overly aggressive interrogation.

A question mark had also hung over Kit's mind on whether or not Wellbeloved was in the pay of one of the London gangs. Yet, life is rarely so black and white. No one is perfectly innocent, nor unblinkingly evil. The space between is occupied by hate and greed but also fear, need and, oddly, duty. Wellbeloved was a complex man balancing a number of different masters, from the police force to the London gangs and, ultimately, to the Secret Intelligence Service which Kit suspected, but had no proof, he was a member of.

'I was wondering if I may be allowed to take a look through the belongings of Mr Gonzalo,' said Kit to Wellbeloved. They were outside the theatre having just seen Chief Inspector Jellicoe off in a police car that would take him to the train station.

Wellbeloved eyed Kit before nodding.

'His things are in a box at the local police station. It's a short walk from here.'

The implication was that Wellbeloved wanted to accompany Kit, so they walked together around the theatre and down a side street which eventually took them into the centre of town. The rain whipped angrily over the pavement. Neither could risk an umbrella as it would have become a hindrance, so they walked with a mute resentment against Mother Nature's malevolent sense of humour.

The redbrick police station was one of the smallest that Kit had ever seen. It was about the size of a large Victorian villa. Wellbeloved led the way inside. A rather elderly policeman greeted the detective with a nod and ignored Kit entirely which appeared to amuse Wellbeloved. The rain had denied the chain-smoking policeman a chance to smoke. He quickly made up for lost time by lighting a cigarette. He took Kit to an office with a sign outside that read: 'Detective Inspector Donovan'.

Kit glanced at Wellbeloved with an eyebrow raised.

'He retired a few months ago. They've not replaced him yet. I've been using his office since the questioning was completed.'

'Nice office,' said Kit, whose teeth were beginning to grit in the cold.

Wellbeloved smirked to acknowledge the fact that Kit was being ironic. He indicated three cardboard boxes sitting on a chest of drawers.

'This is what we took from Gonzalo's room.'

'Did he share the room with Miss Anthony?'

The smirk grew wider on the detective. He said, 'I doubt Mrs Harrison would have permitted this, but from what I gather he was chasing her. Whether he actually caught her is open to question.'

'Shall we?' said Kit. They emptied the first two boxes. The first box contained everyday clothes including undergarments.

'I've been through the pockets,' confirmed Wellbeloved.

The second box contained his stage clothes. This was a mixture of traditional magician garb like evening suits, a cloak as well as character costumes, including the Inquisition outfit that he'd been wearing when tragedy had struck and what looked like a devil's costume. Kit held it up and held it against himself.

'It would suit me more,' said Wellbeloved with a wry smile.

'Did you find any rabbits in the pockets?' asked Kit grimly.

'Not even any coins,' said Wellbeloved, lighting his third cigarette of the last five minutes.

Kit was less interested in the clothes than any letters or diaries that the dead magician would have kept. The two men replaced the clothes in the boxes with all the care and neatness that one associates with the masculine member of the species.

'That box was able to close before,' observed Kit as he looked at the lid of the box sitting at an odd angle on top. Wellbeloved gave every impression that this was a subject of which he could care less. He opened the third and final box. This was a moment both of expectation and sadness for Kit. A man's existence had been condensed into three physical containers. It all seemed so pointless and cruel. He stared at the three boxes for a moment then Wellbeloved broke the spell with a cough that started from his feet before slowly working its way up. Kit doubted that the detective would ever be called upon by Players Navy Cut cigarettes to endorse their product.

The big detective inspector carefully emptied the contents onto the table. There was a roll of paper which Kit unfurled. It contained playbills for other magic shows. Among the artistes were many men that Kit had heard of but not seen. The first one displayed Harry Houdini in handcuffs; the next showed Howard Thurston performing an act of levitation on a young woman; the final one showed Harry Kellar cutting off his own head. Kit showed the playbill to Wellbeloved. The smirk returned.

'Be careful what you wish for,' was the detective's only comment.

Aside from the playbills there was a scrapbook containing reviews of his recent shows, but nothing on the Brothers Grimoire. There was also an accounts book. Kit looked inside and he saw listed in very neat handwriting, a list of the engagements Gonzalo had performed that year, where and for how long, along with how much they had earned in each. It was clearly an industry that required performers to work continuously. The remuneration was not great and, furthermore, Gonzalo would have to share with Jane Anthony and Barney, possibly even the Monteverdi Brothers too.

Aside from his wallet and a few personal articles for his toilet, there was little else that Gonzalo had kept with him during his stay at the digs. Kit stared at the items for a minute or two hoping that something would inspire an idea. Nothing came. Yet a thought was nagging him that something was missing.

Wellbeloved looked at Kit expectantly. Sadly, he was going to disappoint the detective.

'No, nothing here of interest. Perhaps we should return to the theatre,' said Kit.

As Kit and Wellbeloved made their way back to the theatre, Mary was just finishing rehearsing the final numbers for the show that evening. She left the stage accompanied by Daisy and made her way over to Tristram who was standing in the wings.

'It might be a full house tonight,' announced Tristram.

Mary smiled brightly at the news. She said, 'I'm glad ticket sales have gone well.'

Tristram was happy although a little less surprised by the interest.

'Sadly, tragedy engenders a certain morbid curiosity in the public. It's almost as if they are expecting someone else to die.'

'How lovely; let's hope they're disappointed,' replied Mary.

Tristram peered sideways at Mary and said, 'Have you seen Eddie Matthews' act?' This was followed by a rueful grin. 'At least I know that I can count on you. That was marvellous. You really have a lovely voice and all the rest.'

Mary's eyes narrowed at this comment, but she smiled gracefully, 'Well I hope they appreciate the music.'

'This is show business, my love. Trust me, you have it all.'

Mary went to join Daisy once more and they walked back to the digs together. Daisy appeared drawn to Mary, which was great for the investigation, but did prompt some feeling of remorse. She took Mary's arm, and they braved the stiff breeze and the spray of rain.

'Will Mrs Harrison have made us a full meal?'

'Oh yes. She's very good in that regard.'

'And apple tart?' added Mary with a giggle.

'Oh yes. Always apple tart. How are you feeling about tonight?'

Mary paused for a moment to examine her own feelings. There was no question she felt some trepidation. Singing to an audience was not something that she did often, especially one so large. If there was nervousness then there was also excitement at what lay ahead. The only problem lay in the fact that she was not sure that they were any further forward in the case. There was no question that Daisy felt that Mary was someone she could trust. Was it now the time to test that trust.

And then betray it?

'I'm fine I think,' smiled Mary. 'How about you, Daisy? You've been through so much.'

There was just a trace of hesitation then Daisy replied, 'Oh I'll be glad to be back on stage. You miss it even after a few days.'

They were silent for a few moments. Mary waited to see if Daisy would add anything to what she'd said. This was a tried and trusted technique for the police, according to Kit.

It worked.

'You won't tell anyone Mary,' said Daisy suddenly. 'I've heard from Bert.'

Mary gasped. It was a difficult balance to achieve between faked surprise and a desire not to seem like a hammy actress. She seemed to carry it off.

'Yes. I had a telegram.'

The most obvious question to be asked by anyone might have been: where is he?. Mary deftly avoided such an indelicate approach.

'Is he all right?' asked Mary. It was probably this question, more than any, that made Daisy feel that Mary was just the sort of person in which she could confide.

Daisy did not respond immediately. They walked on for a few moments then she stopped and looked at Mary. This was far from ideal as it was definitely not the sort of weather for dilly-dallying, but Mary held a stiff upper and lower lip in order to stop them chattering.

'Bert and I didn't really split up. He's done nothing wrong Mary; you must believe me.'

'I do, Daisy, but the police will wonder why he ran off like that. They might assume he killed Mr Gonzalo and leave the real killer to go free,' pointed out Mary.

This appeared to throw Daisy. Tears glistened in her eyes. She shook her head as if by doing so she could throw away the creeping sense of guilt that she was feeling.

'But they can't think he did it. He was in the pub at the time with Billy Benson,' she replied, panic rising in her voice.

Mary took her hand, 'Look we can't worry about that now. And I'm wet. Let's go back and have some apple tart.'

Daisy laughed through the tears and the two young women hurried back to the digs for a pre performance meal and, yes, apple tart.

22

Harry Miller's taxi drew up outside a small cottage located in the southern tip of Manchester where country and city slowly blend. This is where Andrew Harper's twin sister had lodged. The cottage was white but was slowly being submerged under a jungle of plants growing on the walls. Miller could recognise the roses framing the doorway whilst the clematis and wisteria would have been names only, to him.

Miller walked along the garden path to the door. He rapped the brass knocker a couple of times, careful not make it seem too impatient. There is an art to rapping doors and Miller, who had made so many uninvited visits to houses over the years, was aware that an indelicate approach to alerting houseowners to your presence could be counterproductive.

He waited a few moments and then, through a small, panelled window saw movement from within. Moments later, the door opened to reveal an elderly woman. She frowned when she saw Miller.

'If you've come here to sell me something then...'

Miller smiled and held his hand up. This was a sparky character; he guessed she might respond to a little bit of her own medicine.

'Keep your hair on love, I'm a special investigator attached to the police. My name is Harry Miller. I just wanted to ask you a few questions about a young woman who used to live here by the name of Harper, Mrs...?'

The woman frowned once more, leaving Miller unsure if she was thinking, angry or confused. There was a hint of amusement in her eyes which led Miller to think that his feeling that she appreciated a bit of cheek was well placed.

'Mrs Lanchbery, I don't know anyone by that name, Mr Miller. When was this?'

'She would have lived here around just over a year ago. Perhaps earlier,' explained Miller.

The woman shook her head and replied, 'No, means nothing to me, but then again I only purchased the cottage a year ago.'

This would explain why she did not know Harper's sister. It meant he still needed to find Miss Harper's housemate.

'May I ask the name of the person you bought the house from?'

'What happened to the young woman you are after?' asked Mrs Lanchbery.

'She died last year. Her brother has just died on the south coast. The circumstances are suspicious enough to warrant further inquiry.

This startled the old lady or, more likely, pricked her curiosity.

'You better come inside. I've just made a cup of tea.'

Miller was a little torn. The taxi was waiting, the train was booked for two and he was gasping for a cup of tea. He excused himself for a moment to ask the taxi driver to wait and then entered the cottage.

The lady certainly liked flowers. The curtains and the sofa both had flower patterns and there were half a dozen vases with one weed or another filling them. The scent in the living room was overpowering. Miller sat down as Mrs Lanchbery had disappeared off into the adjoining kitchen. She reappeared a couple of minutes later with a tray of tea in a bone china tea pot with matching cups and saucers adorned by black roses.

'Now, tell me. Was it a murder?'

'Which one?'

'Two murders?' replied the old woman, eyes widening not so much with anxiety as with excitement. It was enough to make Miller wonder what appeal murder had for the older generation. He was thinking of Aunt Agatha, but this old lady could easily have been her best friend. She was like a willowier version of Betty Simpson.

'No, we believe that Miss Harper passed away due to a natural causes.'

This seemed to disappoint Mrs Lanchbery. She sat back in her armchair and said, 'Oh.' Conscious that he had somewhat pricked the mood of inquisitive animation, Miller threw in his ace.

'Her brother was decapitated, though.'

The timing of this was unfortunate as Mrs Lanchbery was just imbibing her tea. She did not quite spit it out, but a close-run thing it was in Miller's view. He would have to time these bombshells a little better in future.

Mrs Lanchbery looked at him archly, 'Next time warn me when you're going to say something like that.'

'I'm sorry,' said Miller and meant it. 'Mr Harper was a magician. He met his death following a tragic accident on stage.'

'I read about it. Gonzalo was his stage name. I thought it was an accident. Your presence suggests foul play. It does seem a bit of a coincidence if his sister died last year.'

Miller ate a piece of the Victoria cake that Mrs Lanchbery had put on a side plate. It was delicious. He replied, 'There is enough suspicion to warrant the investigation. Can you tell me a little about who you bought the house from?'

'Yes, it was a Mrs Hill. She was a war widow, poor girl. She said she was going to move to be closer to her sister in London. She was an attractive girl. I've no doubt she had other ideas in mind. A fairly well-off widow, especially one still young and pretty enough to marry, will always find a gentleman.'

'You have had no further contact with Mrs Hill?'

'No, the sale went through quite quickly and she left no forwarding address. She instructed me just to destroy any post.'

'I don't suppose you kept any of it?' asked Miller hopefully.

'As it happens I did keep one letter. It came from London.'

Miller leaned forward and said, 'May I see the letter?'

'By all means,' came the reply, 'but I'm not sure if it will be much use to you.'

Mrs Lanchbery rose from her seat and went to a bureau at the other end of the room. She opened it and rustled around some papers before extracting an envelope. She held it up to Miller and brought it over. Miller noticed it had been opened. He took out a piece of paper from the envelope and read it.

It was a request from The Strand magazine if Mrs Antonia Hill would like to renew her subscription. Mrs Lanchbery was correct. It wasn't much use. The trail was growing colder by the minute. Or perhaps there had been no trail to begin with. It seemed that he had embarked on a wild goose chase and now he risked missing his train down to London.

Miller thanked the elderly lady for her help. There was a hint of regret in the lady's eyes as he left. Loneliness was a terrible blight that affected most people from time to time. Seeing the widow in her beautiful cottage made Miller realise just how much it was a malady that particularly affected you as you grew older. Miller stopped at the gate and turned around to wave goodbye to the lady. Something was on his mind but, frustratingly, he could not quite sense what it was. It hit him just as he was stepping into the waiting taxi. He told the driver to wait a moment.

'Mrs Lanchbery,' he shouted.

The lady in question was just closing the door when Miller shouted. She opened it again and stepped outside.

'One more question. What was the name of the law firm that handled Mrs Hill's sale?'

23. Intermission IV – The Coward

March 1915

He held the white feather in his hand and stared at it. Then he looked at the young woman who had handed it to him. Only seconds before he had contemplated approaching her to make conversation. They were in a park. She was walking alone. Isn't this why she was here? Her dress was not that of a wealthy woman, but she was clearly not a woman of the night, the *demi-monde*.

One moment he was planning how he would attract her attention, the next she had all but called him a coward. Their eyes had met momentarily when she had approached him suddenly. He wondered if she knew him or he, her. Then it had happened. The white feather was thrust into his hand. Then the expectant silence. Somewhere behind him, he heard a child cry out.

The anger in her eyes was unmistakeable. It blazed with such intensity that he was struck dumb. Anything he'd wanted to say was lost in the whirl of thoughts that submerged him. He was drowning. Words caught in his throat. She glared defiantly at him. Up close he saw how beautiful she was. Then she spun around and went.

In her hand he saw other white feathers.

The flare of shame that had gripped him gave way to anger. For a moment he considered chasing her. He wanted to explain. Yet what was there to say? He'd been passed unfit for service. Men were going out to France and losing their minds to the terror of war.

He'd lost his long before.

What was it the doctor called him? A schizophrenic: that was it. He'd offered to join up. It would have been the perfect solution. Perhaps he would have made a good soldier. Lord knows, death would have been welcome, preferable even to the misery he felt just at that moment.

He slumped off in the opposite direction. Just because he was not over there didn't mean he wasn't contributing. Wars are not just won by men dying on a battlefield. He wanted her to see that. You could still play your part while working in a factory. You could still play your part entertaining the men about to go out to France or coming back on leave. He *was* part of the war effort.

He wanted to believe it himself.

24

Kit stood with Tristram and Rufus watching the queue of people snake into the auditorium. Ezra smiled at people as they entered through the double doors. He was dressed in the livery of a doorman as he collected the tickets and chatted with the customers.

'It's a good bill and no mistake,' he said to anyone that would listen. 'We used to have some great turns here and this is as good as any of them.'

Tristram had to control his emotions as he listened to their aged stage door man speak.

'I hope he's right,' he murmured. He felt Kit's hand grip his forearm reassuringly.

A small bar in the foyer was doing good business with Annie Watts belying her three score and ten years with an energy and enthusiasm that appeared limitless. She lived for nights like these. Her cheeks glowed with the effort. This may have been partly influenced by the fact that she liked to have the occasional stiffener with members of the audience. The bar always closed ten minutes before the performance began in order to allow the good lady time to make her way down to the orchestra pit.

The closing of the bar was the signal for Kit and Rufus to take their seats at the front of the stage while Tristram went backstage to manage the artistes. Ezra remained at the door until the last moment before charging upstairs to man the spotlight.

Hector Goulding appeared on stage to tumultuous applause. He bowed to the crowd and cast a sardonic eye towards Kit and Rufus. He walked slowly to the side of the stage, down the steps that diverted off into the orchestra pit.

Kit could sense the anticipation in the audience. It was like a separate presence in the air or perhaps it was just the nerves he was feeling on Mary's behalf. Or guilt. So far, their amateur theatrics with Mary going under cover had provided nothing of note. Kit felt himself struggling to grasp something that he knew was tantalisingly close. Hector Goulding, meanwhile, was not helping Kit's thinking processes by a rather robust version of *It's a Long Way to Tipperary* overture. Beside Kit, was an empty seat that they were keeping free for Mrs Walker to watch her son.

If Kit was feeling nervous, it was as nothing compared to a mother looking at her son step away from her into a new, unknown world. In this particular case, it was a dressing room, but the point remained. It had been decided earlier that rather than dress Joshua up in finery he should retain his dungarees, boots and baker boy cap. He would walk onstage wearing this ensemble as if by accident. The idea was that he would see a pair of new shoes and try them on. The rest was up to the young boy.

Mrs Walker could not hide her anxiety, but she welcomed the hand that gripped hers. It was Tristram Watts who had come backstage to hurry the performers along. He smiled at her and said, 'Normally, I feel a degree of apprehension when we have new performers. Not this time. Your boy is fearless. What's more, he's talented.'

'Thank you Mr Tristram. You're very kind. If it's all the same to you, I'll stay backstage while he performs.'

'I understand. I have a better idea. Why don't you go underneath the stage and greet him when he's finished,' said Tristram. He led her away from the dressing room area to the area underneath the stage.

Mary and Daisy were sharing a dressing table and mirror. Neither minded the arrangement. They chatted about the evening ahead. Daisy risked a glance at Mary as she applied the lightest touch of lipstick. There was no question that Mary could have sounded like a hoarse duck and still had the men in the audience lapping up her performance. Mary noticed her staring at her and frowned a question.

'The men will love you, Mary,' said Daisy laughing. There was no artifice in her voice or the look she gave Mary. Her compliment was sincerely meant.

'Let's not count our chickens,' replied Mary. 'My knees are shaking.'

This was a surprise to Daisy as Mary had showed no trace of nervousness. Just then a figure loomed over the two ladies. It was Jane Anthony.

'Jane,' exclaimed Daisy and leapt to her feet to give her a hug, 'this is a surprise.'

Jane's eyes were wet, but she was smiling.

'I just wanted to come along and, well, you know. You too, Mary. I think you'll be a star by the end of tonight.'

Mary stood up and hugged Jane. She was quite moved by this and could not speak. There was something about women supporting other women that always seemed to move her. It gave lie to the idea, probably spread by men, that they were incapable of anything other than backbiting and jealousy. She cast her eyes over to the other table where Susan Parrish was sullenly puffing on a cigarette. Jackie Rutherford, meanwhile, caught Mary's eye and winked.

'She's right Mary. You could stand up there and break wind and they'd still love you.'

'It would certainly have them laughing,' agreed Mary.

Eddie Matthews was in no mood for laughing. He was barely in a mood for joking. He picked up the bottle of whisky. The same sense of dread rose up within him that he'd felt every night for the last forty years of performing. It never left him. The pressure to be funny; to make people laugh. No one really understood what it was like. He wasn't pretty. It was easy for the likes of Daisy or Jane or Mary to win affection. They were born to be pleasing to the eye with their soft feminine voices that made men lose all sense of reason.

He had to make people laugh. Yet there would be men and women out there with one job. The word was out. Probably from Billy Benson: give Matthews the bird. They were picking the performers off one by one. First Gonzalo. They killed him. He would die too, but in a different way.

Maybe, he'd decide how.

'This way young man,' said Tristram. He was speaking to Joshua, who was sitting at the dressing table once used by Javier Gonzalo. Barney Hallett was with him, helping apply some greasepaint.

'Thanks Barney,' said Joshua with a beaming smile.

'Just make them smile, son,' said Barney. He patted Joshua on the back as the boy rose to follow Tristram out of the dressing room. They walked in silence along the corridor towards the area underneath the stage. They passed through a door where Joshua could hear the music of Hector Goulding's orchestra. Playing *Daisy, Daisy*. He was more excited than he could ever remember being in his young life. Then he saw his mother. Just at that moment he wanted to run over and hug her. He saw her nod to him. He nodded back.

He was ready.

They passed Mrs Walker without stopping. Soon he was climbing the steps. The music in front of the curtain was reaching a crescendo followed by enthusiastic applause. Joshua heard a whispered 'off you go Joshua.' He walked out onto the stage. In front of him, the curtain would rise in a few seconds.

He held his breath and waited.

Kit was not alone in finding the act of ventilation a challenge at that moment. Joshua's mother, Mrs Walker sat underneath the stage gripping the chair Tristram had given her as if the act of letting go would see her plunge into an abyss. The music had stopped now. The audience were applauding, but the sound of her heart drowned it out.

The level of clapping changed suddenly. In fact, it had turned to laughter. She heard the sound of Joshua's feet clumping above her. The laughter died down for a few moments. Then it rose again. This was when Joshua would have seen the shiny new shoes.

It quietened again and then Annie Watts' piano began to play *Alexander's Ragtime Band*. Gradually the rest of the orchestra picked up the melody. As if by magic, a new sound could be heard above the music. The tap, tap, tapping of shoes on the wooden stage. The syncopated rhythm blended with the music like a new instrument in the orchestra.

Mrs Walker became aware of a figure standing over her. She turned around. It was a tall man dressed in a white suit with plus four trousers. He had a thin, dark moustache.

'Is that you boy?' he whispered politely.

Mrs Walker nodded proudly. They both listened in silence for a moment. Then the man said, 'He's good.'

'Thanks Mr Miller,' said Mrs Walker.

The comedian left her and walked back towards the green room. Another man came through. It was Eddie Matthews. He ignored Mrs Walker and made for the steps up to the stage.

The music overhead was nearing its finale. It stopped suddenly, leaving Joshua to finish his turn with a series of steps completed so rapidly they were like rain battering a window in a storm.

Then silence.

Mrs Walker felt sick with anxiety now. Her hands were sore from gripping the chair. Then the auditorium erupted into deafening applause and cheers. Mrs Walker doubled over and the dam burst. Her body wracked with sobs of relief, pride and happiness. The fear subsided like waves on a beach. It would return, of course, but something had changed which she could sense but not understand. She waited for Joshua to join her below. The clapping, meanwhile, had not stopped.

Nor had her tears.

Eddie Matthews felt like crying as he saw the acclaim with which Joshua was being greeted. Joshua was grinning broadly as he marched off the stage to a reprise of the ragtime music. He grinned up at the comedian but was met with a vacant stare. Moments later, the music changed to *I Do Like to be Beside the Seaside* and Eddie Matthews stepped onto the stage, shaking his hat and grinning. Rarely had he received such an ovation. He wanted to believe it was for him. A comic survived on confidence; once that was gone, it was over. Forty years on the boards counted for something, though. He pumped the air and threw his arms out in the direction Joshua had left the stage from. The crowd cheered wildly. Such a generous acknowledgement of the previous turn only added to the general mood of genial acclaim.

Time to work.

Matthews paced back and forward like a tiger in a cage. His nose seemed even redder than normal. There was despair in the comedian's eyes; in the audience's too from what Kit could see, despite the kind reception which probably owed more to Joshua than the new arrival. Hector Goulding played a bit of music and Matthews performed a silly little dance.

Laughs. He still had it, he thought.

"I'm exhausted,' began Matthews. 'Just chased a thief down the high street. We went past the fire station, past the butcher's shop, past the tailor's. Eventually, I caught him – by the cobblers.'

More laughs, but the volume was not so loud this time. Don't think about it, he thought. Too late. It was there now. The fear. Try Bert Cooper's joke. He started it off as the sweat started to soil his greasepaint. Picking out a middle-aged man in the crowd who was sitting beside a woman he took to be his wife, he asked, 'Here sir, are you married?'

A few minutes later the mood of joy had been well and truly punctured as Eddie Matthews laboured ever more desperately through an act that had aged as badly as he had. He could see the sour faces in the crowd. No one was giving him the bird yet, but it would come. Just you see. They were out there, Waiting. The word was out. He glanced to the side of the stage and saw Tristram gesturing to Hector Goulding. He was making a movement with his hand across his neck.

End this now.

Yes, it was over all right. He could see that clearly.

The bird started just as Hector Goulding waved his baton; the music only just managing to drown it out, but Matthews had heard it. He danced off the stage like he hadn't a care in the world, ignoring Tristram and Daisy Lewis as he went past. He ran down the stairs, past two people underneath the stage who were hugging, past Lucien Lemaire who was standing in the corridor smoking a cigarette chatting to Jane Anthony and burst into the dressing room where the younger Monteverdi brother was massaging the neck of the older one seated in front of the mirror.

Matthews made straight for his table and threw Romeo off his seat.

'Gerroutofit,' he roared angrily. 'Bloody cat.'

He sat down and grabbed the whisky. He stared into the mirror for a few seconds, holding the bottle of whisky. He couldn't stay there any longer. The theatre meant only one thing to him now: humiliation. He rose from his seat, spun around and stalked out of the dressing room without a word to the brothers, almost bumping into Tristram who was in the corridor.

'Where are you going?' demanded Tristram.

Matthews response was brutally short. He shoved the stage door open and went out into the darkness.

Kit and Rufus watched the show reclaim the goodwill of the audience with the succeeding acts. Daisy Lewis was an outstanding performer with an engaging voice and a gently comedic manner that immediately relaxed and charmed the house.

The Wyman Sisters had the whole of the theatre laughing with Susan's droll quips and Jackie's big-hearted ingenuous innuendo before they were singing along to a rather risqué song by Irving Berlin called *Try It On Your Piano*.

The Monteverdi act was perfectly timed to vary the pace of the show. It contained just enough peril to thrill the crowd with their acrobatic turn. After the intermission, much to Kit's dismay, Lucien Lemaire proved to be a capable ventriloquist who played nicely on the amiable friction between France and Britain with his own French accent and a dummy called Charlie who was English and rather bigoted against the Gallic race.

The next act was the comedian that Tristram had been so effusive about. Max Miller strode onto the stage. The confidence of his posture, the couldn't-care-less smile, the loud suit with the plus fours and a hat at a jaunty angle suggested he was a natural born, funny man and knew it. He resembled nothing more than a mischievous teenage boy to Kit and he settled back in his seat to enjoy the turn. Then he began.

I like the girls who do.
I like the girls who don't.
I hate the girl who says she will.
And then she says she won't.
But the girl I like best of all
And I think you'll say, "I'm right"
Is the girl who says she never does
But she looks as though...

'ere listen!' exploded Miller wagging his finger at the audience. He stalked forward just stopping at the edge of the stage and surveyed them with mock disapproval. When the laughter began to subside he said, 'You'll get me banned you will.' From that point on, he had the audience in the palm of his hand. They laughed when he moved his head or twisted his body, hand on hip; it wasn't what he said, although the jokes were rapid fire. It was just that they wanted to be in his company and he with them. The shared pleasure of this was enough.

The final act saw Daisy Lewis return with Mary. Kit glanced at Rufus with an uncertain smile.

'I'm not sure I was this nervous when I was facing our German friends.'

Rufus grinned and said, with a malicious glee in Kit's discomfort, 'I think the men in the audience are going to enjoy every second of this act.'

'Your sympathy is duly noted,' replied Kit. Mrs Walker was sitting beside Kit now. She turned to him with a reassuring smile. Then Hector Goulding and the orchestra began to play the opening number, *A Pretty Girl is like a Melody*.

Kit gazed proudly up at Mary who was dressed in an off-white evening dress. He caught her eye. Mary's smile widened in a manner that suggested as much excitement as terror at what was to follow.

Just under fifteen minutes later, the duo closed the show with *After the Ball* which had the whole audience happily singing along. They had been utterly entranced by the two young women. Soon they were on their feet shouting for an encore. At this point and much to Kit's surprise, Joshua Walker, Lucien Lemaire, the Monteverdi's and Max Miller returned to the stage and the troupe joined the audience in a rousing finale of *I'm Forever Blowing Bubbles*. There was no sign of Eddie Matthews, noted Kit and he wondered if he had been warned by Tristram to stay below.

In fact, Eddie Matthews was lying dead in an alleyway a hundred yards from the theatre.

25

Tristram Watts was standing in the foyer of the theatre as people streamed out. He smiled resignedly at the many people who recognised him and offered their congratulations. Even Lysander Benedict stopped briefly to assure him that his review would be positive. Tristram took this to mean that he would not completely butcher what he'd seen. Billy Benson trooped past giving him a rueful nod. The show must have been a success. Among the last to enter the foyer from the auditorium, principally because they had been in the front row, were Kit, Rufus and Mrs Walker. Kit only needed one glance at Tristram's face to see that something had gone wrong.

'Eddie Matthews is dead,' whispered Tristram, ushering Kit, Rufus and Mrs Walker into his office.

'What happened?' asked Rufus, who was stunned by the news.

'We don't know. His body was found half an hour ago. Detective Inspector Wellbeloved has sent word that no one from the troupe is to leave the theatre.' He looked at Mrs Walker before adding, 'I think that we can exclude Joshua from this diktat. Wellbeloved is one hundred yards up the street in an alleyway with poor Eddie. There's no sign of violence. He seems to have collapsed and died on the spot. He was holding a bottle of whisky.'

'Poison?' asked Kit.

'I don't know,' admitted Tristram. 'He asked that you join him there, Kit. Mrs Walker, perhaps you can take Joshua home.

'Actually, can you let Rufus do that,' said Kit, eyeing the little police artist. 'You don't mind Mrs Walker?'

In truth, Mrs Walker did mind and had no earthly idea what was afoot, however, she trusted Kit. After a few moments consideration, she nodded her head.

They separated at this point. Kit received directions on where he would find Wellbeloved and the late comic, while Rufus and Tristram made their way backstage to break the news to the troupe.

Kit and Mrs Walker walked along the front until they reached a crossroads. At this point, Kit peeled away while Mrs Walker continued on. Out of the corner of his eye, Kit saw a group of young men considering their options with regard to the American lady. Kit stopped and looked at them. Mrs Walker continued on her way until she disappeared out of sight. Kit turned away and walked up the street towards a group of people standing near an ambulance.

The late Eddie Matthews was being loaded onto the ambulance just as Kit arrived. He saw Wellbeloved turn around with what seemed to be a look of relief on his face. It was just him and one other uniformed policeman on the scene trying to hold back the crowd of onlookers. Another man, dressed in a tweed coat with grey whiskers that Kit assumed was a doctor, was climbing into the ambulance.

'Hello, sir,' said Wellbeloved.

'Poison?' asked Kit.

'I suspect so,' said the detective, handing Kit the bottle of whisky with his handkerchief. Kit sniffed the mouth of the bottle. The tell-tale scent of bitter almonds made him jerk his head away.

'Cyanide,' said Kit handing the bottle back to Wellbeloved. The big policeman nodded without adding anything to Kit's conclusion.

'We've had a look around but there doesn't seem to have been any sign of a struggle. No witnesses.'

'Who found him?' asked Kit.

Wellbeloved pointed to an elderly man. Kit approached the man and thanked him for reporting his find. Then he asked what he'd seen.

'I just came out of a quiet little pub that I like, the Docker's Fist and was on my way home when I saw a pair of feet sticking out onto the street. I went over to check on him. Dead he was. Didn't have to check his pulse.'

'Did you see anyone around before you found him?'

'No one,' said the man firmly.

Kit thanked him and nodded to Wellbeloved that the man could leave. Kit strolled back over to the detective. The ambulance was departing now, leaving the crowd with nothing much more to do than to stare at an empty alleyway.

'I'm not sure there's much more we can do here,' said Kit. 'Shall we return to the theatre?'

The two men walked together along the front. Wellbeloved confirmed that Chief Inspector Jellicoe had been informed of the death. He would be on the first train from London.

'We'll take statements from the performers,' said Wellbeloved in the manner of a man who was about to have his prostate examined. In fact, Wellbeloved looked miserable. He had a night and day ahead of him without much sleep.

At the theatre, Wellbeloved went back stage while Kit headed for the office. Tristram was there with his mother. Both were sitting either side of Tristram's desk in silence. Neither could muster anything to say to Kit as he entered, although Mrs Watts tried to smile a welcome.

'I'm sorry,' said Kit immediately. He knew that the show would have to close once more. A pall had fallen over the theatre. Tristram was despondent and with good reason. The future of the Empire was now in question.

"I don't know how we're going to survive this,' said Tristram at last.

Mrs Watts took her son's hand but could find no words of comfort.

'We need to find the killer,' said Kit. Tristram's head jerked up.

'You haven't heard?' he said.

'Heard what?' asked Kit.

'They found a suicide note at his table.'

Mary sat with Daisy and Jane Anthony in the women's dressing room while the Wyman Sisters were giving their statements. The two women were in shock at the latest turn of events.

No one was shedding any tears for the death of Matthews, though. He had not been a popular figure. Instead, Mary detected a mood of despondency more akin to fear for the future than any fear surrounding murder. The show was over. That much was clear. They could not continue with such a cloud hanging over them all. What this meant for the Empire Theatre was secondary to their more immediate worry around being paid for the season they had contracted to do and what would happen afterwards. Would they forever be tainted with association with these tragedies?

Few places of employment were as superstitious as theatres: peacock feathers, wearing blue, saying "Macbeth" or "Good Luck" – all portended disaster. Although no such symbols of catastrophe had been present at the Empire, it did not seem so remarkable a jump to believe that people would be seen as jinxed. The unspoken fear hung like a mute accusation in the air.

'Do you think your boyfriend will still want to invest in this theatre, Mary?' asked Jane Anthony. Nothing in her voice suggested she thought it likely.

'He's not superstitious,' said Mary truthfully.

'We've had one horrible accident and now a suicide,' said Jane, shaking her head. 'This place is jinxed if you ask me.'

'Did anyone see what the suicide note said?' asked Mary. She remained sceptical that the death of Matthews was as a result of his own hand.

'Lucien found it,' said Daisy. 'Apparently it was quite short: something like, "*It's over. They're out to get me. Well, too late. I'll do it for them.*" Something like that.'

Mary listened intently. The note certainly had the sour turn of phrase that characterised the man she had come to know, albeit briefly, on the stage and at the digs. Eddie Matthews was a bitter man; an unhappy man who, it would be all too easy to believe, had decided to end his own life in a final act of truculence against a world that had never taken to him. There was a knock at the door.

'Come in,' said Jane.

Wellbeloved peeked his head around the door along with the police constable.

'Do you mind if we take your statements now?' said Wellbeloved. Susan and Jackie entered the room. They both seemed pale and drawn. Susan took immediate support from a cigarette. Her hand was shaking.

Meanwhile, in the men's dressing room, recently vacated by Wellbeloved, Kit was staring at the handwritten note purportedly from Eddie Matthews. It was written in rather rushed block capital letters, which Kit found odd. It read:

IT'S OVER. THE WORD'S OUT. GET EDDIE MATTHEWS. WELL TOO LATE. I'LL BEAT YOU TO IT.

Kit looked up from the letter at the sound of a door opening. Lucien Lemaire, Barney and the Monteverdi brothers were leaving the dressing room having given their statements. Max Miller had already departed because he had a train to catch back to Brighton. Rufus and Tristram stood either side of Joshua Walker. The young boy seemed fearful; Kit couldn't blame him.

'Perhaps, Rufus,' said Kit meaningfully, 'you should take Joshua home.' Rufus nodded. Kit put his hand on Joshua's shoulder, 'I'm sorry your big night has been ruined. If it's any comfort young man, from what I could see, this won't be the last time you hear such applause. You were marvellous.'

'Hear, hear,' agreed Tristram.

Rufus also put his hand on the boy's shoulder and said, 'Well, come along young man. Time to bring you back to your home. Are you ready?'

Joshua smiled at this. He followed Rufus out into the passage then out the stage door, nodding to Ezra on the way past. The raw cold of the night chilled them both as they ambled along in amiable silence towards the end of the street which led onto the front. The only sound was that of Rufus' cane clipping on the pavement and the hiss and roar of the waves in the distance.

'You really were remarkable tonight, young man,' said Rufus, breaking the silence.

'Thank you Mr Rufus. I enjoyed it. Every second.'

'It certainly looked that way from where I was sitting,' agreed Rufus. His eyes, meanwhile, were scanning the road around them. His hand clenched the cane tightly as he saw the orange glow of a cigarette in an alleyway off the road.

It would come any moment.

Three young men appeared from the alleyway. It was the same gang that had abused Joshua earlier. Jez Barker stepped forward first, while Stan and Mick stood either side of him like the three musketeers.

'Is that your boyfriend?' sneered Jez. This brought approving chuckles from his two friends. They were now standing on the pavement which meant that Rufus and Joshua were headed directly for a collision.

'Let me handle this,' murmured Rufus, stepping in front of the boy. He was no stranger to their sort. No less than Joshua or his mother, he had spent a lifetime listening to their insinuations. Their insults. Their threats. They would attack. It had happened before, and he was always ready.

Jez laughed at the little artist as he stepped in front of Joshua. 'Wot you going to do, queer? Hit me with your handbag?' Stan and Mick would have collapsed laughing at this point were it not for the fact that it would have earned a reprimand from Jez. He was pushing his luck, though. How are you supposed to appear threatening when it's all so funny?

'You are a lovely boy,' said Rufus sardonically. 'Your mother must be very proud of you. Is this what you do for entertainment when you have ceased manipulating one another's genitals?'

Jez's mouth dropped open. He had no idea what the little man had just said, but there was something in the tone, which combined no little fearlessness with a great deal of mockery, that suggested this was not going to go to plan. A more intelligent thug might have read the runes, so to speak, and staged a strategic retreat to regroup and rethink tactics. Although the thought did, briefly, cross Jez's mind, the presence of Stan and Mick either side of him emboldened him both in the sense of how humiliating a retreat would be as well as offering the reassurance that superior numbers can provide. He stepped forward grinning like a hyena in front of his dinner.

'And just wot do you think you're going to do queer boy?'

Rufus took off his hat and handed it to Joshua. He pulled a stray lock of hair back behind his ear. Before dispensing summary justice, one should look one's best. The next movement was so quick that Jez had no time to react. One moment he was contemplating smacking the effete little man across the mouth, the next he had a thin blade scratching at his throat. Painfully.

'You were saying?' asked Rufus calmly. This was met with silence. 'Cat got your tongue?' continued the police artist, holding the blade with deadly stillness.

Stan and Mick were nothing if not loyal. Insofar as they were capable of calculus, they reckoned they still had the little man outnumbered.

'Leave him alone,' roared Mick, the braver if not more articulate of the two. They stepped forward to engage Rufus. This was an unwelcome development from the point of view of Jez as his throat was moments away from being turned into salami.

'Nnnnhhhhhh,' said Jez, his eyes fixed on the blade.

'I think he wants you to stay where you are,' suggested Rufus in a dangerously jocular voice. 'Is that what he said, Joshua ?' Joshua was too stunned to reply. He merely widened his eyes in agreement.

Although none of the boys was likely to trouble the Nobel committee for any prize, Stan and Mick had enough native guile to circle around Rufus and the boy. Jez, thanks to the thin sword perched perilously on his gullet, was a little less enamoured by the sudden show of courage from his friends. His eyes screamed terror.

'Put that sword down,' said Mick. Even he knew this was a rather futile request. This was his early shot at a strategic retreat.

'Let's do 'im,' said Stan, who was not quite on the same page as his friend, or anyone else for that matter.

'I wouldn't do that,' said a voice from behind the two boys.

All eyes, except those of Rufus, which remained fixed on the first young man, turned to the source of the voice.

Kit Aston was standing on one side of the boys, blocking their escape route while Tristram Watts was standing on the other side. Both were brandishing swords rather similar to that of Rufus. Kit and Tristram closed in on the two louts.

'I saw you abusing this young man the other day,' said Kit indicating Joshua. 'I don't like bullies. Never have. Do you know what we do with bullies in the army?' It must be reported at this point that Kit's tone of voice had altered in character somewhat to sound like a sergeant major in a particularly bellicose battalion of the army.

The three terrified ruffians shook their collective heads.

Kit stepped back and did an impressive swishing of the sword that almost had the two Watts brothers choking with laughter. The three louts were certainly choking with fear courtesy of the proximity of the swords. By now, the appeal of racial abuse was fast losing its lustre for them.

Kit ceased his demonstration partly because he was becoming embarrassed by how ludicrous it must have looked to his friends. There would be a degree of teasing coming to a theatre near him soon.

He stepped menacingly close to the boys who were now penned in tight together thanks to some judicious sheep herding from Tristram. In a voice dripping with malign menace and sounding a little bit more Cockney than he'd initially intended, Kit said, 'Don't let me see you near this boy again.'

The swords were withdrawn in one unified movement. The three ruffians needed no second invitation. They scarpered stage left leaving Kit with Joshua grinning broadly and the Watts brothers guffawing loudly.

When they had finished, Rufus turned to Kit and asked in a broad London accent, 'How much for a pound of jellied eels guv?'

26

The next morning, Rufus and Kit were once more having breakfast at the hotel. Rufus who, despite his slender frame, had a hearty appetite, only picked at his food in silence. There was little point in asking why. The death of Matthews was on both their minds. Rufus felt an overwhelming sense of guilt. He had never liked the man in life; his presence had only added to the pressure on the theatre; in many senses, Rufus and Tristram had wanted rid of him. He stared out of the window onto the sea front. His eyes followed a lone seagull swooping and soaring near the water.

'What is to become of us?' he said finally. Then, with regret in his voice, he added, 'I hated him so much. Everything about him. He begged us to take him on. Tristram didn't want him, but he could see that he was desperate, so we did. You can't be like this in business. You can't have pity. And I still hate him, Kit. He's killed us.'

Kit listened in silence. There was nothing he could he say that would lift his friend's mood, but he knew that there were things he could do. The previous night had brought absolute clarity to him that two murders had taken place. One in Manchester and one at the Empire

Theatre. He would find the killer. This had to happen soon.

As they were finishing breakfast, a waiter arrived carrying a message which he handed to Kit. It took a few seconds and then Kit gasped, which broke Rufus' reverie.

'What's wrong?'

'It's from Chief Inspector Jellicoe,' said Kit looking up from the note. 'He's just arrested the Monteverdi brothers.'

Half an hour later Kit, Mary and the Watts family were sitting in the theatre office with Chief Inspector Jellicoe. He had arrived an hour and a half earlier on the train and immediately gone to the digs to arrest the acrobats. They were now being held in a cell at the local police station awaiting an interview with Wellbeloved.

'We sent word to the Italian police a few days ago to give us any information they had on the Monteverdi brothers. They had no record of such an act. Of course, we asked that they investigate. They came back to us last night. While they knew no one called Monteverdi, they were looking for two men, one of whom they knew to be an acrobat, in connection with the murder of a policeman in Milan. Mario Barella and Stephano Ricci have been on the run for a year now. They were believed to have left the country, possibly for England as both spoke the language. The descriptions we sent tallied with the men they suspect of having killed the policeman. They are not brothers according to the Italian police.'

Jellicoe paused at this point and glanced at Kit, then Mary. He seemed a little embarrassed to add anything else to the story. Rufus, however, was in no mood for dancing around this topic.

'I'm sorry chief inspector, but I think that public school education is not what I thought it was, if we do not understand what we are talking about here.'

Jellicoe frowned at the man, who was technically his subordinate, but rarely acted in such a subsidiary manner.

'Thank you Rufus,' murmured Jellicoe, drily. 'Detective Inspector Wellbeloved is at Mrs Harrison's house searching the rooms of the late Mr Matthews and the two suspects. I'm going there now.'

Kit glanced at Mary and asked the question on both their minds, 'Do you mind if we join you?'

This was met with a nod. They set off immediately on the short walk to the digs. Along the way Kit updated Jellicoe on Harry Miller's investigations in Manchester.

'The other twin died of tuberculosis, apparently. He is trying to locate the landlord of the house where she died to find out more about Harper or Gonzalo and his sister. He's been to the grave of Miss Harper, so I think we can rule out any foul play there from a twin. He had to delay coming down yesterday as the lawyer of the lady in question was playing golf apparently.'

'Lawyers,' said Jellicoe, enigmatically.

They arrived at the digs. Outside, a charlady was cleaning the doorstep. She regarded the new arrivals with ill-concealed disapproval.

'Wipe your feet. I've spent a morning cleaning the corridor because of you lot.'

'My apologies madam,' said Jellicoe raising his hat and edging past.

They went straight upstairs and found Wellbeloved in Eddie Matthews' room. It was quite a bit larger, if no less welcoming, than Mary's. The detective inspector was sitting on the bed. Beside him on one side was a cardboard box filled with notebooks. On a bedside table were sheaves of paper. Wellbeloved glanced up at the new arrivals then reached over to the pieces of paper. He handed them to Jellicoe who quickly scanned each of them. When he had finished he showed them to Kit and Mary.

The first note had a single word on it made up from letters cut from a newspaper. It said:

DESERTER

The second note was similar in style. It read:

PROSTITUTE

The third note read:

QUEER

The final note:

COWARD

'What do you make of this?' asked Jellicoe to Kit and Mary.

Kit did not answer immediately. Instead, Mary said, 'Well, I suppose given what we heard today, he's talking about some of the people in the digs. Do you thing he was blackmailing the people in the troupe?'

Kit went over to the box containing the notebooks. He picked one up and leafed through the pages. It was a bit tattered around the edges. From what Mary could see, it was filled with handwritten comments. There were three other notebooks of varying degrees of newness. All were filled with the same scrawled handwriting.

'Jokes,' said Kit, handing one of the books to Jellicoe. Kit shook his head and stared out the window. 'I'm such a fool,' he said.

Mary frowned at this. She said, 'Why? What are you thinking?'

Normally, when women ask this question of a chap, his first instinct should be to run for the hills. The lady is either seeking an opinion on a matter of some import to her or she yearns to have an insight into the deepest recesses of his heart. In all likelihood, the chap has been pondering such profound questions as should he chip or putt from the side of the green or if W. G. Grace or Jack Hobbes was the better batsman. Thankfully, unlike most men, Kit was actually listening to his wife. He turned to her with a look that Mary recognised, and which never failed to stir excitement within her, even if the immediate message was somewhat self-deprecating.

'You married a complete dolt.'

'I do wonder sometimes,' commented Mary.

Kit turned to Wellbeloved, 'Detective inspector, did you find any notebook amongst Gibbons' belongings? You know, with the illusions described or plans for other illusions?'

Wellbeloved shook his head.

Kit exhaled loudly, 'There should have been notebooks like this with Gonzalo's things. If they are not there then someone else has them.'

'The murderer?' asked Jellicoe.

'I imagine so. Yet it doesn't quite make sense. Why kill someone for the notebooks?'

'When you can steal them,' added Mary in answer to the question.

'Exactly,' agreed Kit. 'There's more to this, but we are missing something important.'

'What if we find the notebook or books that you refer to among Eddie Matthews' belongings?'

Kit looked sceptical at this. He shook his head before replying, 'I doubt Eddie Matthews was contemplating a change of career to be a magician, but I can see him as a blackmailer. I have no doubt that the notebooks of Gonzalo would be worth something to some people, but certainly not enough to justify murder.'

'That's if they are his notebooks,' pointed out Mary. 'What if…?'

'The notebooks belonged to Andrew Harper? You're right Mary. Harry said that he was the one who designed the tricks. If anything, it was Gonzalo who was the thief. In fact, it might suggest that Gonzalo played a part in Harper's death.'

'That still doesn't explain who would kill Gonzalo or steal the notebooks,' pointed out Jellicoe. 'Remember, the person with the most obvious motive to have killed Gonzalo was Harper's sister. She's dead now.'

'What if Andrew Harper had a lover. She would have had a motive for revenge if she thought Gonzalo had killed him,' said Mary. She sounded far from convinced.

'I think that it might be an idea. Chief Inspector, if you have not already done so, will you be able to obtain a warrant to search the rooms of the remaining members of the troupe?'

Somewhere from beneath the moustache of Jellicoe, a smile appeared.

'I requested this first thing. I hope by this afternoon we shall be able to conduct a search.'

Kit turned once more to the window. There was a thin film of dust on the inside. His thoughts were swirling around inside his head, although both he and the sea, a few hundred yards in front, seemed outwardly calm. He sensed that the silence in the room meant everyone was looking at him. He turned around to find that this was the case. He smiled and said, 'Sorry, my mind has been turning over the nature of the crime and something that Lysander Benedict said.'

'Which was?' asked Mary, not without a hint of amused sternness in her voice.

Under her penetrating eye, Kit relented, as husbands must do in order to maintain the easy life that they so desperately seek.

'Magicians depend on deception. Few illusions are original; it's all in the presentation. The misdirection here is clearly to make it seem as if a tragic accident occurred. This is not an original idea, but putting the victim in a cabinet and murdering him in front of a live audience probably is a first.'

As Kit was speaking, Henry entered the room through the half open door, curious to see what the fuss was all about. This momentary interruption was greeted with smiles all around. He departed none the wiser.

'The killer feels as if they have a cast iron alibi. Reviewing the evidence, they all do. No one can point to another and say, "I saw them do this". Most of the time you can deduce the killer from the motive. It's not so easy when none appear to have one.'

'The blackmailing letters?' asked Mary. 'What if Eddie Matthews was murdered and the killer planted the letters in his room to make it appear that he may have been our man all along? Perhaps the suicide is yet another piece of misdirection.'

Kit nodded at this.

'I agree. Perhaps we are taking the death of Eddie Matthews too much at face value. And yet...' said Kit, ending the thought with a hint of his own doubts. Suddenly, he became more animated. 'What if it's not a smokescreen? What if Eddie Matthews was a separate person performing a separate crime, specifically blackmail? Don't you see? If this is the case then the murderer still thinks they are being blackmailed. I think we should speak to them again, chief inspector. I do have some thoughts, though, on how and where we do this. I hope you don't mind.'

27

'It's rather a nice day outside, for once,' said Kit. He looked towards Mary meaningfully. She took this to mean that he wanted to talk to her in private. It did not require much thought on Mary's part to guess what the subject would be.

Outside the theatre, the sun shone in a cloudless sky. Of course, in England this does equate to heat, particularly in October. Still, it was a welcome break from the unremitting charcoal skies. They walked across the road, away from the theatre, onto the boardwalk.

The moment that Mary had been dreading was rapidly approaching. She had always known it would be so, but the knowledge did not provide an ounce of relief. The act of pretending to be a performer, worse a friend and a confidant to those she was seeking to disbelieve, seemed immoral. On one level, she understood that her own feelings towards the deception she had engaged in were meaningless. What she had done was in the service of a higher ideal: justice. Nonetheless, she still gazed at what she had done through a glass darkly.

Sensing her turmoil, she felt Kit's arms encircle her. They were standing at the sea front watching in sun-soaked silence the waves lapping up onto the beach. They remained like this for a while. Sometimes, she found Kit was at his most intuitive when he said nothing and just held her. Finally, she looked up at him and said, 'I should tell them soon. They have a right to know.'

'Let me come too. It'll be a blessed relief not to have to act out the part of Chauncey Alston and that wretched southern accent.'

Mary laughed and clung a little harder to Kit. Throughout all of this, some compensation had been gained by seeing the man she loved suffering in a role of her making. Oddly, she felt not a modicum of guilt about this, principally because she knew that Kit would have appreciated the joke too. It seemed like they were stumbling between romantic comedy and tragedy without achieving the merits of either. However, in the midst of such sordid events, whilst trying to uncover the truth through means that were nefarious, possibly immoral, they had a duty to themselves: to retain that which made them human, which made them husband and wife.

'Thank you,' said Mary. 'However, I think that I shall do this myself.'

They stared out at the grey sea in silence.

'Do you know who the killer is?' asked Mary, dreading the answer.

Kit peered sideways to her with a rueful smile.

'No,' he said truthfully. 'I have some suspicions, but nothing that I am certain about. It feels appropriate we are dealing with magic because I have a very strong feeling this is one grand deception. I'm rather hoping that Harry can help us learn more about what happened in Manchester. If the story begins there then almost certainly the solution lies there, too.'

They returned to the theatre, just before the performers were due to show up for the next round of questioning. Rufus greeted them in the office with an envelope containing a telegram.

'It looks like it's from Manchester. Perhaps Harry has come up with something.'

'Let's hope so,' said Mary grimly. 'We could do with a break.'

Kit tore open the envelope and read the brief note inside. He looked up and a smile crossed his face. Even Jellicoe sat up at this. Mary and Rufus crowded round Kit to take a peek at the message.

'Has Mr Miller found something?' asked Jellicoe.

'He has,' confirmed Kit, before adding wryly, 'and through entirely legitimate means too.'

'Wonders never cease,' commented Jellicoe.

'I must say, he's definitely showing promise as a detective,' said Kit, reaching over to hand the note to Jellicoe.

'Interesting,' agreed Jellicoe, reading the note. 'Very interesting, indeed.'

The interviews with the troupe of performers began in the early afternoon. At Kit's request they took place on the stage, rather than at the police station or Tristram's office. There was a simple reason for this. It gave Kit and Mary the opportunity to sit underneath and listen to the questions and the responses. Furthermore, the stage was the natural habitat for the individuals. It was where they performed. They would feel at their most comfortable there.

Kit was counting on this.

He held Mary's hand as the first of the performers crossed the stage. By the heavy tread, they guessed it was Lucien Lemaire. Mary was unconcerned about Lemaire. She did not think him a killer and certainly had no feelings towards him. The same could not be said for any of the women. Despite the short space of time in the digs, she had felt quite drawn to both Daisy and Jane, even Jackie. Susan Parrish remained a cold presence in an otherwise warm house.

Jellicoe's manner of interrogation, unlike Wellbeloved, who had also just arrived to join the chief, was a model of restraint by comparison. He barely seemed to ask questions. Instead, his approach was a variation on the give-them-enough-rope model.

'You didn't fight in the War, I see.'

'No,' replied Lemaire coldly. 'What has this to do with either death?'

'You were an objector?'

'No,' snapped Lemaire. 'I tried to enlist. They didn't accept me.'

Silence.

Most people feel uncomfortable and generally reveal more than they had intended.

'I was deemed too unwell to participate,' said Lemaire. 'Look, Jellicoe, where is this leading? Is there a point to these questions?'

'Unwell,' said Jellicoe. It was more a statement than a question.

This was followed by a sigh and then a shrug. Then Lemaire answered sharply, 'If you must know a few years ago I was unwell. I had some episodes that were deemed schizophrenic. It was a short period of my life and I have since enjoyed a full recovery.'

Below stage Mary turned to Kit with the raised eyebrow of one who had said as much. It was always the way with ventriloquists. Aunt Agatha would have said the same.

The interview concluded soon after, as Lemaire had nothing new to add to his statement on his movements on the night of the murder, nor anything new to share on how he and Gonzalo had met, as well as their feelings toward one another.

Susan Parrish was the next performer to face Jellicoe. The clip of her heels pattered rhythmically across the stage. She sat sullenly in front of the detective, a cigarette clamped between compressed lips. A few questions on the night Gonzalo died were answered in a bored voice. Eddie Matthews' death prompted little by way of sympathy. Then Jellicoe changed tack.

'Had you performed much prior to the death of your husband?' asked Jellicoe.

'Not much. I didn't have much else I could do. I started work as an extra on moving pictures when a friend fell ill. I suppose it started from there. I met Jackie in nineteen seventeen. That's when it really began. Before we knew it, we were in France doing shows for some of the boys over there.'

'That must have been painful,' said Jellicoe gently. Tears glistened in Susan's eyes. It was the first show of emotion since Jellicoe had first seen her. 'Take your time,' urged Jellicoe.

'It was difficult, yes. Then I realised that I would go home to England the next day, while most of them would be facing…'

She couldn't finish the sentence.

'I gather your husband was a performer himself; before the war,' stated Jellicoe when Susan had finally composed herself.

'Yes. I suppose that's why I knew some people in the trade.'

'May I ask what he did on stage? Was he an actor?'

Susan shook her head and dragged deeply on her cigarette.

'No, nothing like that. He was a magician.'

Jackie Rutherford's heavy tread across the stage seemed to shake dust from the rafters. Her arrival to be interviewed coincided with the appearance of Romeo the cat. He wandered over to Mary and brushed against her legs. A moment later, after surveying her legs and deeming them fit for sleeping purposes, he hopped up onto her thigh and settled down for a quick forty winks.

'Romeo by name,' murmured Kit to Mary. 'Let's hope he doesn't start bringing you gifts.'

Mary giggled, 'That's all I need - a large dead rat.'

'You can add it to your collection.'

Up above them, Jellicoe had been through the early formalities with Jackie. The tone of the questioning had hardened slightly as they addressed her relationship with Gonzalo.

'I gather you had a number of arguments with Gonzalo in the week before his death.'

'He treated Jane horribly,' answered Jackie. Her response was forthright which was very much in character. Mary liked Jackie. She was an open girl. Unlike Susan, you knew where you stood with her, and Mary suspected you would have no more loyal friend if she liked you.

'What makes you say that?' asked Jellicoe.

'Gonzalo was a bully. Not that Jane is a shrinking violet, but she is sweet-natured; she's not one for arguments. She's classy but without being a 'nob'. I just gave him what for whenever he was taking liberties with her. Don't ask me when. It was all the time and before you ask, it doesn't mean I killed him.'

'I wasn't going to ask,' said Jellicoe which made Kit smile as he listened beneath the stage. 'I understand that Mrs Harrison found you in Gonzalo's room the day before he died.'

This was news to Kit and Mary. Both leaned forward to hear better. Romeo began to purr loudly which was delightful and unhelpful in equal measure. To Mary, this got to the very nature of cats.

'Jane asked me to bring her a deck of cards from Gonzalo's bedside table.'

'Why did she ask you to do that?'

'I'd said I was going up to my room anyway. We usually leave the doors open. I didn't mind as it was Jane. I think Mrs Harrison just happened to walk in when I was there. I explained why.'

'Why would Miss Anthony want the cards?' asked Jellicoe.

'She does magic tricks too. Not like Gonzalo of course,' replied Jackie before she remembered a rather important detail. 'Well, I should say, "like he did". He won't be performing magic where he is now.'

'Where is that?' asked Jellicoe, curious to hear what Jackie would say.

'I shall let the good Lord decide on that.'

Barney Hallett was the next performer to be interviewed. He fidgeted with his shirt button as Jellicoe fixed his eyes on him. Barney avoided the policeman's eyes. In Jellicoe's experience, this often happened even when the person being questioned was entirely innocent. Perhaps it was something that dated back to one's childhood. Certainly, he had made good use of this implicit power over the years. Sometimes, when in a reflective mood, he might even have a moment of remorse at having done so. This feeling rarely lasted very long. He consoled himself with the knowledge that the alternative, as represented by his colleague, Detective Inspector Wellbeloved, was a lot less agreeable.

'Can you tell me what you remember of the moments leading up to the death of Gonzalo?' asked Jellicoe.

Kit leaned forward again. Every detail was important, and he wanted to be sure that he'd not missed anything that had been said earlier.

'I was waiting at the bottom of the chute,' began Barney. 'I was dressed and ready to go. I heard the music start and waited for my cue. Then I heard stamping. At first, I wasn't sure what it was, then I realised Javier had not come down. Eddie Matthews was nearby. That's when he said, "Something's wrong, Barney." I knew he was right. So, I ran up the stairs leading to the side of the stage where the boys were.'

'Did Eddie Matthews go with you?'

'No, it was just me and Lucien who went up to the stage. Eddie didn't come.'

As Kit was listening to this, he sat back and stared up at the hatch in the stage. This was a crucial fact he had not considered. At least, he felt it was crucial, but he did not know why.

'What's wrong?' asked Mary. Her movement woke Romeo who jumped down from his soft seat.

Kit shook his head. These moments were frustrating. The shape and dimensions of the tragedy were in front of him, but he could not yet see through the fog in which they were shrouded. He willed his mind to think through everything he had heard and seen, to negotiate the jagged, narrow path that would lead to the truth.

28

While Kit struggled to give definition to the thoughts swirling around his mind, Daisy Lewis took her seat in front of Jellicoe. The stern cast of her features became even sterner when, for a change, Wellbeloved posed the first question. If it surprised Daisy it caused amazement to Kit and Mary just below.

'Have you heard from your husband?'

'Good Lord,' whispered Kit, as his attention returned once more to the interviews.

'Did you know?' asked Mary.

Kit shook his head. This was a surprise. Whether it meant anything was another matter.

'Did you?' whispered Kit.

'No, but now that I think of it...' said Mary, leaving the sentence unfinished.

Up above on the stage, Daisy Lewis had regained the power of speech.

'What do you mean?' she asked, stalling while her disordered thoughts unscrambled themselves.

'Exactly that, Mrs Cooper,' said Wellbeloved. 'It says here that Albert Cooper and Daisy Lewis married six months ago, at a registry office in Gretna Green.'

'Why did you marry there, Mrs Cooper?' asked Jellicoe. His voice was conversational.

Daisy was silent for a few moments then she said, 'What has this to do with what happened here?'

'We'll see about that,' said Wellbeloved, not hiding the edge in his voice. It made Mary uncomfortable. She liked Daisy. It had not been an easy life for the singer. Like so many others, a widow before she was twenty-five. Mary had lost her own father in the War and an uncle. What would she have felt like had she lost Kit? The answer did not bear thinking about.

'Where is this leading?' she asked Kit.

Kit glanced towards her but had no answer to her question. The two policemen were trying to unsettle Daisy, this much was clear. What this had to do with the murder was open to question, but there was also the matter of a man who was, in all likelihood, an army deserter. This could not be dismissed lightly, even if it were subsidiary to the main investigation.

'Is your husband a deserter?' asked Wellbeloved. He was not a man to beat about the bush. His patience for stalking suspects was next to non-existent. Jellicoe winced slightly as he bored in on his quarry.

Tears stung her eyes, but anger transferred the sting into her words.

'He did his bit. He was there. Where were you while he was being shot at, bombed and gassed?' she snarled. Moments later she was on her feet. Her staccato footsteps echoed underneath the stage.

'I'm not sure what that achieved,' said Mary angrily.

Kit put his hand on hers and, much to Mary's amazement, chuckled. She looked aghast at her husband. He and his senses appeared to have temporarily diverged.

'How can you laugh at this?' asked Mary, her anger had tapered somewhat as she suspected that another game was in play at that moment. 'What is going on?'

'I could be wrong,' said Kit 'but I think that very wonderful man, Chief Inspector Jellicoe, has just told Daisy that she is not under suspicion for the murder and that she should consider exiting stage left as soon as is practically possible.' Mary nodded slowly at this. Kit was holding her hand and looking into her eyes, willing her to make the next leap. She did and soon she, too, began to feel the sting of tears in her eyes.

'I suppose I was not the only one putting on an act,' she said, relief cascading through her.

'No, my love,' said Kit just as footsteps began to reverberate around them.

Jane Anthony was the last of the ladies to be interviewed. As she walked across the stage, Kit whispered to Mary, 'What do you think of Jane?'

'I like her,' said Mary immediately. 'I think she's still in shock over what has happened, but she's very sweet-natured, as Jackie says. The others told me that Gonzalo used to be a little bit overbearing with her.'

'And they were in a relationship?'

'Jane says they weren't,' replied Mary. 'According to the others, Gonzalo acted like they were. It certainly wasn't like Daisy and Bert Cooper. They made no secret that they spent the night together. Mrs Harrison didn't much like this but pretended not to notice. According to Jackie, none of the girls minded this, but they would have said something to Jane if she and Gonzalo had started to become more romantically involved.'

'They disliked him so much.'

'Yes.'

Up on the stage, Jellicoe regarded Jane Anthony and found it difficult to imagine her as a killer. Yet he knew that even a fragile beauty such as Jane Anthony's was no guarantee that she was innocent.

'I gather that you are also a magician,' said Jellicoe.

'Hardly,' said Jane. She tried to smile as she said this but gave it up as a bad job. 'Graham taught me some card tricks. We have a lot of time off, so I used it to practice. I wouldn't call myself a magician, chief inspector.'

Jellicoe asked in as gentle a manner as he could, about her future plans.

'I might return to acting. I'm not sure I could face being a magician's assistant again,' said Jane.

'Perhaps you could be the magician,' said Jellicoe, a trace of a smile on his face.

Jane laughed at this.

'I think this is another area where society dictates what a woman's role is.'

Below stage, Mary sat up a little straighter at this and nodded. She and Kit listened as Jane continued to explain what she meant.

'Women magicians on stage are rarer than women Members of Parliament. Magic offers the chance for women to be seen in the power of men. You cut us in half, you make us rise into the air, you make us disappear. It's all a reflection of the power that men wield over women socially, politically and economically,' said Jane. Then she laughed and added, 'I don't suppose you were expecting that answer, chief inspector?'

Jellicoe laughed too before replying, 'I wasn't, but I shall never look at a magic act in the same way again. Although you seem to be forgetting witchcraft.'

'I'm on the side of the witches, chief inspector,' said Jane.

'So am I,' said Mary, from below the stage.

'You've certainly cast a spell on me,' replied Kit and tried to ignore the eye rolling that greeted this.

Romeo reappeared once more near Mary. He was in a fight to the death with a piece of wood. The cat was winning. Rolling on his back he grabbed the piece of wood and began to claw it with his hind paws. A door wedge was on the wrong end of a mauling.

'Looks like I'm not the only one who's been hexed by you,' observed Kit.

Mary picked up Romeo and gave him a kiss. Then she added, 'Thank you. Such a thoughtful gift.' Then she looked at Kit. He was staring at the ground.

'Of course,' said Kit. 'How could I have not seen it?'

Following the conclusion of the interviews, Jellicoe joined Kit, Rufus and Tristram in the green room near the stage while Mary went to join the other members of the troupe. Tristram was the last to arrive. He was about to shut the door when Kit said, 'No Tristram. Could you leave it open?'

They waited in silence for a few minutes and then they heard some of the performers passing them in the corridor. Still no one said anything. The silent ticking of the clock on the wall was the loudest noise in the room. More performers passed them, then they heard Wellbeloved's voice.

'After you,' he said, as he held the door separating the dressing room area from underneath the stage.

Kit began to speak immediately.

'The key is the journal containing the magic illusions. If we're able to search the rooms of the performers then we are bound to find it. Whoever has that journal is the killer. It's as simple as that. When will we receive confirmation, chief inspector?'

'I'm hoping the telegram will arrive this afternoon,' said Jellicoe, a little too loudly.

He grimaced slightly as he said this and did not dare look at Rufus Watts who was smirking at the hamminess of what he was listening to.

The men in the room waited a moment and then they heard the sound of footsteps walking away from them towards the stage door. Rufus went to the door and glanced out into the corridor. He nodded to the group inside.

The trap had been set.

29

Harry Miller's extended stay in Manchester had involved an additional night at the theatre, to see another revue. A chat at the stage door had confirmed that the Brothers Grimoire had played there also. Memories were vague, but the stage door manager had quite liked the act but did not have a high opinion of either man.

'Mr Gibson had a high-handed manner while Mr Harper was a bit too much to himself, if you know what I mean. I don't think he liked Mr Gibson much.'

The next morning, Miller made his way to the law firm. The office was in the south of Manchester in Stretford. The taxi dropped him off outside a terraced house with a sign above the window read: Thomas Bennington.

The lawyer met him at the door.

'Mr Miller, you are very prompt,' said Bennington who was probably nearer seventy than sixty. He had a kindly air about him and ruddy cheeks. His eyes sparkled with a good humour that had Miller immediately liking the man.

Bennington took him into his office which looked as if it was a converted living room. There seemed to be no other staff. Paintings adorned the wall. Miller gazed at them unsure if he liked them much. A couple of them showed childlike drawings of men heading towards the factory gate. Bennington smiled when he saw what was engaging Miller's attention.

'A local artist named Lowry. Do you like them?'

'I'm not sure,' said Miller honestly. 'They're unusual.' He stared at them a little more and then smiled, 'Actually, they're growing on me.'

Bennington spent a few moments studying them also. 'Yes,' he agreed. 'They do that.'

Miller declined the offer of a cup of tea and instead got down to business. He explained the background to his inquiry and requested more information about Mrs Antonia Hill.

Bennington took off his spectacles and cleaned them on his handkerchief. Then he said, 'Yes, I remember Mrs Hill. Very nice woman. I sold her house for her. Very sad, I gather she lost her husband during the War. Then she had the young woman you mentioned board with her, and she died, as you say. It's very sad when they die so young. I can never quite fathom the reasoning of the Almighty.'

Bennington went to his filing cabinet and opened one of the drawers from which he took a manilla envelope. He opened it and removed a sheaf of papers. Among the papers was a small photograph. Miller's eyes immediately alighted on it, but he said nothing.

'I gather she went to live with a sister in London,' said Miller, hoping that the lawyer would be able to find the address.

'Really?' said Bennington, looking up from the papers. 'News to me. I thought she and the other young woman were both without any family.'

'What about the family of the man she married or her own family?'

'Oh no, Mrs Hill was another one who came from Barnardo's Children's Home; just like the unfortunate woman who died. The man she married had no family, but apparently was quite wealthy. She met him when she was nursing during the War. They married when it became apparent he would not survive his injuries. It happened a lot, you know,' said the lawyer.

Miller's heart lurched as he listened to the story. It was an almost identical situation to the one he had experienced when he fell in love with a young nurse in Paris after the War. She had agreed to marry a young officer who was dying in order to ensure the young man's fortune went to her rather than people he did not know. Miller nodded grimly and then pointed to the photograph.

'Is that a picture of Mrs Hill?'

Bennington picked it out from the file and handed it to Miller. The photograph was no more than three inches high. It showed two young women, both with light brown hair, standing in a garden. It was a summer's day. Both were squinting as the photographer had positioned them looking into the sun. Miller turned the photograph over. There was writing on the back: Eliza and me, January 1920.

'Which one is Mrs Hill?' asked Miller.

Bennington pointed to the taller of the two women. Miller thought her quite beautiful. The other unquestionably looked unwell. There was something in her posture and her expression.

'Did you know Mrs Hill well?' asked Miller.

'No,' replied the lawyer. 'I hadn't met her before. I handled the sale of the house and then she left. I have her address here.'

Miller looked at the address Mrs Hill had written down. He doubted she was still there, but he would check anyway. Miller went to hand the photograph back to Bennington, but the old lawyer held his hand up.

'Keep it. I don't have much use for it.'

'One last question, do you have Mrs Hill's name from before she was married?'

'Yes,' replied Bennington. He checked through a reef of papers until he found what he needed. 'Here, it is. I knew it was somewhere. Antonia Scott. This may have been a name given to her by the Barnardo's. It sometimes happened like that if they were foundlings.'

'Where is the Barnardo's?'

Bennington wrote down the address along with the address that Mrs Hill had gone to in London. Miller thanked Bennington and departed soon after. He wasn't sure how much use any of this was in terms of the investigation. The taxi was waiting on the street. He had just enough time to make it to Stockport station to catch the train down to London.

'The station,' ordered Miller. He stared at the photograph in his hand and then put it in his wallet. Then a thought struck him. He groaned and tried to ignore it, but it wouldn't go away. 'Change of plan,' said Miller leaning forward to the driver.

'Where to?' asked the driver.

They travelled across the city to the address supplied by Bennington. The Barnardo's home was much larger than Miller had expected. It dawned on him that what he would see inside might also be heart-breaking. He steeled himself to walk along the path and into the reception area of the home. As he entered the small reception area, he saw a woman dressed as a nurse with a long wheelbarrow with four toddlers sitting in it. They all had smiles on their faces. Miller wasn't sure whether to be happy or sad about what he saw. On balance, he was relieved to see that the children were well cared for. At the same time, he felt a sense of shame. He'd never given any thought to this world. While his upbringing had not been privileged in terms of wealth it had been altogether a fortunate one because he had a family. Such things, he realised, should never be taken for granted.

An elderly woman greeted him at the reception. She smiled hopefully. Miller felt a stab of guilt. He was not here to inquire about adoption or fostering. He smiled back and explained the purpose of his visit. A cloud passed over the face of the woman, but she quickly recovered her polite manner.

'I shall check our files,' she said. 'Will you take a seat?'

The lady returned a few minutes later. She had a few sheets of paper in her hand. Miller went over to her.

'We had the three people you mentioned stay with us for many years. It's sad when they cannot find a home. It says here that the young man was a morose sort of boy. When they are like this it's very difficult. His sister, apparently, was very bright, but she would not be separated from him. It's a pity for her, it says here that she would easily have found a place to live with a family.'

'Was she sickly?' asked Miller.

'There's nothing about any illness here. Antonia Scott was apparently very close to the two Harper children.'

'Did you know them?' asked Miller.

'I didn't, although I'm sure we have staff here who would remember them well.' As she said this a tall, rather elegant lady dressed in black came into the building. She had two young girls, no more than ten, either side of her. She glanced towards the lady on reception. Miller detected a slight shake of the head from the receptionist. Once more a wave of sadness engulfed him.

'Miss Waterhouse, Mr Miller is inquiring about some young children who used to be in the house from before the War. Do you remember the Harper children and Antonia Scott?'

The lady turned to the two children she was with and told them to "run along". Then she came over to Miller. The woman had a school mistress air about her, and Miller already felt himself becoming ten years old once more.

'I'm helping in a police investigation, Miss Waterhouse. Sadly, the two Harper children are no longer with us.'

'Yes, I know,' said Miss Waterhouse, there was just the hint of a catch in her voice. 'Such lovely children. It was very sad.'

She led Miller out to an office, and they sat down. Miller declined the offer of tea. He waited for Miss Waterhouse to explain more. Miss Waterhouse took a few moments and then began to tell Miller of the children.

'Andrew was a brooding, introspective boy. Not like Eliza.' Once more, Miss Waterhouse paused.

'I'm sorry if this brings up sad memories for you, Miss Waterhouse,' said Miller gently.

'Eliza was exceptionally bright. Such a lovely young woman she became. I missed her when she left. I miss her now. Antonia, too. Andrew, as I say, was not an easy child, but he was devoted to his sister and Antonia. He was good with his hands. Always making things for the girls. They loved creating magic tricks. He and Eliza used to spend hours with Antonia dreaming them up. Eliza used to write them all down in that big book of hers. I remember she showed it to me once. I couldn't make head nor tail of it.'

'Why was that?' asked Miller.

Miss Waterhouse smiled at the memory.

'She wrote it in code. Only she, Antonia and Andrew understood it. Then they would perform the tricks for us here.'

'What kind of tricks did they do?' asked Miller, fascinated by what he was hearing.

'Oh all sorts. Just like a proper show. They did mind reading, escapology, card tricks, everything really.' Her voice trailed off as she remembered a time long past. 'It's sad when they go,' she added wistfully.

Miller could think of nothing so say to this. A thought occurred to him, and he took out the photograph.

'I'm trying to locate Antonia Scott. I gather she married a soldier. I believe she's a widow now.'

'How sad,' said Miss Waterhouse. 'Such a waste of youth.'

Miller nodded mutely at this but couldn't speak now. He hoped that Miss Waterhouse could not see his eyes misting over. However, you did not become the head of a Barnardo's House without having eyes that would have an eagle running to buy spectacles. He felt her hand take his. She regarded him with great tenderness.

'I'm sorry Mr Miller. You were there, weren't you. I can see it in your eyes. It must have been a dreadful time.'

'It was,' whispered Miller.

'Is that a photograph you have there?' asked Miss Waterhouse peering down at the photograph.

'Yes, that's Eliza and Antonia. They were quite beautiful really. I was so sad when I heard that she'd passed away. Strange that Antonia never contacted me. I heard it from a lawyer called Bennington.'

Miss Waterhouse seemed very sad for a moment. Her eyes moistened and she looked away. Then she handed the photograph back to Miller. Miller thanked her and was about to put the photograph back in his pocket when it occurred to him that there was one more thing he needed to confirm.

'Sorry, Miss Waterhouse. I realise that this must be painful. Can you confirm which of the young women was which?'

Miss Waterhouse indicated the woman that was standing. She said, 'That's Eliza.'

Miller was stunned. She was pointing to the woman that Bennington had identified as Antonia Hill. He had to let Kit and Mary know as soon as possible.

Evening was drawing in when Miller's train pulled into Euston station. He was tired and the temptation to return home and sleep for a week was overwhelming. However, he could not get over the feeling that one last call had to be made. He trooped over to a taxi outside the station. He pulled out the address that had been given to him by Thomas Bennington. The driver looked at the address and read it out loud.

'36 Vance Portman Street, Camden, London'.

'Do you know it?' said Miller.

'Yes, my mum lives there. What do you think? Get in.'

Miller smiled at the driver. British customer service was second to none in its cordiality. Soon, they were off in the direction of Camden. It was a part of town that he did not know very well. He was a south Londoner. It didn't look very different from where he'd grown up.

Street upon street of miserable terraced houses passed by. It made him think once more about his own life. His existence in Grosvenor Square had a dreamlike quality to it. He hardly worked if truth be told. Yet, he lived in surroundings that were another world away from what the car was passing now. Guilt enveloped him once more. How could he have such a sense of dissatisfaction when he led such a privileged life? He'd enjoyed the trip to Manchester as a break from this and a chance to do something useful once more.

Ten minutes after departing Euston they turned into Vance Portman Street. Each side of the street had four storey houses in a better state of repair than many he'd passed earlier. The taxi driver slowed down and kept his eye on the numbers of the houses. Miller too. Something seemed wrong to him. The cul-de-sac was not a very long one, yet the address suggested that there were more houses on it than were evident before Miller's eyes.

'Can't find number thirty-six. Are you sure you have the right address?' asked the taxi driver.

Something told Miller that this was not something that the kindly old lawyer in Manchester would get wrong. There was only one explanation that seemed likely: Antonia Hill, or Eliza Harper, as he now knew her to be, had lied.

'Stop at number twenty-six, please,' ordered Miller. This was one of the last houses on the street. Miller stepped out of the taxi and went to the front door. The cold of the night stung his face. He wanted to be home now with a warm cup of cocoa. The door was answered by a middle-aged man eyeing Miller suspiciously.

'I'm sorry to bother you at this time in the evening sir,' said Miller. 'I'm looking for a Mrs Antonia Miller. I was told she lives at thirty-six Vance Portman road but there doesn't seem to be a house with that number. I was wondering if it was, in fact, number twenty-six.'

The man shook his head, 'No one with that name in this house or any of the ones around us. This street only goes as high as number thirty, and I can tell you that she isn't there.'

Miller thanked the man and returned to his taxi. With something approaching a sigh of relief he said, 'Take me to Grosvenor Square.'

Miller wasn't sure what to make of the day's discoveries. He would have to send a message to Kit about what he'd found out. It was Antonia Hill who had died of tuberculosis, that much was clear. Far from being dead, Andrew Harper's twin was still alive. She had taken the name of Antonia Hill no doubt to inherit the house from her friend. The question was: where was she now? And under what name was she going by?

23

Very early the next morning, Kit walked along the cramped dirty grey street. The weather had changed overnight. Rain threatened the town like an enemy army massing on the hills. He gazed up at the black cloud drifting towards him. The solution had come to him the previous evening. It was so obvious and yet everyone had missed it.

A wet wind caressed his face as he stepped onto the pier. He leaned over the side to watch the swell slap against the metal stilts of the pier. The waves creamed and crashed against the sea shore. He stared at them as the minutes drowsed on. It was time to return to the hotel. Mary would be awake soon. She had returned the previous evening. There was little point in pretending that the show would go on. It would not. That much was clear.

At that moment, he felt a hollow yearning for something he could not identify, never mind articulate. Somewhere as the case had progressed the line between illusion and reality had become blurred. The cold began to gnaw at his gloved-hands, and he was glad to be back in the warmth of the hotel.

Mary was lying awake in the bed. She sat up and rubbed her eyes as he opened the curtains.

'How was your walk?' she asked.

'Well, I might not be able to feel my fingers again for a year, but aside from that it was perfectly charming.'

'Are you ready for this morning? Do you think Daisy will have absconded?'

'Who knows?' replied Kit.

'How do you feel about deserters?' asked Mary, suddenly curious.

Kit sat down on the bed. Although they rarely spoke of the years that Kit had been at the front, it was not a subject that was entirely out of bounds. Mary had spent a year nursing at the front and had seen the impact of the carnage at first hand.

'I don't know if I'm honest. You saw how horrible things were. Things we were asked to do…' Kit paused at this. He felt Mary's arms encircle him. 'I'm not surprised people deserted. Perhaps the only surprise is there weren't more of them. There was a very good reason to do it, I suppose and I'm not talking merely about avoiding death and suffering. It was the failure of our leaders. In that sense there was a legitimacy to what they did. I suppose you could say that I deserted too. The first chance I had to escape the carnage, I grabbed it with both hands. I'm not in any position to judge those that did not have the opportunity to do as I did. It was not the right thing to do. If every soldier did it…'

'There would be no war?' suggested Mary.

'Sadly, there would be,' replied Kit gently. 'Order, rules, duty matters. Without such restraint, far from being free we would be oppressed. Sadly, we need armed forces, and we need those who compose them to obey orders.' Then Kit smiled and added, 'But I hope he escapes. That they both can make a new life together somewhere. I wouldn't be in his shoes.'

They went down to breakfast to find Jellicoe and Rufus already there. Of Wellbeloved, there was no sign. Apparently he had stayed the night at Mrs Harrison's digs.

'I hope he enjoyed the apple tart,' said Mary.

Rain began to fall outside, and they watched it for a few minutes in resigned silence.

'What time is Harry's train due in?' asked Rufus, while buttering some toast; this giving lie to the calumny that men can only concentrate on one task at a time.

'He said around ten. So we have half an hour or so,' replied Kit.

A few minutes later, a waiter came over to the table with a message. He handed it to Jellicoe.

'Telegram?' asked Rufus.

Jellicoe shook his head before handing the note to the police artist.

'Detective Inspector Wellbeloved has just phoned the hotel. They found the journal containing the illusions. It's in his possession now.'

Mary leaned forward; her eyes narrowed.

'Which room?' she asked.

'Eddie Matthews room, I'll wager,' said Kit. This was met by a half-smile from Mary.

'You're not going to be beaten by a mere man, are you, Mary?' asked Rufus. Mary folded her arms and sat back.

'Do we know if it is the original one?' asked Mary.

'It may not be but that probably matters less than the fact that it was there,' said Kit, taking the note. He read the note before adding, 'Under a loose floorboard, I see. Did we check that before?'

'We did,' confirmed Jellicoe.

'So there can be no doubt then. I wonder what Harry has to show us.'

Thirty-five minutes later, Miller arrived in the hotel restaurant. He was shown to the table by the waiter. Four pairs of eyes were fixed on him expectantly as he sat down. Sensing this was not the time for chatting about the inclement weather nor how he had found his trip down to the coast, Miller fished inside his breast pocket and removed his wallet. He took out the photograph and displayed it to the table.

'This is Eliza Harper,' said Miller, pointing to the standing figure. The table drew closer. They studied her face, her smile. Life would change dramatically for the young woman within a few weeks of that moment.

'Good work, Harry,' chorused the table. It had been, too. Jellicoe looked thoughtfully at the little Londoner and then turned to Kit. Nothing was said between the two men, noted Mary, yet so much had been communicated.

Mary put her head on Kit's shoulder. Her heart still felt as if it had been twisted and her body ached with a sadness as the case drew towards its conclusion. A part of her knew that she would miss the excitement that she felt when they were involved in these situations. Another part felt more than a little haunted by the various tragedies that had led to this moment.

'Shall we?' said Kit. His moment to take centre stage had arrived. The audience awaited him.

30

'Would you like a drink?' asked Tristram, holding up a glass of sherry to his brother.

'Thanks, I've just had breakfast,' pointed out Rufus.

'How disciplined of you,' said Tristram pouring himself a little bit more. He seemed keyed up. They all were, as far as Kit could see.

It was mid-morning. Harry Miller had arrived from London and now sat with everyone in Tristram's office as they waited for the performers to arrive. Mrs Watts popped her head in from the small kitchen behind the office. One look at Tristram's sherry earned a frowned rebuke, but nothing was said on that subject. Tea was offered and accepted by all. They knew better than to refuse and it was normally accompanied by rather delicious buns or sandwiches.

Much to Kit and Mary's surprise, Daisy Lewis had not absconded overnight. Mary watched her walk through the foyer of the theatre. She glanced into the office and saw Mary sitting between Jellicoe and the man she knew as Chauncey. Her face showed neither approval nor disapproval, yet Mary sensed there was sorrow in her eyes. A feeling that she had been misled by Mary but, perhaps, also recognition that she was a sinner too, in this regard.

Henry, the St Bernard belonging to the Wyman Sisters was also with the performers. He trooped in quietly like the others as they went through to the auditorium followed by Detective Inspector Wellbeloved. The big detective glanced through the window and received an approving nod from Jellicoe in the manner of a shepherd acknowledging a sheep dog. The last to arrive were the Monteverdi brothers, accompanied by two policemen. Unsurprisingly, both were handcuffed and seemed none too happy about life.

Writers all too rarely share the snack arrangements before the revelation of whodunnit. Forging into territory all too rarely explored, your chronicler can confirm that tea was served along with some home-made scones. Suitably replenished, it was now time to join the performers on the stage to perform the final act.

As they entered the auditorium, Kit noted that there were a couple of other policemen present - one at each exit. If the troupe were in any doubt about what was about to take place then this, more than anything, would have provided a rather large clue. They sat in a horseshoe shape around a table which had four chairs. Everyone stared at the group climbing the steps to the stage, bar Henry. The effort of walking the short distance to the theatre had evidently tired him and he was taking the opportunity to grab forty winks at the feet of Susan.

Mary sat with Kit, Jellicoe and Wellbeloved while Miller stood behind them. The ladies fixed their eyes on Mary. Once again, she sensed sadness rather than condemnation. Her role over the last few days was all too clear to them even before Kit rose to his feet to speak.

Perhaps aware of the light that would be cast on Mary, he began on this point first.

'Good morning everyone. Thank you for once more returning to join us. I can see on your faces that you are wondering what has become of Chauncey Alston. As you will have guessed by now, he does not exist and for that I would like to apologise. Alas, the subterfuge was necessary and, I'm afraid, it involved my wife, Mary, also. My name is Kit Aston.'

A few of the troupe looked up sharply at him as they recognised the name.

'Over the last few years, I have had occasion to work with the police. In particular, I have worked with Chief Inspector Jellicoe and Rufus, on a number of cases. We were asked by Rufus to investigate the vile letters that were sent to you last week, little realising what would follow. As you know, tragedy struck twice, and it is to this I will turn now.'

Kit was silent for a few moments to allow what he had said to sink in.

'The only way to understand a crime truly is to have caused it. Otherwise, in criminal detection, you need to assemble the evidence, sift through it, separate the irrelevant from the material and form a conclusion. For the criminal, rather like the magician, you need people to misunderstand the evidence of their eyes. Illusion and deception are threads that run through why we are here today.'

'Graham Gibson, otherwise known as Javier Gonzalo, was murdered. This was not a tragic accident. It was murder. Now, all of you had met Mr Gonzalo before at one time or another. He was, I gather, a very charismatic performer. A showman. However, what one sees on stage and off can be two very different things. I gather that Mr Gonzalo was not universally popular. In fact, many disliked him. However, few people are killed because they are unlikeable. Gonzalo was murdered for a reason. That reason was revenge.'

'Before I say more about this, I want to turn now to the death of Eddie Matthews. If you did not already know it, and I think many of you did, Eddie Matthews was the source of those threatening notes that were sent to you last week. This was a prelude to a second series of notes that would have been specific as to the nature of what he knew about some of the individuals here. To put it bluntly, Eddie Matthews was a blackmailer. He was a man at the end of his career, a man who knew that he had no future in variety and who was desperate to cash in on the one thing he did have. Knowledge and a long memory.'

Kit paused for a moment to cast his eyes around the stage. No one had said anything. It was as if they were collectively holding their breath. This anxiety was based on what Eddie Matthews knew and if Kit would share that now, in public.

'I won't say any more on what Eddie Matthews had on individual members of this group. I'm not in the business of blackmail and nor is the chief inspector. We are, however, here to catch a murderer: the killer of Javier Gonzalo and of Eddie Matthews.'

'But surely Matthews killed himself,' said Lucien Lemaire.

'No,' replied Kit. 'He was murdered.'

Susan was in tears now. She was comforted by Jackie. Even Daisy Lewis seemed close to the edge now. It was time to move matters to their conclusion.

'Eddie Matthews died because he was in a place he shouldn't have been and then, because he was a blackmailer, decided to take advantage of what he knew.'

As Kit said this, the curtains in the middle of the stage were raised to reveal the black cabinet where Gonzalo had met his death. Kit nodded his thanks to Ezra.

Kit walked over to the cabinet. All eyes followed him as he surveyed the ominous coffin.

'I don't wish to upset you, but I think it is worthwhile reflecting on what happened that fateful night.'

Kit turned to Mary who hopped up from her seat and strode over to join him by the cabinet. Suddenly, from the orchestra pit a piano began to play. All eyes swung in the direction of Annie Watts. She was playing the piano with Hector Goulding on violin. They were playing the Paso doble that accompanied the Inquisition act.'

'This is in very poor taste,' said Lucien Lemaire. He was comforting Jane Anthony who was crying now on his shoulder.

Kit ignored him. He waited a moment for his musical cue then nodded to Mary. She stepped inside the cabinet. Kit closed the door and swung the cabinet around to reveal to the audience that the door was shut. As if on cue, the music stopped.

'Javier Gonzalo is now inside the cabinet. He needs to release the trapdoor to escape below stage. It's at this moment he realises the door cannot open. He tries again. And again. The door will not open because…'

Ever the consummate actor, Kit paused at this moment for dramatic effect. From his pocket he fished out a block of wood. It was a door wedge. The same door wedge that Romeo had offered as a gift to Mary the day before.

Kit walked around the back of the cabinet and slipped the door wedge underneath to prevent the trapdoor opening. He reappeared a few moments later.

'That is what killed Gonzalo.'

'But there was no wedge when we went to the cabinet. The trap door opened without a problem,' said Enrico Monteverdi.

'Yes, I know,' said Kit.

At this point he pushed the cabinet away from the hatch in the stage and opened the door. Mary stepped out from the cabinet and returned to her seat. All eyes fell on the wooden wedge as it sat beside the hatch.

Slowly, Kit walked over to the wedge. He stood looking at it for a few moments then, without warning, he kicked it into the hatch.

'That's all our murderer had to do,' said Kit. 'Like all illusions, it seems so banal when you know what happened. The only problem in this illusion, the only unforeseeable element for the killer, was that Eddie Matthews was standing directly underneath the hatch and saw the wedge fall through. He didn't see who had kicked it, though, that would come later.'

'So, who did it?' asked Lemaire, irritably. The screaming silence was broken by the sound of Jane Anthony sobbing. Lemaire put his arms around her and glared at Kit.

Kit extracted a journal from his pocket. It was the book with notes on illusions and diagrams of the equipment that would be needed to create them. He held it up for everyone to see.

'We found this in Eddie Matthews' room. It's a journal containing magic tricks, illusions, diagrams on equipment. I glanced through it. If Eddie Matthews had been able to sell this it might have been worth a lot of money.'

'Was this stolen from Gonzalo?' asked Gian Luca Monteverdi.

Kit raised his eyebrows at this.

'That's what the murderer wanted us to think. In fact, that's why they planted it in his room. It's a fascinating book, but it's not what all of this is about.'

'What is it about, then?' asked Lemaire in a bored voice.

'I told you. Revenge. It's revenge for a murder committed over a year ago in Manchester. A murder committed by Gonzalo but disguised to look like a suicide. Gonzalo murdered his partner in an act called the Brothers Grimoire.'

A few heads jerked up at this.

'I can see that a few of you were familiar with them. The second member of the duo, the murder victim, was a young man named Andrew Harper. He was, by all accounts, a morose, rather depressed boy. The police thought that he'd taken his own life, but at least one person knew this was not so.'

'Who?' called out Lemaire.

'His twin. Eliza Harper. She was convinced her brother had been murdered and she knew who the murderer was and why. Gonzalo did not come up with magic tricks. He was a showman, not a creator. He stole from Andrew Harper the journal of illusions. But Andrew Harper did not create the illusions either. He made the equipment, but he did not dream up anything. No, it was Eliza Harper who did this. She created the illusions for her brother and then saw Gonzalo steal them and try to pass them off as his own.

'Where is she now?' asked Jackie Rutherford.

'There is a grave in Manchester with her name on it,' replied Kit. 'She died of Pulmonary Tuberculosis a few months after her brother.'

This was greeted with shock. All at once the troupe began to talk at the same time. Kit held his hand up to silence them.

'Yet, there was one last illusion that Eliza dreamed up that was perhaps her greatest trick of all. She rose from the dead.'

Kit brandished the book again and opened it.

'This book is the book we found in Eddie Matthews' room. It's not the one that Gonzalo stole. How do I know this? Well, it's written in plain English for a start. This was the problem that Gonzalo never considered when he stole the book. It was written in code. This code was devised by the remarkable young woman for just such a scenario. Yet, we found this book in Eddie Matthews' room. Only one person could have known to plant this book in the room. It's the same young woman who is in this photograph.'

Kit took out the photograph and showed it to the group. They were too far away to see the faces.

'This is the killer of Javier Gonzalo and Eddie Matthews,' said Kit.

'They deserved to die,' said a voice from the group.

Everyone turned to the source of the voice. Jane Anthony glared defiantly at Kit with eyes that glistened with tears. Lucien Lemaire, meanwhile, almost fell over in his effort to disentangle himself from the woman who had just confessed to murder.

Jane Anthony rose to her feet and walked towards Kit. She reached out. Kit handed the book back to her.

'Gonzalo murdered my brother,' said Jane. 'I only did what the hangman should have done.'

'And Eddie Matthews? He was blackmailing you?' asked Kit in the manner of two people chatting in a tea room.

Jane laughed mirthlessly at this.

'Do you really think all he wanted was money? He was a rapist. Ask around Liverpool or Manchester or Birmingham or London. Ask the women that worked with him. They'll all tell you the same thing. He preyed on them. He found out their secrets and then he would strike. Money was the last thing he wanted. He enjoyed the power. Ruining the lives of women. All young women, of course. Young women who had made mistakes or needed money. While Graham Gibson got away with killing my brother because of an incompetent policeman, Eddie Matthews was ruining lives all over the country.'

'So you murdered them,' said Kit.

'No, I executed them,' came the unrepentant reply from Jane Anthony.

31

An hour later, Kit sat with Tristram and Rufus in the theatre office. Outside, it seemed as if it was the end of days. Rain lashed the windows of the theatre with an appalling malevolence. The three men watched the rain bounce off the pavement, while further in the distance waves white-whipped the sand with spray.

'Do many people come out on a night like this?' asked Kit.

'Not any more they don't,' said Tristram glumly. 'They'll listen to the radio.'

'It doesn't seem to affect Billy Benson. They were queuing outside earlier.'

'Douglas Fairbanks,' came his brother's mournful reply. It was difficult to compete against a carelessly good-looking pirate, or a demure southern belle or vampish femme fatale. This was variety of a different kind, and it was taking over.

Kit looked thoughtful at this before turning his attention to Romeo. The theatre cat, in the absence of Mary, was curled up on his knee and purring loudly.

'The hero of the show,' said Kit, stroking the black cat behind the ear. Romeo looked up sideways at Kit as if he understood that the reviews were in, and he was now a star. There was a knock at the door and Harry Miller entered the room.

'They're all away now,' said Miller, closing the door.

'Take a seat Harry,' said Tristram. 'We owe you a great deal young man.'

Miller waved his hand trying to evade any credit.

'It's true Harry,' said Kit. 'It was your doggedness in following up on the death of Andrew Harper and the apparent death of his sister that helped provide the crucial piece of evidence. My piece of chicanery may not have held up in court.'

Miller sat down and opened a bag which contained some rolled-up playbills. He took them out and unfurled them on the desk. For the first time, Kit was able to see the posters advertising the Brothers Grimoire.

'That's Andrew Harper,' said Miller pointing to the devil character. Kit glanced at it, but his attention was drawn to the name at the bottom of the bill: Madame Svengali, the witch of Metis. He glanced at Miller. At this point, the words of Nathaniel Magwitch came back to Miller.

'She was a mind-reader. She didn't speak to anyone except Andrew Harper apparently. Never appeared in anything other than her stage garb.'

Kit smiled at this. He looked up at the others and said, 'I wonder what the odds are that this was Eliza Harper? This is how she would have been aware of the relationship between her brother and Gonzalo. I suspect her friend, Antonia, was in the audience feeding her information about people through some form of sign language. Interesting she used the word, Metis. In Greek mythology, this was the wife of Zeus. She was known to change her shape at will. '

Kit paused for a moment and reflected on how it must have felt to have lost both a brother and best friend within a matter of a few months. He felt a wave of sympathy for the young woman, and it surprised him. She was a murderer. Yet what he had heard from Mary about the woman she knew as Jane Anthony as well as the certainty he felt that she was avenging the murder of her brother was unsettling. What would he have done if someone had cold-bloodedly killed Mary?

Kit shook the thought from his mind before saying, 'At this risk of repeating myself, she is a remarkable woman. To have spent six months with the man who killed her brother, planning for the moment when she would take her revenge.'

'Why wait so long?' asked Tristram.

Kit shook his head in admiration, 'It was all part of the misdirection. More than that, it was part of the show. Horrible and yet…'

'Remarkable,' said Rufus, finishing the thought. 'They really are deadlier than the male, aren't they?' There was going to be no argument from the other three men on this point. Rufus eyed Kit shrewdly. 'Do I detect a certain admiration for the young lady? Surely you don't approve of vigilantism?'

Kit did not immediately respond, then he said simply, 'No. No, I don't approve of vigilantism. The law is there to protect us all. Yet, I'm struck by what I would have done in similar circumstances. If we assume that Gonzalo did kill her brother and I am willing to believe this is so, then are there moral grounds for acting as she did, given the fact that the police failed to do their duty.? She will argue that she had no other recourse. The Monteverdis claim that they were acting in self-defence. That the death of the policeman was a tragic accident.

'They were acting in self-defence,' said Rufus firmly. For once the usual barb was absent from his comment.

'Returning to Jane or Eliza, what about the murder of Eddie Matthews? ' asked Tristram.

Kit shifted in his seat. This was even more troubling.

'One could argue she was protecting vulnerable people, which could be grounds for some form of vigilantism although her actions were hardly proportionate in this case. I'm not a supporter of capital punishment, so I would say they were not proportionate in the first case either.'

'You're not a hang 'em or flog 'em advocate then?' asked Tristram.

'Have you ruled out drawing and quartering also?' asked Rufus, his eyes twinkling once more.

They chatted for a few minutes although Kit, to Rufus's eyes, seemed on edge. Kit noticed Rufus looking at him strangely and this brought on a rueful grin. He pointed to the grandfather clock.

'I do wish you would have that fixed,' said Kit. 'Can I interpret loosely from it that we are near two in the afternoon?'

Rufus drew a pocket watch from his waistcoat. He tapped it twice before saying, 'Bloody thing never works.'

Tristram sighed before confirming that it was almost two o'clock.

'I invited someone over for a chat. I think you should hear what he has to say,' said Kit. He was facing the sea and saw the visitor arriving at the theatre. It was Billy

Benson. Moments later, he entered the office with an air of bonhomie that contrasted markedly with the brothers.

'Hello boys,' said Benson. 'I gather from his lordship that the case has reached a successful conclusion.'

'You're still free,' said Rufus, 'so perhaps that is premature.'

'Very funny, Rufus. Now, what do you think?' said Benson, ignoring the usual sniping from Rufus.

'Think about what?' asked Tristram.

Benson turned to Kit and looked at him meaningfully. All eyes, which is to say, Rufus and Tristram both turned to Kit.

'We hadn't reached that point Billy,' said Kit, 'but now that you are here it's as good a time as any to discuss this. I hope you don't mind Tristram, Rufus.'

'Mind what?' asked Tristram, suspicion clouding his face like a mother standing by an empty biscuit tin and a boy with crumbs on his face.

'Your mother kindly loaned me the books of the theatre yesterday. I had a chance to review them. Some interesting arrangements in there, I noticed. You appear to have some regular customers who pay you with groceries. I saw chickens mentioned more than a few times,' said Kit.

Tristram and Rufus exchanged glances before Tristram said, 'We have, shall we say, understandings with some of our regulars. Paid in kind. You know.'

'Indeed. Not a bad idea,' agreed Kit. 'Neatly avoids tax.' He was smiling at the arrangement.

'We could send them a chicken leg, I suppose,' suggested Rufus helpfully.

'I'm sure they'd appreciate that. Anyway, that was of less concern than your ticket sales. It looks as if you may as well not be open Tuesday for all the business you have that night. Basically, you are highly dependent on Wednesday through Saturday. Four days a week where you can earn an income. It's hardly sufficient, is it?'

There seemed to be no answer to this that would not make the responder seem an idiot, so Rufus and Tristram wisely remained silent.

'I think there is an alternative opportunity here,' said Kit turning towards Benson who was beaming broadly.

'You're not suggesting we sell up?' exclaimed Tristram.

'No,' said Kit. 'That's the last thing I would ever do. My idea is simpler than that. You go into partnership with Billy here. For two days a week, Monday and Tuesday, when you're either shut or business is low, you can show moving pictures.'

This suggestion was greeted with silence. Outside a dog was barking at a seagull. It seemed to bark a very long time before Billy Benson broke the silence.

'It makes sense boys. I'm turning people away Monday and Tuesday nights sometimes. If we go fifty, fifty then we can both make a bit. I don't want the theatre to stop showing variety. I love all that. Always have. Give it some thought.'

Kit sensed that any reluctance on the part of the brothers was a desire not to be seen to break ranks first. Just then, they heard the muffled sound of music gently wafting in from the auditorium. A thought occurred to Kit. He rose from his seat. 'Shall we go in and listen?' he suggested.

Despite a certain amount of foot dragging on the part of the brothers, who appeared to be reverting to their teenage selves, they followed Kit, Harry Miller and Billy Benson into the auditorium.

Annie Watts and Hector Goulding were in the orchestra pit playing Mozart. There was no reason for them to be rehearsing. The show would be cancelled. A short break would follow, and a new show would be put together after the unfortunate publicity had become yesterday's news. The notoriety would give them a short boost before business returned to normal.

The five men sat down at the back of the theatre. Near the front sat Ezra and Joshua. Over the next few minutes they watched Mrs Watts and Goulding become lost in the music they were playing.

When Kit turned to Tristram and Rufus he saw tears on their cheeks. Perhaps it was the thought that they would ultimately have to accede to the march of progress. Yet, Kit did not entirely believe this. They, like he, had found the sight of the two elderly musicians unutterably moving. The joy that they took from simply playing was its own purpose whether or not they had an audience. How often, Kit wondered, had they done this over the years? How much longer would they be able to do so?

At end of the piece, Billy Benson, who had been sitting in the seat in front of the Watts brothers turned and said, 'Think of it, boys. A live orchestra playing to the films we show. We could have royal premieres here, Hollywood stars. All of it.'

Tristram sighed then said, 'Look around you Billy.'

Benson did so and he saw what Kit could plainly see. The gold paint had dulled on more than just Sock and Buskin; the stage curtains were being held together by

Annie Watts' needlework and many of the seats had patches over the parts that had become too worn.

'I'm sure we can do something about all this,' said Kit.

'What do you mean?' asked Tristram.

'You know what I mean,' said Kit.

32

Mary's stomach was feeling a little sea sick as she walked on dry land. She ignored the rain pounding the pavement and pressed on towards Mrs Harrison's digs. The performers would all be back there now. All except Jane Anthony, or Eliza Harper as Mary now knew her and the Monteverdi Brothers. They had been taken away to the police station. Tomorrow they would be transported to London. There they would either face trial or, in the case of the Italians, be handed over to their embassy to face justice back home.

Mary knocked on the door of the digs. It was answered by Susan Parrish. The ever-present cigarette was glued to her bottom lip. Her smile was thin and not particularly welcoming.

'Hello Mrs Aston. Come to arrest someone else?'

This wounded Mary. The pain when it came stung her more than she could ever have imagined. Her whole body seemed to freeze, and she began to tremble. Perhaps Mary's anguish was evident because, almost immediately, regret poured from Susan's eyes.

'Sorry. That was unfair.'

She stood back to let Mary come in from the rain. Mrs Harrison appeared in the corridor. She did not look any more pleased to see Mary than Susan had been. Her reason was all too clear. In the next couple of days she would lose everyone from the house. They would move on to their next engagement or somewhere a little bit cheaper.

'I believe I owe you some money,' said Mary attempting a smile. She couldn't get her lips to form the required shape so gave it up as a bad job.

Mrs Harrison left to find her accounts book. Jackie Rutherford appeared at the top of the stairs just as Mary began to climb. When Mary reached the top Jackie enveloped her in an enormous bear hug. After a what seemed like a lifetime, Jackie released Mary. They both began to giggle.

'Thanks Jackie. I think,' said Mary, checking to see if her limbs and body were still attached to one another in the traditional way.

Jackie gently rubbed Mary's arm. She said, 'It was lovely to meet you Mary. I love your voice. Fancy that man of yours more, mind. I wasn't very impressed with that Chauncey Alston, but that Kit Aston will do all right.'

'I wasn't too impressed with Mr Alston either,' admitted Mary. 'I much prefer Kit.'

'Well, if you ever grow tired of him, not that I think he'll ever be tired of you, then…'

'I'll send him over directly,' said Mary, taking Jackie's hand. Then she glanced towards Daisy's room.

'She's packing up. No doubt off to see Bert.'

'You knew?'

'Yes, we all did, I suppose. I hope they, well, you know…'

'They will,' said Mary. There was a glint in her eye as she said this. She nodded her thanks to Jackie and then turned towards Daisy's door. A few knocks from Mary were followed by a voice inside saying to come in.

Mary's heart was thudding once more. She paused for a few seconds then with a moment of decision twisted the handle and walked inside. Daisy was sitting on the bed. Either side of her were everyday clothes and stage clothes. There was no smile of welcome on her face, but nor was there recrimination.

'Mrs Aston,' said Daisy.

'Mrs Cooper?' asked Mary, attempting a smile.

This question was met with silence and then Daisy's face transformed first into a smile followed by tears. Mary was over beside her in an instant. She hugged the young woman tightly, joining her in feeling that curious mixture of guilt, sadness and relief that can only find true expression through the tears which distinguish women from men and other animals.

It took a few minutes before either was able to speak.

'I'm sorry I misled you, Daisy,' said Mary. 'I hated myself.'

Daisy took her hand, 'I think we are playing a part, Mary. All of us. Goes with the territory, I suppose.'

'You'll see Bert now?' asked Mary.

Daisy paused for a second to size Mary up which brought another guilty smile from both. Then she nodded.

'Yes, I'll see him. They'll probably try and follow me.'

'They won't,' said Mary. 'Trust me on that. The chief inspector promised Kit. He's a man of his word.'

Daisy was, once more, moved by this. Silence fell between them for a short while. Then Mary reached into her handbag. She took out a white envelope. It looked rather thick to Daisy's eyes. After a few moments it dawned on her why.

'No, Mary, I can't. I won't'

'Take it, Daisy,' begged Mary. 'There's a letter. A letter of introduction to my uncle, well, it's Kit's uncle, I suppose. We'll let him know. He lives in California. You can make a new start. You and Bert.'

Daisy was crying once more.

'His name's Arnold, not Bert,' said Daisy. She saw Mary looking at her and then it dawned on her what she was wanting to ask, 'Not quite so glamorous. I'm Daisy. Lewis was my married name but, well, it's a different one now. It's actually Daisy Chatwin if you must know.'

With hands that were trembling, she took the envelope from Mary, but could not express how she felt. Instead, she let Mary give her a hug that stretched out wonderfully. Finally, Mary glanced down at the clothes around the room.

'Let me help you pack.'

33

A policeman ambled along one side of Grosvenor Square with the unhurried gait of a man who had no particular place to go nor any reason to rush there. He saw Kit and Mary looking out at them and he offered a salute. They always acknowledged him. Nice people. They had invited him in for a cup of tea once when it was raining. He remembered things like that. The old woman before them had done the same. Tough old bird that one.

It was the evening after the arrest of Jane Anthony / Eliza Harper. Kit and Mary had returned with Harry Miller earlier to Grosvenor Square, the house that Aunt Agatha had gifted to Mary. They were sitting in the drawing room which overlooked the square. Sam, Kit's Jack Russell, was snoring on another seat. The room was dimly lit with only two lamps on. It reflected their rather sombre mood. Mary picked up the evening newspaper to read for at least the seventh time the story of the arrest. Simpkins, the black cat who had adopted Kit, hopped up onto the seat to join Mary and inspect the paper. In fact, he sat on top of it.

'I'd read it anyway, Simpkins,' said Mary, beginning to stroke him behind his ear. 'It's not like the chief inspector to be so late,' observed Mary distractedly.

'No, he's usually very prompt. I hope everything's all right,' agreed Kit. He was staring out the window. The square was empty now, as the policeman had disappeared.

'Anything of interest out there?' asked Mary.

'Not really,' said Kit. He turned to Mary and tried to smile. She took his hand and sighed.

'Perhaps we should call Harry in and speak to him. I'm not sure I can stand this much longer.'

'Nor can I,' replied Kit, rising to his feet. There's nothing quite so impressive as a man of action. A man, who once decided on a purpose, faithfully and doggedly pursues said purpose to its bitter end. How many model aeroplanes, or playing card castles would have remained unbuilt had the male of the species not been sanctified by such resolution?

Kit went to the door and called out into the corridor, 'Harry, have you a minute?'

A muffled voice responded that they would be along presently. Kit went over to his seat by the window with Mary. The door opened and Harry Miller appeared.

'Harry, can you join us for a few minutes. There's a matter we would like to discuss with you. We're expecting Chief Inspector Jellicoe in a few minutes, too.' Miller chuckled at this as did Kit. 'Don't worry, I think your past has long since been accounted for.'

'That's a relief, sir,' replied Miller, taking a seat at the table. Kit glanced at Mary. Her heart felt a pain that she knew her husband shared. What else could they feel? In a few minutes they would agree to part company with a man that Kit owed his life to. A man who had risked his own life in order to save Kit's. 'Was there something you wanted to see me about sir?' prompted Miller.

'Yes, Harry. As a matter of fact there is. Mary and I have decided, in a manner of speaking, to fire you.'

Mary had just that moment taken a drink of water to steady her nerves. The timing, she realised, was ill-judged as she proceeded to spit out the contents of her mouth, dowsing the sleeping Simpkins in the process. He leapt off Mary's knee and stared up angrily at her.

'Sorry, darling,' said Mary.

'Darling?' said Kit. 'Well, I think we've just established the order of preference in this household.'

Miller was smiling uncertainly, 'You said fired, sir.'

'Yes,' said Kit. 'Dismissed. Canned. Sacked.'

'Kit,' exclaimed Mary, one eyebrow raised, but she was half-smiling too.

There was a knock at the door. Miller rose to answer it, but Kit bid him to remain seated. 'Don't worry.'

A few moments later they heard Chief Inspector Jellicoe's voice in the corridor. They waited a minute for his arrival. Kit and Miller both rose to their feet when he entered. He was carrying his hat and mackintosh.

'Aren't you forgetting something, chief inspector?' asked Mary. There was glint of mischief in her eye.

'The light's not very conducive,' pointed out Jellicoe. This excuse was dignified without any response. He stared at Kit, Mary and Miller before shrugging his shoulders resignedly. He walked forward a few steps. 'From here?' he asked.

'Yes, please,' said Mary.

Jellicoe set his coat down on the sofa and then, still clutching his bowler, he spun around and threw it towards the bust of Helen of Troy from the studio of Canova. This was a tribute to Betty Simpson who for forty years had successfully thrown her hat onto the bust.

Jellicoe's hat missed.

'You're no Betty Simpson,' said Mary.

'Indeed,' agreed Jellicoe, joining the others at the table by the window. Drinks were offered and drinks were declined. In truth, Jellicoe appeared a little flustered which Kit suspected was not a consequence of missing the bust.

'We've informed Harry that he's surplus to requirements,' began Kit.

'Kit,' laughed Mary. Even Miller was quite enjoying this.

'I promise I'll return the cutlery,' said Miller.

Mary shook her head. The ever-unfathomable inability of men to take anything seriously was once more making a spectacle of itself. The fact that Miller was now not only the victim, but a willing participant only added to the sense of affectionate irreverence. On the whole, Mary rather liked this manner of friendship. Was she really so different with her sister, Esther? Probably not.

Miller looked from Kit to Jellicoe, expectantly. Perhaps some idea was forming in his mind.

'I owe you my life, Harry. Nothing will ever change the debt I owe you. I thought that by having you join me in this life that it would go some way towards repaying you. I think we've had some extraordinary adventures.'

Miller nodded. It was true. He had lived a dozen lives over the last few years, faced death on numerous occasions and fallen in love with a woman who he could not see for another three years. Life was never straightforward.

'At the same time, Harry, I've come to realise that this is not the life for you. I think you know this too. I believe that you have a yearning to find your own way, and I do not want you to feel any sense of obligation towards me. There can be none. I owe you everything. Part of this debt is my wish not to stand in the way of you living the life that you desire.'

'Thank you, sir,' said Miller, quite moved by Kit's words. He felt his heart tighten, his body stiffening with tension. This was what he wanted yet just at that moment doubt set in. The idea of being set adrift, away from the security, the luxury of Grosvenor Square now seemed like a forbidding prospect.

'Chief Inspector Jellicoe is here for a reason. Perhaps you can guess,' continued Kit.

All eyes turned to Jellicoe.

'Your work in Manchester was outstanding, Harry,' began Jellicoe. 'No man could have done better. I want you to join us, Harry. Become a gamekeeper, not a poacher. Will you, Harry? Will you join us?'

Jellicoe's eyes bored into Miller's. His countenance was both serious but also, at that moment, kindly. Miller felt an enormous rush of relief. The effect of the words spoken by Jellicoe, profound. His answer would change his life. He was ready to give that answer now.

'Yes, chief inspector,' said Miller, glancing towards Kit and Mary briefly. He received a nod from Kit and then added, 'Yes, I'd like to join you.'

Jellicoe and Miller shook hands to seal the commitment made. Kit clapped his hands while Mary leant over and gently kissed Miller on the cheek.

Jellicoe consented to join Kit, Mary and Miller in a drink to celebrate. Kit went over to the drinks cabinet to fix four gins. As he did so he asked Jellicoe, 'Chief inspector, I hope you don't mind me prying, but it's rather unusual for you to be late. You seemed rather flustered when you entered. Is everything all right?'

The reminder of his tardiness seemed to pain Jellicoe, or perhaps something else was on his mind. He paused for a moment then revealed what had delayed him.

'Yes, I was going to tell you. As you know, Eliza Harper and the Monteverdi Brothers were travelling up to London today to be remanded at Bow Street. I've just been made aware of a rather extraordinary development.'

34 Curtain Down

Twelve years earlier:

Barnardo's Home, Manchester, 1909

The dining room in the house was a whirl of activity. Eliza Harper was everywhere shouting, cajoling, directing and laughing. Around her, half a dozen girls and boys were setting up the stage for the afternoon's performance. Andrew, as ever, had a hammer in one hand and a nail in the other. He was ensuring that the folding panel that covered two of the dining room windows would remain upright through the performance. Second-in-command, Antonia Scott, was overseeing the placement of the banner she had made the previous evening. It read:

MADAME SVENGALI & THE CHILDREN OF METIS

MAGIC SHOW

Happy with the placement, Antonia nodded to a boy who was no more than ten, standing at the top of the ladder. A few belts with his hammer and the banner was in place. He skipped down the stepladder at an unhealthily quick rate causing Eliza to cover her eyes and groan. There was no time to admonish him and anyway, it was hardly her place, given what she was going to do that afternoon.

Even Miss Waterhouse did not know the full scale of the risk that she was potentially exposing herself to. Except that there was no risk. It was all one, great illusion. Eliza had been planning this for weeks. Every last detail had been captured in the old leather-bound book that she carried with her. It was written in the code that only she, Antonia and Andrew could understand, and Andrew had brought her vision brilliantly to life. No sister could have been prouder of a brother.

She glanced over at Andrew. His eyes were fixed on the base of the panels. He brought the same intensity to this that he did with everything. What would happen to him when they left the safety of Barnardo's? She wandered over to him. He was kneeling over the board putting the base block in place. Andrew glanced up towards her and smiled. Eliza nodded in approval and her brother's smile grew wider.

The orchestra arrived to set up. The orchestra, in this case, was a pianist called Katie and a young boy called Eric who played a trumpet that was as big as he was.

By midday, the stage was complete. Eliza directed the setting out of the chairs facing the stage. All that was required was a smile or a frown. She never had to raise her voice. The whole of the Barnardo's home seemed to live for a moment of acknowledgement from their queen.

'Make sure to have an aisle down the middle,' warned Eliza to the young stage hands helping her.

Miss Waterhouse arrived as the last of the chairs was being put in place. She looked around the dining room. She tried hard to suppress a smile while watching Eliza

263

ordering the younger children about. She was a natural-born leader, and they adored her. Not just the children; the staff also. It had been so since the day she arrived all those years ago. It would break her heart the day she and her brother left. In some senses and selfishly, she was glad that Andrew was as he was. It had given her the chance to spend more time and watch Eliza grow. Eliza caught Miss Waterhouse's eye and they nodded to one another.

'It looks wonderful, Eliza. We're all looking forward to the show. Sergeant Dunton has confirmed he's coming along with Constable Tibbs and a gentleman from the press, Mr Ruskin. I hope you'll be ready.'

Then Miss Waterhouse eyes flicked in the direction of a conical metal container. It was an old, very rusted, milk churn. How on earth did they get this? The next thought was more troubling. She didn't have to ask the question as she looked at Eliza. It was in her eyes. Eliza's eyes crinkled in amusement. She took the head of the home's arm and led her away from the stage.

'Don't worry. We're ready,' grinned Eliza.

The show began promptly at four. All of the staff and the invited guests sat in the chairs while the younger children had to make do with the floor, just in front of the seats. Miss Waterhouse was used to seeing shows from Eliza, Andrew and Antonia, but when they had invited guests as they did that day, she could never quite control her nerves. Despite the extraordinary confidence of Eliza, her great fear was that something would go wrong; the illusion would fail. While this would be treated as a joke by

Eliza and Antonia, she worried how it might affect a mind as fragile as Andrew's.

The audience was talking excitedly now, but they hushed as Katie on piano and Eric on trumpet began to play a sombre, atonal melody that was oddly compelling. The piece did not outstay its welcome. As it faded out, Andrew took to the stage dressed in an older evening suit that Antonia had fixed up to fit him. The audience hushed as he surveyed them, his face mournful, almost sorry. In many respects, thought Miss Waterhouse, he would make an impressive stage illusionist. He had such a serious manner. He announced the imminent arrival of Madame Svengali. No one applauded. Eliza was most insistent on this.

At least, not until the end.

Miss Waterhouse never asked how they were able to do the illusions, but she had finally worked out how this particular mind reading trick was performed. She had seen it six months earlier when they had performed the Christmas show. As ever, it gave credit to both these young girls. Young women realised Miss Waterhouse with a stab of pain.

Madame Svengali appeared on the stage following another low atonal announcement from Eric's trumpet. Eliza wore a black cloak, a black wig and heavy black makeup around her eyes. She managed to be both beautiful and terrifying in equal measure. She sat down and stared out at the audience impassively.

Noting her arrival, Andrew Harper surveyed the audience. 'May we have a volunteer,' he asked, fixing his eyes on Constable Tibbs. The audience laughed and Tibbs rose from his seat. He barely seemed any taller standing

265

than seated and certainly no older than many of the children near his feet. Sergeant Dunton, a man at the other end of his police career from the young constable, sat back to enjoy seeing his protégé made sport of.

'We have not met before, sir?' asked Andrew.

The boys and girls laughed at this, and a few urged his immediate arrest. They were silenced, but not severely, by Miss Waterhouse.

'Madama Svengali, what can you tell us about Constable Tibbs?'

Eliza's voice was a cross between German and Slavic. Quite how she had developed this facility was beyond Miss Waterhouse. She immediately began to relay information that Tibbs had shared earlier in the office with Miss Waterhouse when he and the others had arrived for a pre-performance afternoon tea. She then correctly identified what Tibbs had in his pocket. Once again, in the office he'd emptied his pockets to find a key to a pair of handcuffs. Tibbs and Sergeant Dunton were delighted by what they heard.

While Andrew asked for volunteers from the audience, usually the invited guests, Antonia would sit in the crowd, making deaf sign language to give Eliza the answers to the questions that Andrew posed from the stage. It was so obvious and yet it never failed to delight the children. No doubt they had other confederates who had eavesdropped on conversations as the guests arrived so that sometimes even topics only raised minutes earlier were brought up by Madame Svengali.

A series of illusions followed, each more devilishly inexplicable than the last. Cards would be chosen by the policemen or the journalist which would then be torn

266

apart before magically reassembling themselves and appearing in obscure places in the dining room. Antonia Scott appeared to levitate at one point thanks to a hypnotic trance from Madame Svengali. At no point did Eliza's accent drop from character.

Before the end of the show, Andrew appeared dressed in red with a pair of horns and tried to kidnap Antonia. He disappeared in a blinding flash that brought a few delighted screams from the children and utter bafflement from the adults who had no idea where Andrew had gone. Then he reappeared outside one of the windows as if he were locked out.

The three young adults reappeared on the stage at the end for the finale. Eliza had dispensed with her Madame Svengali costume and stood before the applauding audience. An encore was demanded, and an encore was provided. This, as Miss Waterhouse knew, was all part of the show. Tears of pride stung her eyes as she looked at the beautiful young woman that Eliza had become. Sixteen years old and so confident, so mature. She was a credit to the home. Had she thought about it longer or, indeed, had a greater ego, Miss Waterhouse would surely have basked in the shared acclaim she bestowed upon Eliza.

'Sergeant Dunton, Constable Tibbs: I believe that Miss Waterhouse asked you to bring along a pair of handcuffs for this performance.'

Constable Tibbs stood up and shuffled forward towards Eliza. Tibbs was twenty years old and in his first year as a policeman. He was a decent if none too bright boy. The young woman before him was, quite simply, dazzling to him. His face coloured a deep red, so much so that a few of the boys began to whistle. They were silenced with a frown from Eliza.

Miss Waterhouse shifted in her seat and felt her skin prickle. The realisation that the young constable had fallen in love with Eliza somewhere between her arrival on stage and his putting the handcuffs on was a cold awakening to reality.

Eliza now had her hands cuffed behind her back. She slowly twirled around for the audience to see that the handcuffs were on.

'Constable Tibbs,' said Eliza. 'Are you satisfied that these handcuffs are good and tight?'

Tibbs nodded to her and returned to his seat. Katie and Eric began playing the slow, strange-sad melody that they had opened the show with.

Miss Waterhouse's heart was thudding now. Realisation had dawned on her about the purpose of the metal milk churn. Moments later, her fears were confirmed when Andrew Harper took the wooden screen back to reveal its presence at the back by the window. Part of her wanted to stand up and stop the show, but she was stopped by Sergeant Dunton's name being called by Andrew.

'Sergeant Dunton, will you join us on stage for a moment. Perhaps Mr Ruskin also?'

The two men laughed, a little nervously, but acceded to the request. The stepped up onto the makeshift stage and followed Andrew over to the metal churn.

'This is a milk churn as you know,' said Andrew. 'Mr Ruskin, can you tell the audience, what is inside.'

Ruskin was, like Tibbs, a young man who was in his second year as a journalist. He worked obituaries

268

normally. He felt a cold fear as he looked inside the churn. It was half full of water.

'Water,' stammered Ruskin. He glanced at the calm young woman who he now realised was going to step inside the churn. He wondered how she would fit. Yet, at the same time, he was not unaware, like Tibbs, of her slenderness and beauty.

Eliza gave her hand to the young man. Her hand was so small and soft that it was all he could do to stop himself shouting 'don't do it', but Eliza was already stepping inside. He watched her slowly sink into rusted metal. Some water was displaced. Andrew sealed the churn by spinning the top.

Eliza was now locked in, realised Miss Waterhouse. Worse, there was limited air in the container. Even Dunton and Ruskin looked troubled as they took their seats once more. Once they were seated, Andrew and Antonia put the screen in front of the metal container.

'Are you sure about this, Miss Waterhouse?' whispered Dunton.

'No, sergeant, I am not,' managed Miss Waterhouse through compressed lips. She had seen Eliza perform escapology before but never had the peril been quite so intense. Miss Waterhouse could not breathe. She realised that this made her situation rather like Eliza's. With one crucial difference. Eliza's life was at stake.

The music was louder now. There was no attempt at a melody or any coherent structure. It was a crashing sound. The sound of life fighting for itself. No other sound could better have suited the mood of the audience than what Katie and Eric were performing. Random keys were being thrashed with willful malevolence. Eric was blowing so hard that he was virtually levitating himself.

It was too much.

Miss Waterhouse rose to her feet.

'Open the cannister,' she shouted.

Tibbs and Ruskin were on their feet as if the bugle had blown, which in a manner it had. They surged as if in a race to save the young maiden. Andrew and Antonia moved the screen lest the two men destroy it in their efforts to save the young girl. Comically, they almost wrestled one another to open the lid of the cannister. Finally, the cannister was open.

It was empty.

The two men looked up, dumbfounded. Just as they did so they heard the door at the back of the dining room open. All heads turned around to see who had entered the room.

Eliza Harper padded barefoot up the central aisle. She was dripping wet, with a towel around her. Her eyes were smiling in triumph.

Everyone was on their feet, the room erupted into applause, none louder than the two young men standing on the stage, no longer quite so worried and, perhaps, feeling a little foolish and certainly more than a little in love.

Eliza reached the front of the stage and turned to face Sergeant Dunton. The old policeman was grinning widely. Miss Waterhouse was trying to smile, but could not decide whether she was angry, relieved or proud. Probably all. Eliza had not warned her about this illusion and that was something she would not permit again. Surprises were, at best unwelcome; shocks were unacceptable. Miss

270

Waterhouse had genuinely feared for the life of this young girl who was more like a daughter than any child she'd ever had in her care.

From inside her towel, Eliza extracted a wet pair of handcuffs. She placed them in the outstretched hand of Sergeant Dunton.

'Your handcuffs, I believe, Sergeant Dunton.'

'They are indeed,' acknowledged Dunton. 'Not that they were much good with someone like you. I'm certainly glad that I shall never have to arrest you, young lady. I doubt we'd hold you for very long.'

Eliza consented to a smile. Then, in a matter-of-fact voice without a trace of conceit, she replied to the sergeant. Although softly spoken, her words seemed to fill the room, carrying out into the corridor, then into the garden, travelling like a despatch from the present to a future destination where illusion blurred with reality and became one.

'No sergeant, I don't think you would hold me for very long at all.'

The End

Research Notes

This is a work of fiction. However, it references real-life individuals. Gore Vidal, in his introduction to Lincoln, writes that placing history in fiction or fiction in history has been unfashionable since Tolstoy and that the result can be accused of being neither. He defends the practice, pointing out that writers from Aeschylus to Shakespeare to Tolstoy have done so with not inconsiderable success and merit.

I have mentioned a number of key, real-life individuals and events in this novel. My intention, in the following section, is to explain a little more about their connection to this period and this story.

For further reading on this period and the specific topics within this work of fiction I would recommend the following: Roy Hudd's Book of Music Hall, Variety and Showbiz Anecdotes which provided a fund of stories and jokes that I was able to use in this book. Richard Baker's book, Old Time Variety was also very useful in gaining an understanding of the period. John East's biography of Max Miller provided a great insight into this complex and extraordinary character.

Variety / Vaudeville Theatre

Music hall or Variety theatre in the UK and Vaudeville in the US all belong to the same form of entertainment that had its heyday in the late nineteenth and early twentieth century. In essence it was show featuring a variety of acts including singers, musicians, comedians and speciality acts such as acrobats, jugglers, ventriloquists and, of course, magicians. The two greatest alumni of this wonderful world are Charlie Chaplin and Stan Laurel. British variety stars included the incomparable

272

Gracie Fields and Max Miller (see below). The US also produced its fair share of extraordinary entertainers including the Marx Brothers, Jack Benny and George Burns & Gracie Allen.

Max Miller (1894 - 1963)

Born Thomas Sargent, Max Miller adopted his stage name around 1920 thanks to his formidable wife, Kathleen Marsh with whom he had briefly worked as a double before going solo. After serving in the war, Miller became a comedian, appearing at concert parties for much of the early twenties. By the thirties, his persona as 'The Cheeky Chappie' had been established and his following grew.

From the thirties through to the fifties, Miller was probably the most famous comedian in Britain. His act was famous for being more than slightly risqué. He had a white book and blue book which he used on stage to indicate what type of joke he was going to tell. In fact, Miller was never explicit and often left the audience to work out the punchline before accusing them of putting him in trouble. He did run afoul of the censors from time to time and fell out with major variety show producers, but this rarely lasted long, and his popularity ensured that he was soon topping the bill wherever he performed.

My father actually met Max Miller in the fifties and claimed to have given him a joke which he used in his act. Who knows if it's true, but as John Ford said, "When the legend becomes fact, print the legend."

The playlist of songs

A number of songs are referenced in the novel and if you are interested in knowing more about them I have compiled the following playlist. I think my dad would have approved!

You Made Me Love You (James V Monaco / Joseph McCarthy) – written in 1913 and recorded by Bing Crosby, Aretha Franklin, Al Jolson, among others. There is even an outtake of The Beatles magical Mystery Tour where it is featured.

Let Me Call You Sweetheart (Leo Friedman / Beth Slater Whitson) – written in 1910 and recorded by Bing Crosby and Linda Ronstadt, among others.

I'm Forever Blowing Bubbles? (John William Kellette / James Brockman / James Kenris / Nat Vincent) – written in 1919, this is a popular song among fans of the British football team, West ham United.

After the Ball (Charles K Harris) – written in 1981, this is one of the biggest selling songs of the early twentieth century. It features memorably in the great Jerome Kern musical, *Showboat*.

A Long way to Tipperary (Jack Judge / Harry Williams) – written in 1912, this became a Great War standard, popular among the British soldiers possibly because of its non-military theme.

Pack Up Your Troubles (In Your Old Kit Bag) (Felix Powell / George Henry Powell) – written in 1915, it features in films starring Laurel & Hardy, Gene Kelly & Judy Garland.

For Me and My Gal (George W Meyer / Edgar Leslie / E Ray Goetz)* – written in 1917, it was recorded by Al Jolson and Perry Como, among others. It also featured in the eponymous film starring Gene Kelly and Judy Garland.

Oh by Jingo (Albert von Tilzer / Lew Brown) – written in 1919, it is a novelty song that featured most recently in the Stephen Fry / Hugh Laurie remake of Jeeves and Wooster.

Daisy Bell (Henry Dacre) – written in 1982, this is a music hall / vaudeville standard.

Alexander's Ragtime Band (Irving Berlin) – written in 1911, it launched the career of the great Irving Berlin. It was recorded by a multitude of artists including, Louis Armstrong, Ella Fitzgerald and Ray Charles.

I Do Like to be Beside the Seaside (Mark Sheridan) – written in 1907, this is a British music hall standard.

St Louis Blues (WC Handy) – written in 1914, this has been recorded by a who's who of music including Bing Crosby and Louis Armstrong.

Try It On Your Piano (Irving Berlin) – written in 1920, this was a risqué song but seems rather tame by the standards of today were nuance and subtlety take second place to explicit language and subject matter. And yes, I am showing my age a little!

A Pretty Girl is like a Melody (Irving Berlin) - written in 1919 and the theme song from Ziegfeld Follies.

About the Author

Jack Murray was born in Northern Ireland but has spent over half his life living just outside London, except for some periods spent in Australia, Monte Carlo, and the US.

An artist, as well as a writer, Jack's work features in collections around the world and he has exhibited in Britain, Ireland, and Monte Carlo.

There are now seven books in the Kit Aston series.

A spin off series from the Kit Aston novels was published in 2020 featuring Aunt Agatha as a young woman solving mysterious murders.

Another spin off series is features Inspector Jellicoe. It is set in the late 1950's/early 1960's.

Jack has just finished work on a World War II trilogy. The three books look at the war from both the British and the German side. Jack has just signed with Lume Books who will now publish the war trilogy. The three books will all have been published by end October 2022. See taster after this section.

Acknowledgements

It is not possible to write a book on your own. There are contributions from so many people either directly or indirectly over many years. Listing them all would be an impossible task. Special mention therefore should be made to my wife and family who have been patient and put up with my occasional grumpiness when working on this project.

My brother, Edward, has helped in proofing and made supportive comments that helped me tremendously. Thank you, too, Debra Cox, David Sinclair and Anna Wietrzychowska who have been a wonderful help in reducing the number of irritating errors that have affected my earlier novels. A word of thanks to Charles Gray and Brian Rice who have provided legal and accounting support.

My late father and mother both loved books. They encouraged a love of reading in me. In particular, they liked detective books, so I must tip my hat to the two greatest writers of this genre, Sir Arthur and Dame Agatha.

Following writing, comes the business of marketing. My thanks to Mark Hodgson and Sophia Kyriacou for their advice on this important area. Additionally, a shout out to the wonderful folk on 20Booksto50K.

Finally, my thanks to the teachers who taught and nurtured a love of writing.

Printed in Great Britain
by Amazon